SERIAL INTENT

STEVE BRADSHAW

No part of this publication may be reproduced in whole or in part, or stored in a retrieval system, or transmitted in any form or by any means, electronic, mechanical, photocopying, recording, or otherwise, without written permission of the author, except for the inclusion of brief quotations in a review. For information regarding permission, please write to: steve@stevebradshawauthor.com

Copyright © 2017 STEVE BRADSHAW
All rights reserved.

1st Edition 2017

ISBN: 978-1-937996-98-7

Library of Congress Cataloging-in-Publication Data
SERIAL INTENT
STEVE BRADSHAW

Printed in USA
SERIAL INTENT © is a work of fiction. Names, characters, businesses, organizations, places, institutions, events, and incidents either are the product of the author's imagination or use is fictitious. Any resemblance to actual persons, living or dead, events, or locales is entirely coincidental and fictitious.

Other Books By STEVE BRADSHAW

EVIL LIKE ME

THE BELL TRILOGY

BLUFF CITY BUTCHER

THE SKIES ROARED

BLOOD LIONS

Dedication

In honor of the more than 20,000 federal, state and local law enforcement officers who have made the ultimate sacrifice for the safety and protection of our nation and its people.

http://www.nleomf.org/memorial

SERIAL INTENT

STEVE BRADSHAW

"The dead cannot cry out for justice. It is a duty of the living to do so for them."

Lois McMaster Bujold

SERIAL INTENT

Primary Characters

Babcock, Eldon	Defense Attorney
Crowley, Ben	Homicide Detective
Dario	Patient
Day, Sally	Newspaper Columnist
Dunn, Charlie	Survivor
Fetter, Lindsey	Victim, Survivor
Foster, Winston	ME Field Agent
Hutson, Joe	Homicide Detective
Landers, Louie	Homicide Commander
Marcantonio, William T.	Crime Family Patriarch
Mason, Robert	Survivor
Provost, Leonard, MD	Medical Examiner
Sorensen, Margaret	Wife of Jacques
Sorensen, Jacques, MD	Psychiatrist
Wolfe, Aaron	Homicide Detective
Woods, Barry	Estate Attorney

ONE

"I am going to count to three. When I say three, you will be in your safe place. As always nobody can hurt you, and nobody will judge you. One—"

Dr. Jacques Sorensen had rules. He never met clients outside the office, or after hours, or alone. But this was very different. It was about family. Everything was changing.

Ice crystals peppered the window panes in steady threatening waves, the cold wind found all the imperfections of the tattered shack—whining and humming in each crevice and crack like a brood of taunting night creatures dying to get inside. "Two—"

Now he was having second thoughts. After the change in the weather, he should have insisted on the South Side site—the abandoned Masonic Lodge on 64th Street. It held many fond memories from decades ago. Now it was just another broken-down edifice on an overgrown corner lot invisible to the world, but that made it the perfect place for the prior sessions. It was a place forgotten, convenient, and much safer than the old cabin in the woods.

The accumulation was becoming a problem. The rutted dirt road to the cabin snaked through miles of empty treacherous terrain few traveled, especially in the winter. Tonight, one mistake could be a death sentence.

"—Three," he said with the same authoritative tone he used hundreds of times before. Now all that was left to do was wait. It usually took ten minutes. He had things to say.

"I'm not happy here." The raspy whisper crawled through the room on schedule. It was as if the words came inside through the cracks with the wind.

"I am sorry to hear that," Sorensen said with a slight smile. The complaint was predictable and a good sign—he was coming.

"Don't patronize me!" This time the words climbed the dark walls like a swarm of angry spiders taking over the room.

The fire did little to light the small cabin, but Sorensen would not be sidetracked. Coughing through the arduous process he checked each rope with a smoking lantern. Sorenson did not know if his nausea came from inhaling kerosene or failing health coupled with the cold, late hour. Either way it did not matter anymore.

"You always say that," Sorensen said with an impatient tone. He knew the buttons.

"Yeah, well, this time I mean it."

Sorenson circled a second time for a closer inspection of the blindfold and knots—nothing could be loose. "Who am I speaking to now?" he asked when he finished and walked through his breath back to the window. He set down the lantern and opened the tattered burlap curtain with a shaking finger. Sorenson had stopped watching the transformation years ago. It too made him nauseous. *I should have thought this through better,* he sighed.

"That question only irritates him! He knows you only want him. He knows you don't care about me. I've never meant anything to you." The anger percolated in each word. Sorensen knew the steps. Dario would be arriving soon.

2

"I'm sorry you feel that way. My intentions were never to hurt you. I care about you," Sorensen said in a casual and disconnected voice. He would control the process as long as possible. It was shorter every time. "Now who am I speaking to . . . ?"

After a few minutes of cold silence, the words that filled the room were very different. It was as if another person had entered the cabin. "What time is it?"

Sorensen slid on his glasses and found his watch. His answer had to be precise. If not, it would delay everything. "It is 12:47 a.m." His cuff slid down his arm as he reached up to touch the cold window pane he had been studying. The ice crystals were sticking, building. Soon there would be more ice than glass. He had to push forward. "It is late. If Dario is not coming, I need to go home. We all need to go home." *That should be enough.*

He did not turn when the chair legs creaked and wobbled on the wood floor behind him, or when the gurgling and gasps mixed with the whine of ropes stretching to their limits. Dr. Sorensen knew exactly what was happening—although he could not explain it. His eyes dropped to the weathered wood windowsill—the syringe barrel was full and cap off the needle.

"You impatient bastard," Dario boomed. "Afraid of a little frozen water? Untie me, at once," he demanded as if fully expecting his order to be carried out immediately.

Sorensen stayed at the window with his back to his life's mystery. The first time he had witnessed it, he almost died. Then, on a cold December night in a dark alley, the man he had denied came back home.

"I will not untie you," Sorensen said with the same calm and steady voice.

The night he almost died a second time, Dr. Sorensen heard the same gurgling and gasping for air, but it was in the alley by his brownstone. He entered the shadows knowing what he would find. If he had not broken the hypnotic-like trance, Sorensen would have lost his life at the hands of a monster out of control. The mystery had returned and wanted to be called Dario.

Dr. Sorenson understood the psychological aberrations, but he could not explain the physical changes. Unlike Robert Louis Stevenson's fictional character—Dr. Jekyll and Mr. Hyde—the twisted and contorted manifestations he observed seemed to grow muscle mass in minutes. Physical identity transformed beyond what Sorensen had ever thought was humanly possible. His early hypothesis was the change was accomplished with the redistribution of blood and excessive hormonal secretions. It was the only way to explain the bulking-up of muscle tissue and the changes in strength, agility, and cognitive powers.

When Sorensen returned to the dark alley that night, Dario had gone away. Sorensen knew the man lying there. Over the next several years he would watch Dario return at will and gain even more strength. The host had no chance. Dr. Sorensen rationalized his lack of medical skills and failing health had left him no choice. He had to change his whole strategy.

"I'm not talking to you anymore," Dario growled.

Can you read my mind? Is that what I've been missing all these years? Sorensen wondered. *Do you know my new plan, what I'm about to do? Is that why you now threaten me? Telepathy is another area I'm not equipped to evaluate. It is another reason you must not be permitted to continue like this. I always dealt with the tip of the iceberg. I can't do this anymore. I don't care what Margaret believes. I don't care about any mission. God! Why didn't I just let you kill yourself years ago?*

"Okay, tell me why you've decided not to talk to me anymore, Dario." Sorensen still could not help himself. He had to know. That kept him coming back.

"You're useless to me, Jocko. You waste my time." Dario tugged at his ropes and bit at his blindfold. His chair creaked as he flexed and struggled to break loose—as always. "I demand you take these ropes off me. I'm not an animal. Do as I say." The struggle stopped. Another minute passed. Then Dario said under his breath, "I never liked you either."

Multiple personalities were not new. Over forty-six years at Northwestern Memorial Hospital, Dr. Sorensen had treated dozens with dissociative identity disorders. The day he retired, he quietly moved his files to a small rented office in the city a few blocks from his brownstone and Margaret's relentless needs—the mission. Now, Dr. Sorenson was having his own thoughts. He had his own plan.

The office was his excuse to get out of the house and away from everyone's expectations. He said he was working on a medical paper, researching patient files. He said he would publish in the *American Journal of Psychiatry*. But Dr. Sorensen did not have anything unusual or new to write about. He used his small office to drink scotch, smoke his pipe, and his other lifelong interest. Sorensen should have been a lawyer. Instead of medical books, he preferred to read about criminal law and reformation of the American justice system. He followed homicide cases. Many of the outcomes were detestable. The night Dario came back into his life, he made the biggest mistake of his life.

The time to fix everything had come. Sorensen would use Dario in a much different way. He would present Dario in a controlled state at the annual meeting of the American Psychiatric Research Society scheduled for Chicago in six days.

The "Dario Complex" would rock the psychiatric community, and Dr. Jacques Sorensen would be a medical icon. Acute psychophysiological metamorphic phenomena were limited to horror movies, up until Dario. Sorensen's discovery would be the most significant human metamorphic condition ever observed and documented. Sorensen would introduce Dario to the medical community. His work would become the foundation of new psychiatric research for decades to come. Dario would be Sorensen's crowning achievement—his true mission.

"I'm sorry you feel that way, Dario. Do you want to waste more time complaining and berating me, or shall we get on with things? We both have prepared for this moment."

"I feel as bad as the night I was born." Dario tugged at his ropes.

"You were not born. We've been over this ground," Sorensen said. "You are not an entity. You are a figment of an imagination. You do not exist on your own. You are a compilation of confused emotions housed inside a weak man. The pain and confusion gave rise to an anger so intense that your manifestation was made possible. You have always been a misplaced emotion. You have always been a temporary visitor. It is time."

"He looks nothing like me," Dario muttered. "He does not have my strength. He is not as intelligent as me. You like me more than him. You always have."

"You're out of control. I cannot allow it anymore."

"No," Dario barked. "I have thought about this. I'm not cooperating. I hate you! You don't really know me! *He* is always the victim, the loser. *He* cannot change anything that matters. You've tried to help him, but he has failed to respond every time. He's only jeopardized your mission. That's why I am here."

Sorensen stared into the cold night. Dario told the truth, but it did not matter anymore.

"I'm a part of your mission, the one you don't talk about," Dario said. "You're not stopping me. I won't let you turn me into some sort of circus sideshow to be studied."

"So you can read my mind," Sorensen said. "It does

not matter. You're not on any mission," he said as if he were sending back a sour glass of wine. "You do not understand the big picture. And now you are too dangerous to walk free, Dario."

"We need to talk more," he pushed. "You cannot give up on me, again."

"Talk is over," Sorensen said, his eyes moving to the syringe that would disable Dario.

"I was born to do what no one can or will do. I am needed by you more than ever."

"No, Dario. I don't need you. Joseph does not want you. Margaret will understand. And the group, you terrify them."

A blast of sleet washed over the cabin. The fire popped and the lantern flickered. "I changed my mind, Jocko. I'm not allowing you to put me away again."

Sorensen had crossed more lines in his life than he wanted to think about. He was drowning in the carnage and deception. "You need to sleep now," he whispered into the cold window pane. *You have no missions, and neither do I.* Sorensen reached for the syringe.

"Who will kill all the monsters, Jocko?" This time Dario's words tickled Sorensen's ear. Hot breath lifted Sorensen's sparse, white hair. In the frozen pane Sorensen saw the empty chair and the ropes on the floor. He blinked and Dario's evil eye came into focus above his ear.

Sorensen muttered, "What are you—"

Dario's arm snaked around the doctor's frail torso and tightened like a python. Before Sorensen could finish, the air squeezed from his lungs and his spine snapped like a rotten limb on an old tree. The doctor's paralyzed body slumped to the floor. His cheek pressed onto the cold wood. Unable to move he watched the cabin door open and a black coat lift in the sleet and fade into the night.

In five minutes Dr. Sorensen's eyeballs would be frozen stones.

TWO

"What does Wolfe say about the Fetter shooting?" The commander asked as he poured a cup and walked to the window where he took in the only city he ever knew, but never understood.

"Wolfe's on his way back," Hutson said as he rocked back in the swivel chair. Hutson was built exactly like Wolfe, even had the thick wavy brown hair. But that was where the resemblances stopped. Hutson did not possess Wolfe's savvy intellect, initiative, machoism, or basic physical strength.

"He's not talking," Hutson said under his breath. "You know Wolfe. But if you ask me, I think it's great the Fetter woman killed the bastard. She's been living in hell long enough."

"That's right. I gotta agree. Maybe now her nightmare can be over," Crowley said from his favorite place, the door jamb where he was half in and half out of the boss's office. Like most things in his life, he was not fully committed. Crowley's personality was somewhere between Hutson and Wolfe. He was the glue that held the threesome together. He forced Wolfe to be human and he often stopped Hutson from being an idiot.

"We all knew Ramsey would go after her if he ever got out," Crowley said. "And, in all fairness, we knew we couldn't stop him—too many things in our way."

"That's right," Hutson chimed. "Not a thing we could

have done to stop the man. There's just no rehabilitation for some of these sick people. Ramsey's a monster, mean all his life. He hurt a lot more people than we'll ever know. Now the world's a safer place."

"We're losing the war," Crowley added. "And we're losing damn near all the battles, too. We are overrun by crazies and tied up by laws and rules. We can't get the bad guys off the damn streets fast enough. It feels kinda good when one goes down. But honestly, I never expected the Fetter woman to come out on top of that one."

"Explain yourself," Commander Landers demanded as he kept looking out the window with his nose above his steaming cup of coffee. "What about Mrs. Fetter?"

"I don't have the details. I'm just reacting to Ramsey being shot and Fetter surviving the whole damn experience. I know the guy was in her bedroom when he got nailed."

What you don't know is Ramsey got shot by an unknown assailant, not Fetter, Landers thought. He had other sources at the crime scene. Now he had to wait for Wolfe.

"Okay. I got your input. If you two got nothing to do, I could—" He turned to the swivel chair spinning and door easing closed. Staring at the swinging door blinds his thoughts moved back to Aaron Wolfe—his top homicide detective. Landers knew the city ate up and spit out the good ones. Somehow Wolfe had survived.

Less than five-hundred homicides in Chicago was considered a good year. Crowley was right; the good guys were losing the war in all the major cities. Seemed like more and more of the battles were won by armed citizens desperate to protect themselves. The system no longer kept them safe enough. Something broke.

Another hour passed before the knuckle-rap jerked Landers eyes from his pile to the door. The rangy man with the bushy mustache, heavy overcoat, and gold badge swinging from his neck walked in without a word. The unshaven, rugged face and thick brown hair hung over Lander's desk with an empty stare. Wolfe stood there like a lion looking for raw meat.

"Have a seat," Landers ordered. He could read Wolfe's face. He carried the unbridled contempt in his dark eyes. But this time that was missing. This time Landers saw something new—uncertainty. If Wolfe was confused, it meant he would be talking even less than usual.

Wolfe did not allow distractions to get in the way of his investigations, especially the premature and speculative banter with authority figures. Landers knew the routine. For the next twenty-four hours Wolfe would digest his crime scene, consider the physical and circumstantial evidence, and weigh the truths and lies. Landers usually gave him plenty of room, but this time had to be different. This time the kill was not a routine homicide. This time Landers felt the kill could have far reaching implications.

"This one we're talking about," Landers said in his official voice. He pointed to the swivel chair in front of his messy desk.

Wolfe sat. His .45 long barrel gun pushed up his coat and his knees touched the desk overhang. "I don't have much to say," he huffed as he pushed his gun down and scanned the room like he was looking for something to shoot.

Landers flashed a smile and his eyes got serious on the battle-scarred face beneath salt-and-pepper hair. "Last time I checked, you worked for me Detective Wolfe." Landers sipped his coffee and set his cup down with a deliberate thud. "Tell me what you have."

"Not much more than you already got from your eyes at the crime scene and office scuttlebutt." Wolfe looked at his wrist even though he didn't own a watch anymore. He never replaced the one that stopped a bullet.

"You haven't had a watch for three years, Wolfe. I'm not doing this. You're gonna talk to me." The commander's eyes sharpened as he leaned back in his chair and made a triangle with his hands, the top point touching his nose.

"Not much new here. We have a known felon beating the goddamn system and returning to the scene of the crime six years later. Scumbag Ramsey killed Fetter's husband and raped her. I assume he wanted to violate her once again and kill her this time. Guess we'll never know."

"Keep going," Landers pushed.

"Eric Ramsey was shot between the eyes—back of his head blown off."

"Mrs. Fetter had a gun, didn't she?" Landers asked.

"She did. A Glock 9MM," Wolfe said as he looked away avoiding dialogue.

"Had it been fired?"

"Yes, but missed the target."

"Then who shot Eric Ramsey, Wolfe?"

"That's what I need to figure out." He turned back to Landers with eyes burning. "Our sniper's back. Ramsey was hit with a lot more than a 9MM hollow-point."

"Does that explain a face shot while between Mrs. Fetter's legs?"

"It could. CSI has bullet fragments. Could be a match to the .50 Barrett. They're working on trajectory analysis and blood spatter. There was an open window. CSI will have more for me tomorrow."

"We have enough of the bullet to—"

"—connect with the others? Yes."

Wolfe looked down at his gun. *You don't need to know now that Ramsey was not between Lindsey Fetter's legs when he got shot. I don't even know what she was doing when Ramsey was executed—I sure as hell don't need another thought process screwing up mine.*

But why did she deny the rape kit? And why did she lie about using the gun—her bullet missed by a few feet? All she kept saying was that she was in fear for her life. Lindsey Fetter shot an intruder in her bedroom. She had acted well within her rights. Seemed over rehearsed.

"The Glock, does it belong to Fetter?" Commander Landers asked.

"She says it's hers. We're looking into it. After being brutalized, watching her husband die, and living alone in fear for six years, I expect it to be her gun."

"Where'd she keep it?" Landers asked. Wolfe had the same suspicions.

"Under her pillow, loaded, she said." He eyed the pot. A diversion about now would be good. Their talk had gone way too long. "You mind if I get a coffee?"

"You don't drink coffee, remember?"

"Oh yeah, that's right." *Damn. I gotta do better than that.*

"Did Mrs. Fetter know Eric Ramsey got out on parole last week?"

"She got the courtesy call from the prosecutor's office—Hello, Mrs. Fetter. Your convicted husband killer and rapist paid his debt to society in just six years. Isn't that wonderful? Eric Ramsey is a new man. Oh yeah, he is also a free man capable of coming to see you. This call is just another service provided by your Chicago area justice system. Have a nice life."

Landers stared at Wolfe, his ire understandable. Regardless, the CPD had a job to do. Landers got all he was going to get from Wolfe, for now.

"Find the shooter, Wolfe. When you do, you may solve the other sniper cold cases. And find out how Mrs. Fetter fits into all this. Something stinks."

Wolfe got up and headed to the door reading a new text on his cell. It was from Lindsey Fetter. She had his personal number. The message was short—"WE NEED TO TALK."

THREE

"We've heard enough of the legal mumbo jumbo—due process, double jeopardy, search and seizure, and the exclusionary rule—the end results are the same too damn often. Victims get screwed." Robert Mason pulled off his wire glasses and studied the scratches he had rubbed a dozen times a day for the last three years. "This is all about serial intent."

It was trying to snow. The two sat on newspapers on a cold park bench in Lincoln Park looking at an empty lake across an empty Foster Avenue Beach. Charlie Dunn grew up in the cold—Michigan, the Dakotas, and Illinois. He and Beth preferred cold. Robert Mason came from the south—Texas—but he had lived in Chicago forty-two years, his Susan thirty. He just liked being outdoors. Now the two men were alone. For the last two years they met on the same park bench at the same time every day, but this time was more important.

"I hear what you're saying," Dunn said. "But I'm not comfortable yet." He relit his old cigar and puffed. His worn leather gloves clung to the fat wet stub he'd been working on since they sat down. The diversion seemed to help Dunn's nerves. They both had stayed up later than usual the night before—it was time to talk about it.

"How long's it been," Mason asked.

"Too damn long," Dunn shot back. "I'm starting to forget, Robert." He puffed more. "I guess I can't remember much of anything anymore. I think I'm finally losing it."

"You're not old. You're still in your sixties. Hell, we both workout, eat right, and take our vitamins. I read somewhere that sixty-five was the new fifty. It's not your age, Charlie. You're doing what I do. You're trying to forget the bad." Mason rubbed his eyes and slid on his scratched glasses. "It hurts, that's all."

"Been ten years," Dunn said. "I miss them. It's killing me inside a little every day."

"I know. It's a terrible thing."

"Why didn't they kill me that night too? I hate this."

"They tried," Mason said.

"They made me watch. My Billy tried to help. It was awful. I thought Billy had him, but then the other guy came from behind. He grabbed Billy and rammed his head into the wall. I don't know how many times. Billy was out cold the first time. Then all the blood. He was only fourteen. Why did they kill him? I tried to get loose. The ropes were too tight."

Dunn dropped his head and rubbed his eyes like he had just rolled out of bed. "They raped Beth in front of me." Dunn chewed harder on his cigar. His eyes found the frozen lake. "I didn't come out of my coma for six months. The attorneys kept saying Beth fell down the stairs trying to escape. Said that's what killed her. I don't know how those people came up with that. After the trial my memory came back. I saw them both violate and beat her to death. I saw them throw her down those stairs. How did those detectives and CSI people get it all wrong? Made it look like it was a damn accident, not a brutal act by two monsters. They never charged them for her death, just rape and my son's death. Their high-priced lawyers played all the games. What does someone have to do to get the electric chair?"

"They never got the electric chair in this state," Mason muttered. "Used to be lethal injection. They abolished the death penalty in Illinois in '99. Don't do this to yourself."

"It would have been better for me to die that night, Robert."

Now Mason stared at the empty frozen lake. He wished he had died too, but it didn't happen that way. "It all should have been over when they caught the monsters."

"There's no justice anymore. Victims get screwed everyday by the system."

"I read it in the newspaper, October 21st, 2006. I remember the headlines—*Solid Evidence on Double Homicide in Elmwood Park*. Said the prosecutor had everything—blood, DNA, fingerprints, fibers from clothing, and one of the victims survived—you! They had an eyewitness. The bastards ate your food, used your bathroom, and tracked blood everywhere leaving their shoe prints. It was a done deal. They caught them on the next day."

"None of it mattered in the end," Dunn said flicking his cigar ash.

"Well, the good news is one got killed before the arraignment—stabbed in a holding cell. He got it the old fashioned way, a knife in the gut. I remember the picture of the guy in the newspaper. He looked evil. Those eyes were cold and empty. Why don't people see these killers? They listed the guy's felonies in the paper. He had fifteen years of charges, jail time, and probation. The guy did it all: armed robbery, burglary, rape, and assault with a deadly weapon. Those are just the ones I remember. This is what I'm saying—serial intent."

"Yeah. Intentions are there all the time. But I saw it different," Dunn said.

"What do you mean?"

"For me it was bad news. That guy dying left Pender to face the charges alone. The defense attorneys used his partner's corpse to weave their lies to get Pender the minimum."

"I remember. They made the dead guy out to be the

bad guy. Pender was the innocent and unwilling participant. He was afraid to go against his partner for fear of his life."

"I watched Pender kill my son and attack my wife. I watched him laugh after they threw her down the stairs. They smiled when they came to finish me off."

"The prosecutor said the physical evidence confirmed Pender had raped and killed your wife, not the other guy." Mason knew the story well, but now he wanted Dunn to work through his pent-up emotions. Mason had important business to discuss.

"It didn't matter," Dunn said. "Took four years to get to trial. They threw out most of the physical evidence because of improper procedure. They claimed the other guy was the killer. They sold Pender as being dragged into the whole thing. The poor misunderstood guy was once again in the wrong place at the wrong time. He needed a break."

Mason shook his head in disgust. "Do these defense attorneys have any principles? Is it all about the money and getting someone off regardless of guilt?"

"The prosecutor said my testimony did not matter because I had been in a coma a long time. They said the defense would argue I had lost touch with reality. They would nullify my emotion-charged testimony claiming it had been invented by my brain under duress. They had psychiatrists ready to say—because the dead bastard was not around to pay for the crime I would do anything to get Pender convicted."

"The prosecutor's hands were tied because a lot of the physical evidence got thrown out—the exclusionary rule." Mason muttered.

"Somehow the CPD violated Pender's constitutional rights," Dunn said. "They explained it to me, but I never understood the ruling. I truly believe bullshit legal maneuvers stole justice." Dunn lit a new cigar and puffed off a half-inch.

"What about my son's constitutional rights to not be

killed in our home? What about Beth's constitutional rights not to be violated, beaten, and thrown down our stairs?"

Mason gave him some time to slow his heart rate and breathing. "The prosecution's case turned into nothing more than hearsay," Mason said. "The legal system failed again. It took away the only eyewitness—you—and the most damning physical evidence. This is not how it's supposed to be. Your horrific life experience is another American tragedy. Convicting Pender should have been a slam-dunk."

"I thought the 'plea bargain' was a good thing. The prosecutor threatened to go to trial for murder one—life in prison, no chance for parole. The defense agreed to a lesser charge to avoid the trial. I thought we won, but we lost. The plea bargain was murder without intent to cause bodily harm or death. There was no rape charge. Still, Pender was supposed to go to jail forty years without chance for parole. I said do the deal. But it changed after all that."

"They found evidence of rape later," Mason said. "Wasn't it an oversight, a mistake? They could have gone back after Pender with it."

"They found it three months after sentencing," Dunn mumbled.

"Found what exactly?" Mason asked.

"Pender's semen—his DNA. It was recovered from my wife."

"The one piece of evidence handled according to proper procedure was misplaced?"

"It proved Pender lied about everything. He was not watching. He was an active and willing participant."

"Misplacing the evidence was a prosecutorial error," Mason said.

"Couldn't do anything with it. They call it 'double jeopardy'. Pender could not be tried twice. He was already convicted." Dunn tossed his new cigar into the melting snow. "Turned out the plea bargain worked against my family, too."

Mason cleared his throat and sat up straight for the first time all morning. "Charlie, we need to talk about last night."

Dunn felt his pockets for another cigar. "I don't want to talk about last night. I'm having second thoughts. We need to go back to the group."

"'Crime Victims Together' did not help us. I got worse. It drained me emotionally. I felt even more helpless."

"It's a process we gotta give time. Those people mean well. They help with law reform, strengthen sentencing, and they really try to protect the rights of victims and survivors. Nobody's gonna make us feel better, Robert. It's what we're gonna carry the rest of our lives."

Mason slid his hands deep into his coat pockets and leaned back on the cold park bench. "I read this year there are more than five-million criminals out of jail early. They're on probation or parole. In Chicago ninety percent of the killers are people with criminal records."

"Ninety percent?" Dunn gasped. "That proves serial intent is real."

"There were more than five-hundred people killed in Chicago this year. I'm no expert, but it sure seems like nothing's working right around here."

"Things are getting worse."

"Politicians haven't fixed much for decades. Every day I read about terrible homicides, and I watch convicted killers get pitiful sentences—ten to twenty years for killing someone. Then they get out early. It's like no one's watchin' so let's let 'em out."

"They are animals—predators. Many can't be rehabilitated. They will kill over and over."

"A city crawling with predators, they're getting away with murder," Mason said. "I guess their constitutional rights are more important than ours. The legal system seems to allow blatant manipulation. Solid physical evidence gets thrown out every day because of one legal trick or another—the hell with what it proves! Eyewitnesses disappear—who cares. When they do show up, their testimony is minimized. They are nervous but made to look like fools."

"It's a miracle when a killer actually gets stopped." Dunn huffed.

"And all this crap costs taxpayers millions a day."

"Damn mess," Dunn muttered.

"It's getting worse, Charlie. Don't forget I lost my wife, too. The legal system let me down, too. I'm not looking for revenge. I'm waiting for Whitten to get out. I'm gonna have justice. But now I feel like I gotta do something."

Charlie walked into the snow and picked up his discarded cigar. He slid it into his coat pocket and returned to the park bench. The white morning sky started to spit ice crystals. The forecast said possible snow. "I can't believe I tossed a perfectly good Vintage cigar," he mumbled as he avoided the topic.

Mason waited for Dunn to settle back into his warm spot on the bench and relight his cigar. "You know who's getting out this weekend, Charlie?"

Dunn jerked his shoulders back. Nothing more had to be said. "Are you sure?"

Mason nodded. "James Harvey Pender is getting out on parole after serving six years of his pitiful thirteen year sentence for killing your son and your wife. Is this the kind of justice we gotta accept? Society has dropped the ball, Charlie. You know I'm right."

Dunn turned back to the frozen lake puffing on his Vintage cigar. A gust swept through the empty park flapping their coats. Another veil of light sleet entered from the northeast.

"I'm ready to talk about last night," Dunn growled.

FOUR

"The modern world is an unforgiving place. Hesitation is the path to extinction."

"Did you know there are fifteen-hundred-miles of electric wiring in this building?" Jennings Babcock sat in his wheelchair looking out the window of the Babcock, Boyle & Braden Law offices that took up the 97th floor of the Willis Tower.

"That's good to know. Really glad you shared that factoid, father." Eldon signed another document and slid it into a waiting file. There were a dozen more on his desk.

"Only twenty-five miles of plumbing. They needed sixty times more wire than pipe."

Eldon rolled his eyes as he signed another. "Is there a reason you came in today?"

"Show some respect, son."

"I'm sorry. I meant no disrespect."

He looked over the city of Chicago that—like everything else—had changed so much. "They call me 'Old Man' Jennings around here. I still have ears in the office, yah know."

"I've never heard it. The people respect you. They know you are the founding patriarch."

The sprawling offices of Brayden, Boyle, & Babcock were dark and empty, except for behind the door of the CEO. Typically the partners worked Sundays to catch up.

Weekdays were wall-to-wall court appearances and client meetings. But now they rarely came in on weekends. The staff of forty-two had been cut down to thirty mid-year, and the caseload at BB&B continued to decline. High-priced accountants projected severe financial consequences if revenues did not grow by eighteen percent, or expenses decrease by twenty-two.

"Yes. I'm here for a reason," Jennings said. "The controlling partners met."

"Really? I didn't get the invitation. Rules say the CEO must be present."

"You have ninety days to right the ship, son."

Eldon dropped his Mont Blanc and leaned back in his $5,000 leather chair. His smile melted. "Are you serious? They think eliminating me will fix the problems in the world?"

"You decide what clients we take, son."

"Believe me when I say that is not the root cause of our financial problems. Corporate law is strong—my area of expertise. We have major clients with solid futures—intellectual property management, mergers and acquisitions, regulatory affairs, and branding now represent sixty percent of our revenue stream. It's growing."

"We understand. Unfortunately, growth is too slow with the existing base. New clients in that segment are not coming on board fast enough to offset losses with the other forty percent. This did not happen overnight. We all saw it coming. We've discussed it before."

"Civil litigation, environmental law, bankruptcy, labor relations, and foreclosure law are stagnant. E-discovery is an investment in the future. It will be here in another few years."

"That is still only another ten percent of our portfolio. I noticed you left out the other thirty percent. That omission is the problem. You avoid dealing with—"

"I never liked criminal law," Eldon barked. He

returned to signing documents.

"That's where the firm is hemorrhaging." Jennings tugged at the plaid blanket on his lap and reached for his brandy. As he sipped he studied the man he dreamed would one day takeover the law firm he had built, a lifelong effort that almost killed him. It took every ounce of courage he could muster and a lot of luck. Jennings never considered himself a smart man. He was slower than most. But Jennings was a problem solver. He always found a path to success.

"Criminal law is the high growth segment we are missing," Jennings said. "You can't fix the firm without dealing with it."

"Are we going there again?" Eldon sighed.

"You need to get over your *ethics problem*. I am not old school. It is you who is not being realistic. It is you not being a good businessman in today's environment, and that is why your head is on the chopping block. BB&B must have a CEO willing to make CEO decisions. The modern world is an unforgiving place. Hesitation is the path to extinction."

"We don't want to go backward," Eldon said. "It is time for the founding partners to step aside. The 'modern world' you refer to is very different. Your old ways do not work anymore. We have established a legitimate legal practice in this modern world. We cannot go back to smoke filled rooms to make deals with the devil. Some got away with it in the past, but most did not. Few of those law practices exist today." Eldon poured more brandy and joined his father by the window. "I hope you're not going where I think you're going with this."

Everything about Jennings Babcock was dead or dying. The old attorney lost mobility ten years ago, a fall and failed surgery. He lost weight to stomach cancer. He lost hair and teeth to chemotherapy, and he lost his fourth wife to a younger man with legs. The only things left were his sight, hearing, law practice, and son. He held tight onto all four although they were all fading.

"Sometimes a man's principles can get in the way of good business decisions, son."

Eldon smiled. "There are no more 'necessary evils', father." He sat on the windowsill and looked at the city lights gaining strength as the skies darkened. Ice crystals sprayed the glass, and new ribbons of heat rose from floor vents creating a false sense of security in the cold world.

"We're not dealing with mafia or drug lords," Eldon said. "If I cannot appeal to your sense of ethics, maybe I can educate you on the new world dangers. Today is not like the fifties. Too many people are watching too many things—too many eyes in the sky. There are moles and whistle blowers, advanced technologies, monitoring devices, financial tracking systems, and a new mountain of government regulations. All must be successfully navigated by everyone in the firm. The risk of losing everything we've built at any moment is great. We cannot be stupid."

"I have a way out of our financial problems, Eldon. You need to hear me out." Jennings held out his glass waiting for a refill. He acted as if he hadn't heard a word his son said.

With a grimace, Eldon poured. "You remember the James Pender case, father."

"Of course," Jennings snapped. "I don't want to talk about it. You are missing the point, the opportunity."

"Does it bother you that that piece of human garbage got away with cold-blooded murder?" Eldon waited for some kind of answer.

Jennings sipped. "We followed the letter of the law. We defended our client. That is how it works. Defense attorneys defend. It is not our right to determine someone's guilt or innocence. You know this to be true. Why are you challenging the concept now?"

"Is that how you sleep at night? We bastardized the

law. We tied the justice system into a series of well-crafted, intricate knots that essentially screwed the innocent people. We not only knew Pender committed the gruesome crime, we knew he did so with wicked enjoyment. We knew Pender was an evil man.

"What did we do? I'll tell you. We found loopholes to keep damning physical evidence away from the jury. We silenced the poor man—the father and husband—who Pender made watch as he killed the son and raped and killed the wife. Where is the humanity in that?" Eldon shook his head staring at his face in his spit-polished wingtips. "I'm ashamed of myself."

"Nonsense. We did our job. We put on a vigorous defense, as we are supposed to do for our clients. Everyone is innocent until proven guilty. It is the prosecution's job to prove guilt, not our job to prove innocence. Have you forgotten the fundamentals? Our job is to raise doubt. No sir. It is the prosecution who should be ashamed. They did the poor job. They let a guilty man get away with murder—a ridiculous plea bargain and a ridiculous sentence."

"Pender is a monster." Eldon seethed inside. He had learned long ago to hide his feelings from the crippled man who could justify anything.

"We don't know that, son. You think that."

"God only knows how many other women he violated and killed in his disgusting life. He is not done. We made it possible." With contempt in his heart he leaned into the old man. "You made me take that case. Know this, the day Pender received his pathetic sentence I made a promise to myself. I would never represent a predator—one with serial intent—again."

Jennings looked away as if the declaration did not matter. "I would not turn my back on a friend. The Marcantonio family needed my help. They were there for me when I needed them. In the beginning, I was one of a hundred lawyers in the city struggling to survive. I needed someone to believe in me. William T. Marcantonio was a very big man in the city. He gave me a chance. If he had not, none of this would be here. Your mother would have never married me. You would not exist."

Eldon downed his brandy contemplating his likely removal as CEO. He knew his ethics and business focus would not deliver the kind of numbers the board demanded. He knew it was only a matter of time before he would be moved aside.

Are you that different from me, old man? Eldon thought. *Or is it my success that makes me the ethical man in the room? Does my wealth and position give me false values? Would I have them if I was poor and desperate? I don't even know how that feels. But now, knowing I could lose everything, will I compromise? Will I rationalize? Will I do anything to keep it? God! Is the threat alone enough to generate doubt? Am I a fake? Maybe I'm no better than my crippled father with the twisted values, the man who knew fear and desperation. Maybe I am no better than the man who made everything in my life possible, even my ethics.*

"You need to let it go, son," Jennings said under his breath.

"If Pender had not been employed by the Marcantonio family, he would be serving a life sentence," Eldon said. "We never would have been involved. His victims would have justice."

"You don't know that. Another law firm would have had the same opportunities to dismiss physical evidence and negotiate a plea bargain."

Eldon did not hear his father. "And Pender would not kill again."

"I saw you just got him paroled," Jennings said.

"He gets out in a few days," Eldon said as he blinked back into the room. "I pray he does not kill again. Regardless, your debt to William W. Marcantonio has been paid in full."

"Wires and pipe, son," Jennings said holding out his glass for another refill.

Eldon poured more brandy. "I'm worried about you, father."

"You're focused on wires, son. You need to focus on pipes."

"What in the hell does that mean?"

"It takes sixty times more wire than pipe to get a job done."

"Nice metaphor—the Willis Tower and your opening comments. I'm not quite sure about the relevance."

"William Marcantonio called me last week. He needs our help."

The blowers shut down leaving the rasping sleet on the twenty-foot glass windows of the sprawling corner office. Eldon looked up from his drink, his brow dipped.

"He is willing to pay a lot of money. He liked how we handled the Pender case. The retainer alone will be enough to right our ship. Your position as CEO would be secured."

Eldon got to his feet. "You say Mr. Marcantonio liked our handling of the Pender case? Now I feel a whole lot better. Have you heard a single word?"

"We have a law firm to run," Jennings said. "We represent clients. We defend people. It is our job to build cases and argue in a court of law on behalf of our clients. The prosecutors have their jobs. The judges and juries have their jobs. No. Have you heard a word I've said?"

Eldon returned to his chair and sunk into the soft cushions. Staring into the shadow under his enormous mahogany desk, he rubbed the growing ache in his neck.

"Something's very wrong with our country's system of justice," he said as if he were standing alone looking in a mirror. "It was never intended to hurt the innocent and free the criminals." His eyes found his father. "It's happening too often across the country. The scales of justice are broken. I've been reading about it. Legal scholars are debating the new phenomenon. Many argue the justice system is overdue an overhaul—what once had its flaws is now broken. Too many high-priced lawyers know how to work it. We can tie it into knots. We know how to run the table. We can break the bank. Like Vegas, some of us 'card counters' should not be allowed in a courtroom. We need to be better regulated. And if it can be done without jeopardizing the accused, we need to revisit the concept—innocent until proven guilty."

"You're talking nonsense. We use the legal system we have today. That simple."

"Even the most sophisticated and complex systems in the world need revisions, upgrades, adjustment, rebooting." Eldon said.

"Our legal system is special," Jennings barked.

"Like everything else, it must evolve in this changing world," Eldon said. "Tort reform is too slow of a process. We're all busy playing the game and chasing the money."

"It is what we have to work with today," Jennings puffed as he wheeled over to Eldon's chair. He bumped his knees into the soft leather to get his son's attention. "I know you're uncomfortable. I've been there in my life. It's part of being the top man with the responsibility. I ask you to just meet with William Marcantonio. It is possible the arrangement he seeks can work. It may be nothing like the Pender case."

I never understood why Marcantonio wanted to help Pender in the first place, Eldon thought. *I remember that sick smirk on Pender's face when he told me everything he did to the Dunn family—Marcantonio ordered him not to lie to his attorney. I remember walking out of that cell and puking in the parking garage. I should have gotten in my car and kept driving. I should have disappeared—the hell with the legal profession. Nothing can excuse what I did. Now I've gotta live with it.*

Jennings whispered as he squeezed Eldon's arm. "I

need you to meet with Marcantonio." Eldon blinked back into the present and nodded.

"Good. I will set it up and let you know. I think this can work for all of us."

Eldon's eyes found his father's. "James Harvey Pender is symbolic of a much larger problem we all face. We are at a tipping point."

FIVE

Wolfe stopped at the edge of the light pouring out the back of the ambulance onto the dark field filling with snow. He studied the bloody man in handcuffs sitting on the tailgate surrounded by paramedics and Chicago's finest. The man's eyes were swollen closed like a prizefighter after ten grueling rounds—a fight he lost. Wolfe estimated late thirties. The man sat still except for occasional chest heaves. Each time he sucked in air, it was as if he just remembered to breath. Each time the man's body stiffened like a carp, CPD gun fingers twitched over holsters.

After working hundreds of homicides, Wolfe knew all kinds of killers and missed little. Standing at his latest spectacle, he was the only one who knew the cuffed man did not kill anyone this night. Whoever did was still out there and could be enjoying the show.

The lead paramedic recognized Wolfe—their paths had crossed many times before. He backed away from the medical team and spoke out of earshot. "Looks bad but none of his wounds are life threatening. Most of the blood came from the victim." The medic leaned into Wolfe and whispered, "If you ask me, something else has traumatized this man. He's not acting like a killer caught at the scene of his crime. However, I'm no expert."

"What's your plan Conway?" Wolfe asked with eyes on the catatonic manikin.

"We're gonna take our time. He's on the edge—shock

induced from acute stress."

"What's your plan?" Wolfe asked again with a sharper edge.

"We'll push fluids. He's medicated—will let that take hold. I'll give him ten minutes or so to calm down before we do anything. We could screw things up if we move him now. I want to avoid medical consequences. Been a long day."

Wolfe's eyes followed the IV line from the bloody arm to the bag of Ringer's lactate. "Unless he's dying, the man doesn't leave here until I talk to him. We good?"

"We're good," Conway said as he returned to his medical team.

Before Wolfe could check his phone for messages—something relevant to his next mystery—a bouncing light pushed through the cluster of pines by the ambulance. Wolfe smiled when he saw the man in blue carrying a flashlight and clipboard forging a new trail in the snow. It meant his crime scene could still be intact.

"You Aaron Wolfe, homicide?"

"I am."

"Lieutenant Huddle—first responder." He pointed to the trees. "Wunders Cemetery. You need to come with me before the snow changes things too much more."

They rounded the thick pines and walked Huddle's trail toward the portable floods on tripods. The lights were set up in the middle of the ten acres of tombstones, cement crosses, and stick trees. Long shadows draped over the snow-dusted grounds. Flashlights bounced and dogs barked on the perimeter of Wolfe's next hell. He scanned the markers on both sides of the isolated row pleased the CPD had protected the original route to the crime scene.

The macabre setting only pissed him off more. In silence, Wolfe knelt over the body and took in everything like no other could. Huddle gave Wolfe a moment and then started into the basics. "We have a thirty-eight-year-old white female—Miss Ellen Dumont. She lived in the 3700 block on North Sheffield Avenue—a brownstone two blocks away. At the moment, we don't know what she was doing out here in the middle of the night."

"Walking her dog and visiting her parents," Wolfe muttered. "Where's the ME?"

"Medical examiner's on the way. Should be here any minute," Huddle said. "How do you know about a dog and parents, detective?"

Wolfe moved his penlight from her face to her wrist. "The leather leash." He lifted her coat sleeve an inch and pulled the strap from under her body. Huddle backed away when he saw the attached bloody collar. "Her dog's out there somewhere. A little guy. Probably dead."

"You said visiting her parents." Huddle swallowed hard.

Wolfe aimed his penlight at a nearby tombstone. "We passed it. Marion and Benjamin Dumont, they died three years ago on this day. Most likely an automobile accident—they were both in their seventies. Ellen Dumont took her dog for a walk tonight to say goodnight to them on the anniversary of their death."

The lieutenant flipped a page and kept writing. "If the dog's here, we'll find 'em."

Wolfe hovered over the body with a slow light studying every minute detail. His education was not typical for a homicide investigator. Wolfe had a Masters in forensic science and another in criminology. Another minute with a body and Wolfe would know more than most investigators could reconstruct in a week.

"Miss Dumont was stabbed in the chest," Huddle said.

Wolfe opened the torn coat with a gloved hand to study the wounds without disturbing the evidence for the ME. There were two knife wounds. One was a superficial cut on the neck—the carotid. The other was a deep penetration wound to the heart. Most don't know the near-center anatomical location of the organ. This killer did.

As Wolfe's light stayed on the chest wound, Huddle provided more information. "We are looking for the knife. We think the guy we're holding tossed it out here. We'll find it."

"You have an ID on the guy in cuffs?" Wolfe asked.

"Yes sir. Mr. Barry Woods, an attorney, West Town Legal. He called 911 on his cell. Before he stopped talking, he said he lived with Dumont."

"Did he say anything else?"

"He kept saying over and over—he got away. I think he got in a fight with his girlfriend and stabbed her. He's got her blood all over him."

Wolfe got back to his feet and stood over the body scanning the cemetery. "Mr. Woods is not our guy, Lieutenant."

"How can you be so sure?" Huddle asked.

"The boyfriend got here after the fact."

"I don't understand."

"Woods got into a fight with the killer. Ellen Dumont was already dead. He came upon the guy raping his dead girlfriend. I just don't know his route because of the disturbances."

"You got all that in five minutes?"

Wolfe turned to Huddle with steady eyes. "Ten minutes. Barry Woods has defensive knife wounds on his hands and arms. His face is beaten to a pulp. That enormous egg on the back of his head is probably what saved his life—knocked him out over there." Wolfe aimed his light at a tombstone. "See the blood and torn up turf? That's where most of the fight took place after Woods dragged the killer off his girlfriend. Woods fought hard. He fell. Hit his head on the bloody edge of that tombstone." Wolfe turned away. "Make sure the forensic boys get it."

"I'm no expert, but it seems to me it could be possible Woods and Dumont had a fight."

"Do you think Barry Woods got all those wounds from defending himself against Ellen Dumont's vicious knife attack? Dumont was killed without rage. She had two wounds. One wound held her captive—the knife to her neck. When she started to fight, he knew exactly where to put his knife, the center of her heart, a single thrust—done. That's not rage or passion. That's a cold-blooded murder and postmortem sexual assault."

Huddle rubbed his chin as dogs barked in the distance and flashlights merged.

"If Woods and Dumont lived together, Woods did not need to drag her out here with her dog to have sex with her dead body," Wolfe said as he turned back to the girl. "That little lady did not give Barry Woods the beating I just saw."

"How do you know sex happened after death?" Huddle asked.

"The ME will confirm. For me it's an educated guess. I've seen it before, the way she's laying there. Her arms and legs—it's not a living position. I don't know how else to describe it."

Huddle flipped another page and made another note. Wolfe checked his cell phone. "Mr. Woods was in an intense battle. I suspect he did not know his girlfriend was dead until after he regained consciousness and had instinctively called 911. When he discovered she was dead, he slid into a catatonic state—shock. The man just lost the girl of his dreams in the most hideous of ways, Lieutenant. The young attorney is not a necrophiliac or killer."

"I've heard about you, Detective Wolfe," Huddle said. "Good to know someone can help the rest of us figure this stuff out."

"Appreciate that, Lieutenant. Truth is I'm lost most of the time." Wolfe patted Huddle's shoulder and turned away. "We need a tent over Miss Dumont. Snow's gonna screw up forensics and irritate Winston Foster. The field agent for the ME is good and most particular."

Wolfe scanned the cemetery of shadows and bobbing lights like a wild animal sensing a presence. *Something's just not right*, he thought as he backed away from the crime scene. Huddle and a cluster of blues would erect a tent. Wolfe knelt down behind the grave marker on the next row. From there he moved a slow light and discovered more blood.

It was a few drops on a dry oak leaf protected from the snow behind a gravestone. The drops on the leaf told a story. The tails of the drops pointed Wolfe in the direction of the fleeing killer—that was all he needed. Next he found a boot mark on the next row, again the dry side of the headstone—the assailant made a four foot leap to avoid leaving a print in the snow. *It was snowing when you killed her. You went west staying on the dry ground.*

The police dogs and flashlights merged at the north end of the cemetery. There they formed a line from the east to west borders and moved south sweeping the area. Wolfe followed blood droplets west from Ellen Dumont's body. A row of thick evergreen shrubs came into view and behind them an eight-foot stone wall.

At first Wolfe did not see the man in the shadows. When he looked up from the boot track in the snow, the silhouette of a man took shape between the shrubs, and then a cracking sound filled the cold night air. It was like a single lightning strike on a hot summer night. The sound seemed to roll from the east, and then a sizzle in the air zipped past Wolfe's ear hitting the silhouette. Wolfe dropped to his knees and lowered his head—he had an idea of what happened. He could be next. From behind a large tombstone, Wolfe watched the man fall to the ground. Wolfe aimed his flashlight. The back of the man's head was gone.

SIX

"I think something's gonna happen, Sarge. Maybe something we're not planning on." Officer Stahl typed more instructions and waited. The micro-POD turned forty-five degrees. A few seconds later it zoomed in on the dilapidated hotel less than a mile away.

Sergeant Irwin pulled his coffee mug out of the microwave and blew in it as he joined Stahl at the screens.

"We've been watchin' this place a couple weeks," Stahl said. "I questioned our initial information, but I've got a feeling."

"Convince me we should not abort," Irwin said. "I've got a long list of hot spots and people all over my butt." He checked his watch. "I've got eight hours to put five new PODs into play and to reassign a dozen others. This is one of them."

The experimental police observation devices (PODs) were introduced to the city in 2001—the "eyes in the sky" program. The new technology gave the CPD real-time surveillance capability. They deployed the first PODs in the highest crime areas and saw success. New and improved micro-PODs were released six years later. The wireless systems were bulletproof and had night vision. It allowed the program to expand to another hundred rooftops and towers around the city. Squad cars were equipped with monitors and joysticks for PODs in their areas. The CPD had dedicated staff at each station for 24/7 surveillance.

When the POD program was tied to street intelligence, they experienced a significant drop in crime.

"Sarge, I saw somethin' move in the shadows on the east side of the hotel." Stahl's fingers pecked across the keyboard like a concert pianist. The video feed was one block on the top-right of the giant monitor. It zoomed in on a shadowed section.

Irwin squinted over Stahl's wiry hair. They stared at the shadow in silence.

"Refresh my memory. Exactly what are we doing with POD 1282? Why're we watching this broken down, cheap hotel on West 26th?"

Stahl opened the fat binder beside him and flipped a dozen plastic-sheeted pages. He stopped and ran a finger down the center of one with a squeak. "Actually, we're watchin' the abandoned trailer sitting on the vacant lot behind the hotel. Vehicular access to our target site is on West 27th." He turned back to the screen. "I don't see any activity now."

"So, we're supposed to monitor a parked semi-truck trailer with no cab as a possible new drop site for the South Side?"

"Yes sir."

At any given time there were two-hundred PODs available for operation. Assignment requests for PODs came from all departments and included definition of target sites, observation timing parameters, and objectives. Each POD assignment had to be approved by Sergeant Irwin. He was doing good to remember fifty actives at any given time. Another fifty PODs around the city were available to squad cars on an "as needed" basis. Activation of a POD by an officer required approval of the on duty POD manager—Officer Stahl.

"What's the story here?" Irwin asked as he had a hundred times before. The on-duty POD manager is responsible for knowing all assignments in his sector.

"Illegal drugs: blow, casper, green dragons, apache—"

"Use English please," Irwin huffed.

"Sorry. Crack cocaine, assorted depressants, fentanyl, methamphetamine, and heroin to name a few." Stahl pointed to the trailer in the center of the lot. It was surrounded by a healthy crop of four-foot weeds busting through the crumbling tarmac. Two street lights lit half the trailer and a small area in the back.

"Intelligence thinks it could be the new primary drop site they've been looking for. They can account for about half the trafficking routes into the South Side."

"Is that a fact?" Irwin said into his coffee mug. *Probably just another rabbit hole.*

"That trailer's been sittin' there about two months. We've been watching it for twelve days. As expected, there's been a lot of gang activity in the quadrant. Unexpected, no one got near that trailer. That supports our theory a mafia family is controlling the site."

"You were expecting some gang visits?" Irwin asked knowing the answer.

"Yes. They don't leave new rocks unturned long in their territories. The DEA diversion people confirmed it. The trailer is off limits. They want to see who goes there."

"Narcotic arrests are down forty percent," Irwin said as he pulled a chair up to Stahl's workstation. "People are saying it's gotta be because the DEA is doing all the work or because the CPD narc division is less active. They don't give credit for better training, better intelligence, or better technology." Irwin set his mug on the file cabinet and studied the video feed. The site was well lit for a drug drop site. "Who owns the property?" he asked.

Stahl looked back at his master binder. "The vacant lot behind the South Loop Hotel is one of three lots on that road. They are owned by the Babcock, Boyle & Brayden Law Firm."

"A law firm? Are you sure?"

Stahl unlocked a metal file drawer and pulled out a fat phonebook-like reference manual. He flipped the tissue-paper pages and scoured the small print with a magnifying glass. "Nope. Take it back, Sarge. Owned by William T. Marcantonio."

"Willy Tee, the Chicago mafia kingpin. His name seems to pop up whenever somethin' really clandestine surfaces in the South Side of the city. Been that way for decades."

"His name's on the deed of trust for each of the three properties. He holds legal title as security for an unnamed debt."

"I wonder why the BB&B law firm is in debt to Marcantonio." Irwin got up and looked out the window at the snow swirling under the street lights. "Regardless of how this goes down, I want to know more about that cozy arrangement," he said. "We will need to pass it on to our DEA people."

"I think you need to watch this," Stahl gasped. "What're the chances?"

"Chances for what?" Irwin broke from his daze and spun around to the screen. The two watched headlights turn off West 27th and crawl up to the gate, the beams reaching into the lot and touching the trailer. "Since I've taken over, I've never seen one real time."

"I knew they'd come sooner or later, but not while we were sitting here talking about them," Stahl said.

They watched a man get out of the car. His coat lifted in the wind. He hunkered over with his hands in his coat pockets and flapping tails. Standing at the gate he looked east and west.

"The sleet hitting the city must be coming down stronger there."

"Bet it's stinging," Irwin muttered. They watched the man open the chain-link gate and wave to the sedan. It crawled up next to the trailer and the lights went off.

"The guy who opened the gate has a limp," Stahl said.

"That could be important later," Irwin said. "Go to full screen."

Stahl pounded commands on the keyboard. The video expanded and filled the fifty-inch screen. The POD zoomed in. Night vision flickered and adjusted. Two men got out of the car and joined the limper. The three walked to the rear of the trailer and looked around.

"Okay boys," Irwin said under his breath. "Open the doors. Show us what you got."

"This is the first time anyone's been on that lot since we've been monitoring." Stahl's finger trembled over the mouse. The three just stood there. "What are they waiting for?"

"Better get our people there now," Irwin ordered. *I could use a success this month.* "Tell them we have activity. We'll wait on getting DEA involved. Let's see what we have first."

Stahl picked up the phone as Irwin leaned in for a closer look—a crime was getting ready to happen. His eyes moved down to the rolling numbers at the bottom of the screen—02.14.07.49 and counting. The hour and minutes hung solid. The seconds ticked off methodically, but the milliseconds rolled by relentlessly, like the years of Irwin's life. Just yesterday he had joined the force and started a family. Thirty-five years later he was looking at mandatory retirement and a miserable life in a one-bedroom apartment with only pictures of the family he lost to the shield. His depression—and liver condition—were being treated, but progress had been slow. Drinking was the only escape that worked.

He estimated they had less than five minutes to move. Successful drug operations happen fast to minimize exposure. The operation he studied in the monitor was a drug inspection operation—there were too few to transport. His guess was two drones (workers) and an entry-level wannabe, a family member or junior boss. Irwin was leaning toward a junior boss, a scumbag with a record the family had been grooming, someone who owed them, someone who would commit heinous acts with no hesitation or questions.

"This is Officer Ben Stahl, POD. We have possible criminal activity in progress. Location is South Side, 300 block of West 27th. We have an unmarked semi-trailer parked in a vacant lot and three visitors. We've been watching this target for twelve days—suspected drug drop site. Dispatch three squad cars immediately, no lights or sirens until on West 27th. Activate mobile monitors, POD 1282 to observe in transit."

"They're opening the doors," Irwin barked. Stahl hung up and turned back to the screen. "One went back to the car. He's opening the trunk—looks like they will be taking something with them. How far out are we?"

"They are close." Stahl scanned the screen pecking at the keyboard. He was an expert. The image sharpened. The contrast adjusted. Then he saw it. "Sarge. The shadow. It's back."

Irwin's eyes moved from the trailer to the shadow on the east edge of the hotel. "I got him. Is there a chain-link fence between the properties?"

"A six-footer with another two feet of coiled barbed wire on top. Seems a bit much."

Irwin smiled. "Guess the hotel got tired of guest automobiles getting ripped off."

"I got that impression when I visited the target site prior to approval," Stahl said.

"The guy next to the hotel appears to be quite interested in our three visitors. Give me a quick biometric scan," Irwin ordered.

Stahl worked the keyboard with his fat fingers. Instantly a series of inlaid green circles with graduation marks found the man and proceeded to rotate opposite directions searching for definitive image markers. When the dialing stopped, the brilliant green turned into throbbing red. The info-box popped onto the screen with rolling numbers populating three of the ten lines.

"Only three data points," Irwin whined.

"He's a Caucasian. Six-four and 240 pound range. A mesomorph—someone with a muscular build." Stahl turned from the screen. "I got that with my own two eyes," he boasted. Irwin did not react. "There are no facials and no hair color. I believe the sleet's messin' with the POD lens."

They watched their mystery man leave the edge of the hotel like a lion stalking its prey. He crouched down at the fence. "I need a facial," Irwin demanded.

"That's the best we can do. Bad weather and the target's almost a mile from the POD."

"We gotta have one closer. Find it now."

"We do, but it is not the ideal view or it would have been selected."

"Just find me one." Irwin clasped his hands and squeezed.

Stahl searched on another monitor. "I do remember DEA asking for a view from the south. I did not ask why."

"I know the protocol," Irwin barked. "Look fast, Lieutenant. We don't have time." He leaned closer to the monitor as if he would see the mystery man's face better. "He's not spying on them," Irwin muttered. "I think he's waiting to pounce."

"Got one—a closer POD. A tower a quarter mile away, but it is east of the property. I'm bringing it up now." Stahl typed a flurry of commands. The large picture on the neighboring monitor flickered and transformed into a split screen. The new video joined the other and came alive. Stahl's fingers crawled across the keyboard. The eastern view zoomed and focused on the coordinates.

The crouched man jumped the chain-linked fence and coiled barbed wire. He disappeared in the tall weeds twenty yards from the trailer. The three heads turned and froze.

"Did you see that?" Irwin whispered. "Is that even possible?"

Stahl didn't blink. His lips did not move when he spoke. "That guy cleared eight feet from a squatting position. I don't understand it."

The second POD followed the movement and auto-adjusted resolution. When the picture cleared, another sheet of sleet crossed the lot moving toward the hotel.

"We need to know who that man is, Stahl. This is not going to end well. Where in the hell are our people?"

"They gotta be very close. It's been almost five minutes."

On Lieutenant Stahl's last word, the east POD flickered and went out.

"What the hell happened?" Irwin boomed as he straightened his aching back and rubbed his aching neck. "It went out fast. That was an instant failure. Something hit that POD."

"Maybe a bird or large hail ball hit it." He typed a flurry of commands, but kept his eyes on the original POD video feed.

"There's no hail out there, Stahl. It's sleet."

"I think the three guys see him. Our people just turned onto 27th."

The mystery man exploded out of the tall weeds and charged the three men standing behind the trailer. Stahl's fingers stopped pecking. Irwin's hands dropped to his side.

"Oh God," Stahl sighed.

Seconds later the original POD video stream flickered out. Both men stared at the black monitor in silence.

SEVEN

"When was the last time you saw him, Mrs. Sorensen?"

Detective Joe Hutson sat in the small living room of the old brownstone surrounded by antiques and faded colors and perfume smells that reminded him of his grandmother and his childhood—nobody would ever hurt Pop and Gram. He watched the one log smolder on the pile of scattered embers. It sizzled in the fireplace moments away from being engulfed.

Margaret Sorenson did not look at the fireplace. She stared out the window and halfway listened to the third visitor from the police department. She had called them Saturday morning. Jacques was not in his room. He normally stayed up late, but he was always the first one out of bed. Jacques was one of those who only needed a couple hours of sleep. Margaret had learned to live with his twenty-hour days, but she still needed her eight hours. The difference worked in the beginning. Fifty-two years later it had led to separate bedrooms.

This time breakfast was ready before she knocked on his door. The bed had not been slept in. There were no notes. Jacques rarely used his cell phone. Her calls went directly to messages. But she had an idea where he was . . .

"Mrs. Sorensen, I'm sorry to go back over ground you may have covered with others," Hutson said. "But I've been assigned. This is an active 'missing persons' case. It's official. Everything you say is important. I will stay on this until we find your husband."

"I'm sorry. What did you say?"

Hutson smiled, again thinking of his grandmother. She too had trouble focusing. Hutson was accused of many things—selfish, distracted, uncaring, and slow—but he always had a soft spot for old people. It also made him feel superior for a change.

"Mrs. Sorensen, you said you last saw your husband on Friday afternoon. You got up Saturday morning and discovered he was gone. He had not slept in his bed. Is that right ma'am?"

She smiled at the detective as if he was a son visiting. "Yes dear. That is right." *You really don't know me, do you?* She thought. *You don't remember anything . . .*

"Can you tell me what Dr. Sorensen was doing before he disappeared?"

"Certainly dear," she said and turned back to the window.

Hutson smiled again. "That's great." He opened his small leather notebook with pen in hand and reframed his question. "Please tell me what your husband was doing Friday."

"He was with *him* again."

"Him?"

"Yes. Him," she whispered.

"Who was your husband with, and where, Mrs. Sorensen?"

"Jacques has an office downtown. It's not much. One room on the third floor four blocks away. He walks there every day. Jacques retired four years ago—should have ten."

"He's retired. I see. Please continue, ma'am."

She pretended she didn't know him. She could play the game, too. "I suppose all doctors think they can keep doing what they do no matter how feeble-minded they get." She passed Hutson a crumpled card. "The address of the office is circled, in case you need to go there."

"Thank you, Mrs. Sorensen." He noticed her trembling hand. *Is that because of your age, or are you nervous about something?* "Did Dr. Sorensen see patients?"

"Not officially—his medical license expired years ago. I know different."

"What do you mean, you know different?"

"Jacques was too old to practice medicine, although he was just a psychiatrist. He wasn't doing surgery or anything important like that." She turned to Hutson with a stern gaze. "Jacques is a good man no matter what anyone says," she declared. Then she softened. "He was not a great doctor. That weighed heavy on him. I wish he had not been so hard on himself."

"You have suggested your husband was seeing a patient on Friday. Since he had only one patient, do you know the name? It could be helpful."

"I don't want to get my husband in trouble. He's not certified anymore, you know."

I know. You said that already. "I don't think it will be a problem, ma'am. We just want to find him for you. If he saw this patient, it may be the last person he was with."

She brushed off the arm of her chair as if she had spotted a small spider. Staring at the floor by her feet she whispered, "He had one patient. He's been seeing him for a while. Friday was an important day."

Finally. "What is the name of his patient?" Hutson asked again.

"Jacques came home for lunch as usual Friday. He was excited, nervous, and afraid. I know that is a strange combination of emotions, but I've seen it before."

"You've seen it before?" he prodded.

"When he has made a decision about a patient."

"When the patient has a breakthrough, gets better?"

"No. Not always. I mean it is when Jacques decides to let go. Some patients don't make progress. For Jacques, the therapy is over. He can do no more. They are on their own."

Hutson stared at her boney fingers and bulbous purple vessels pulsating under paper-thin skin. *He doesn't refer the patient to another doctor? He abandons them? Seems odd,* he thought. "So, on Friday you husband possibly released a patient he may or may not have helped."

Her eyes darted from the window to Hutson and back. *You really don't know, do you?* "I'm afraid I cannot—"

"I need that patient's name, Mrs. Sorensen. Your husband had one patient for several years. Surely you heard a name. This could be important."

I will try it this way. "I heard part of a name—Dario. Jacques never meant to tell me. It sort of slipped out one day. He tried to cover it up. He said he meant Dr. Rio. Well, he doesn't know a Dr. Rio. I checked. There's no Dr. Rio listed in the international registry of psychiatry. I knew he made it up. I just left it alone."

"Dario. Okay. We never know what's going to be important, Mrs. Sorensen. Now, can you remember anything else out of the ordinary on Friday?"

"Jacques was going to Algonquin, the cabin. I haven't been there for years. It's in the middle of nowhere. The dirt road off Miller is terrible. It goes through Peter Exner Marsh. Nobody goes up there. It's an awful place—mold spores." Without a word she got up and disappeared into the kitchen.

"Mrs. Sorensen," he yelled. "We're not done here yet."

"Last time I went up there I told Jacques I'd never expose my bottom to that bumpy dirt road again." She poked her head out. "That's been at least ten years or so. Would you like a cup of coffee?"

"Sure. That would be nice." *Why does that place seem familiar?*

He pulled out his cell and sent a text to Detective Crowley—CONTACT ALGOQUIN PD. SEND CAR TO

SERIAL INTENT

JACQUES SORENSEN CABIN. DIRT ROAD OFF MILLER ROAD TO PETER EXNER MARSH.

He tapped maps and typed Algonquin and route from Chicago. "Algonquin's an hour northwest of the city, Mrs. Sorensen," he yelled across the empty room. "Weather was gettin' bad Friday afternoon—started to snow. Forecast for the weekend, not so good. What makes you think your husband would risk going up there?" *He could be snowed in the cabin—simple as that.* Hutson closed his notebook and watched the fire pop and sizzle.

She approached with a silver tray and two steaming cups. "Jacques took his winter coat. He never wore that heavy old thing unless he was going to the cabin. Always bitterly cold up there in the winter, the winds whipping off all those little lakes and that miserable marsh. There's no insulation. Jacques said the fireplace was good enough. Place never got warm." She gave Hutson his cup. "And Jacques took his ropes."

Hutson stopped the cup at his lips and stared at the old lady. She looked familiar to him but why? *Ropes? Did he go to your cabin in a snowstorm with ropes? Am I looking for a missing person, or did I just find a missing body—a suicide?*

His next set of questions had to be carefully crafted, or he could push the old lady into shock or fall down another rabbit hole. He would lose hours chasing purple butterflies. "Mrs. Sorensen. Why did Dr. Sorensen go to the cabin? Why did he take his ropes?"

She sat and stared out the window still holding the tray.

What are you thinking? Hutson wondered. *Maybe she knows he ended his life.*

A log popped and sprayed tiny sparks across the hearth. Hutson watched the fat glowing embers devour the underside like a school of piranha devouring fresh meat. Soon the log would be gone, nothing left but a pile of nondescript ashes. Its existence was but a small meaningless memory carried to the grave by him and the old lady. Why does anything matter?

"Dario told me he was at the cabin," she said. *Maybe that will trigger something.*

Hutson's phone vibrated. The new text message was from Crowley. SORENSEN DEAD. BROKEN ROPES. HOMICIDE. BE CAREFUL!!!

Maybe Hutson should have taken Dr. Sorensen's disappearance more seriously. He visited the brownstone alone and failed to do the walk through. *Did you say Dario said?*

The wood floor creaked. Cold eyes watched the dying log long enough.

# EIGHT

"I couldn't get here sooner," Wolfe said. "My text message should have been sufficient."

Lindsey Fetter opened the door wider and nodded looking at the floor. The homicide detective brushed snow off his shoulders and walked in as if he owned the place. Stopping him in the entry, she held out her hands for his coat. "I'll take that." Her tone revealed pent-up emotions only Wolfe would be able to detect. He did not respond to her the way he knew he should. Waiting three days was inexcusable. The delay meant much more.

Winged gargoyles were perched on each corner of the rooftop of the exclusive downtown apartment building. The single residence on the top floor had ten-foot arched ceilings, ornate carved molding, and colors from the dark end of the light spectrum. Tall shrouded windows stopped lights from the sprawling city below. Dark wood floors, black marble halls, and large rooms with sparse furniture transported one back in time to a cold mansion out of a Dickens novel. The two sat at one end of the long dining room table. They were surrounded by giant oil paintings of rogue stallions running wild in night storms. Like attentive ghosts, a dozen chairs were positioned at the table draped in linen reflecting candle light. On the tray between them was an opened magnum of Petrus—2008 and two Baccarat Chateau crystal wine glasses.

"You know I don't like $8,000 wine," Wolfe said with

a hint of sarcasm.

"Why didn't you come when I texted you?" she asked.

Wolfe never explained himself, but this time he would make an exception. Lindsey Fetter was more than a victim to him. "You killed the man who dared to return to the scene of his crime. The ME took the miserable carcass away. The crime scene had been worked and released by CSI. No need for a judge, jury, or executioner. My work was done." He picked up the $400 glass and held it to the nearest candle—money meant nothing to him.

Lindsey Fetter was a naturally attractive woman. The one-time Illinois beauty queen and Paris model did not need to marry money. She came from a wealthy family of land barons and commodity traders, and had a law degree from Harvard. After Paris she pursued her passion. She signed on with the Cook County State Attorney's Office and served five years. There Lindsey met Malcolm P. Fetter, an oil & gas entrepreneur. Malcolm's first wife had been killed by a multiple felon. The then Lindsey Nolan prosecuted the case. She lost. Pesky legal technicalities. The two shared the trauma and married six months after the dust settled. He was a broken man and she was hopelessly guilt-ridden.

Wolfe had met Lindsey in her Cook County days. Heinous crimes he investigated were handled by her office. Their time together grew into more. In the beginning it was a shared disdain for the darkest elements of society. Then it evolved into a frustration over the limits of due process. Their impossible missions in a dark world, and their growing angst over injustices had created a shared oasis, a place to escape the pain. Entangled feelings turned into passionate love, but their future was too frightening to entertain for even a moment. How could a burned-out homicide detective and disenchanted county prosecutor ever have a life together? Unspoken fears grew. They backed away. Weeks turned into years. Then Wolfe saw

Lindsey had married. It was the last time he smiled—the girl he loved had found peace. He sunk into his dark world.

"Don't be that way," she whispered. But he was too alone and too thick-headed to know Lindsey Nolan had never stopped loving him, and that she was too afraid to ever tell him.

He rubbed his chin and sidestepped the moment. "Are you pouring, or shall I?"

Her eyes spoke. She took the glass from him and poured. "We need to talk, Aaron."

"What about?" he quipped.

"About what happened here," she said and then sipped her wine. He stared. She set her glass down and touched his hand with one finger. "You are a smart man, but you don't know what happened here. You think you know, but you don't"

"Really! I guess Eric Ramsey did not die here, the man who killed your—"

"Say it, Aaron."

He pulled his hand back and stared at her perfect face. "—killed your husband."

"That wasn't so hard, was it?"

"I'm sorry he is dead," Aaron muttered.

"It's been three years," she whispered. "You never came to see me. You never—"

"Never what . . . ?" Wolfe shifted in his seat. *I don't know what to do, how to be,* he thought. *I was sad for you and mad for him. I stay confused.* He looked at the shrouded window as if he could see through the thick curtains. He whispered, "This city swallows me. Staying away is best for you. When you see me, you see the world that takes life, the one that haunts us both. I bring you pain. You've had enough for one life."

She touched her handkerchief to the corners of each eye as she studied the only man she ever truly loved but could never be with. "There's more going on here than you know, Aaron. What you think happened is not what happened."

He picked up his wine glass and drank half. "You don't know what I know."

"I didn't kill him. I mean I did but there's more."

"Stop talking now," he ordered. "This is why I did not come the night you texted. I want you to have time to think carefully. You are talking to a Chicago Homicide Detective. You do not want to give me information I must act on. Do not make me do this." He drank the other half of his wine and slammed the crystal Baccarat on the oak table rattling the tray.

"There's an organization," she said.

"Please stop."

"They are like me. They are like you. They know our justice system is failing. They know it is not going to change for a long time, if ever. Bad people are winning too often, Aaron. Innocent people are dying. Victims are losing. Justice is failing one case at a time."

Wolfe stared at the woman he adored since the day they met. He would do anything to protect her, but he was a rule man. Rules got him out of a shattered home. Rules got him through college and post graduate studies and into the police academy. Rules got him to the pinnacle of his profession—homicide investigation. He would fix a broken world by taking the monsters off the streets. Soon he despised the justice system—it had failed his victims. Too often predators were put back on the streets to hunt again. Too often the law and due process were the enemies of the innocent.

"Please, Aaron. You must listen to me with an open mind."

Wolfe had to justify his world. He knew the law was not working in all cases, but it was working in many. The law had become the delicate infrastructure he built his life around. Without compliance, he would lose the line between good and evil. He could not have this conversation with Lindsey Fetter. He had to avoid the whole topic.

"Did you know there are only 25,000 bottles of 2008 Petrus on the planet?" he said as he studied the label. "The low yield is only a part of the story. This is a wine of great intensity and unique blend—perfume of mocha, caramel, black cherries, black currants. After five years of cellaring it's good for twenty-five more." His eyes found her rapping fingernails. "If I were you I'd save the rest of this bottle for a more important occasion." He started to get up.

"They came into my bedroom before Eric Ramsey," she said. "I was petrified. They stood in the dark. They were shadows like vampires. One stood on each side of my bed." Her eyes sharpened. "At first I thought it was a bad dream. Maybe I was reliving that terrible night when Malcolm was tortured and killed, and I was—"

"Don't do this. Don't say any more." Wolfe started to stand the rest of the way, but Lindsey pushed him back down. He yielded and sat.

"You listen to me. I will not let you run away again, Aaron. You must deal with this." She grabbed her glass and took a sloppy swallow of wine with her eyes locked on him. At that very moment she realized he meant even more to her. He was her true love and her rock—the only man she could show everything, the man that made her safe.

"I won't leave, but you need to stop talking," he said in a firm whisper.

"You must hear this, Aaron. They told me Ramsey was coming."

"Who told you?"

"The two men in my bedroom. They said they had been watching him, following him, listening to him. They knew his plan. They knew the date and the time. They knew he was going to attack and kill me this time. Ramsey bragged about it, Aaron. He had evil intentions."

Wolfe did not move. His mind raced through all

possibilities—he could not stop it.

Lindsey took another swallow of wine. "I got the phone call a few weeks ago. The state prosecutor called. He said Eric Ramsey would be released from prison. He explained it as a combination of the plea bargain deal and a new work-release program."

Damn system makes zero sense sometimes, Wolfe mused.

"How could they do that? He killed my husband, Aaron. He raped and beat me. How could they let that man out of prison?"

"I remember legal procedural problems that threw out the DNA," Wolfe muttered. "The plea bargain deal put the bastard behind bars twenty years before parole consideration. I know nothing about work-release programs. Still, I can't imagine that dirt bag being eligible."

"His attorney pulled strings and made him eligible," she sighed.

"Who were the guys next to your bed?" Wolfe asked.

"I don't know names. I don't even know what they look like. They wore ski masks and long black coats. Their existence had to be denied. It was their only condition."

"Their only condition for what?" Wolfe puffed.

"I had a choice, Aaron. They are part of a movement to fix the criminal justice system. They represent victims of the most heinous crimes where justice did not prevail. They said they have one mission."

"And what is that?" Wolfe asked.

"Serial intent. They remove these predators from society when the criminal justice system does not," she said.

"Serial intent. Predators. Well, that sounds just wonderful."

"It's not what you think."

"Oh. You mean they are not fanatics," Wolfe shot back. "You're telling me they are not taking the law into their own hands."

"They are not fanatics, Aaron."

"Come on now," he exploded. "They seek their own justice. You know better. You're a lawyer. These people are no different. They hunt humans without a license. They are criminals. They operate outside the law."

Lindsey looked over at the flickering candle and stopped the argument. "I was laying there, the two standing beside my bed. I thought Eric Ramsey would murder me this time. One of the men spoke. It was an elderly voice. He said they came to help me. I didn't move. He quoted a Supreme Court Justice. 'Guilt or innocence becomes irrelevant in criminal trials when we flounder in a morass of artificial rules poorly conceived and impossible to apply.' Warren Burger said that back in the '70s, Aaron."

"I want to know how they got on the tenth floor of this secured building without being detected."

"Stop and listen to me," she demanded.

"I think you're lucky they did not hurt you," he muttered.

"They were old men—articulate, gentle, and soft spoken. They know they're operating outside the law. I think they were survivors. I think they lost someone they loved and now they want to do something about it, Aaron. They said they have no intentions of getting involved in every murder case."

"Great. They have principles," Aaron scoffed.

"Their focus is on the most heinous crimes committed by serial offenders who beat the legal system. They believe these people are born with twisted minds." Lindsey walked to the window and opened the thick curtain. The night light fell into the room touching Wolfe's face.

"They said there are Bengal Tigers walking the streets. They said these animals look for people to kill. They will never stop on their own, because there are no cages strong enough, or systems smart enough to contain them, they must be terminated."

"According to their rules, any felon acquitted of murder could be designated a monster and be terminated," Aaron said. "These fanatics could kill an innocent person, Lindsey. We know people are wrongfully accused all the time. Who are these people to think they could get it right more than us? In this country, a person is innocent until proven guilty. It's the prosecution's job to prove guilt, not the defense's job to prove innocence."

Lindsey returned to the table and sipped her wine waiting for the lecture to be over. She not only had heard the argument a hundred times, she had made it often. "Why didn't you practice law after passing the bar, Aaron?"

"I had other interests," he snapped back.

"Stop. You're talking to me. We both know why you chose law enforcement over the courtroom. Why can't you just admit it?"

"Fine. The legal system is broken. Too many assholes are getting away with murder. But that's still not justification to take matters into your own hands. People have bias, especially when they are close to pain. They do not make good decisions. In the end, an impartial judge and jury are our best shot to get it right."

"I used to believe that too," Lindsey said. "But then it happened to me. It's different when you are victimized and the monster gets away with it and returns."

He could not argue the point. Although he witnessed a lot of injustices and saw many victims, he did not have the personal experience. If he had, would he see more? Would he demand more? Would he be less tolerant of the justice system? Would he support another avenue to justice? And most importantly, could Aaron Wolfe step outside of the law?

"They offered me a gun. It had been registered to me. They took care of everything the day Eric Ramsey was prematurely released from prison. They said if I wanted to stop him I could shoot him with my gun in my bedroom that night. They said he was on his way."

She looked down and wiped her tears. "They understood I might not be able to shoot a man regardless of what he had done. They also warned that killing a man would change me forever. They said the decision had to be mine. They respected my decision either way."

"Nice set up. They scared you into only one possible action," Wolfe muttered.

"No. I didn't have to kill Ramsey. They said they would divert him but could not assure he would stay away. If I chose diversion, they advised I leave Chicago and not return. There was a good chance he would not look for me outside the city."

Wolfe stared at his empty glass.

"They would support my decision either way, but they would not execute Eric Ramsey for me. Their mission is to give victims a level field for justice to prevail on the victim's terms."

"You chose the gun," Wolfe said with piercing eyes.

"Yes. I did."

"Did they stay?"

"No. They left."

"Ramsey came," Wolfe said, "and then what?"

"He came just as they said he would. I shot him."

"You know your bullet did not hit Ramsey, right?"

"I missed. When he saw the gun, he waved his knife daring me to shoot."

"Who shot him between the eyes?" Wolfe asked.

"I don't know. I do know one of the men in my room went to the window while the other was talking. I thought he just opened the curtain to let some light in. He opened the window. I didn't realize it until later, although I was cold. I guess I was scared waiting for Ramsey."

"After you missed Ramsey, what happened?"

"The window sheer moved, like a gust of wind

entering the room. Ramsey got knocked backwards and dropped out of sight. I didn't move for a while. I had no idea what happened. I just held my gun. When I got out of bed, I saw him on the floor. I realized my window was open. I checked. The sheer had been torn. The ledge outside my window is too narrow for someone to stand on it. The bullet had to come from far away."

Wolfe left the table and returned to the shrouded window on the same side of the building as Lindsey's bedroom. He opened the curtain and felt the white sheer. He scanned the skyline of Chicago, the stark shadows reaching into the night above the city lights. He saw a cluster of buildings a mile away. They were in line with the bullet trajectory, information he did not share.

"They helped me, Aaron. Once I pulled the trigger, they made sure Eric Ramsey could not hurt me ever again.

Your action was a green light, their justification. These people leveled the playing field alright. They knew you shot and missed Ramsey. Wolfe rubbed his neck struggling with the reality that Lindsey Fetter was alive only because someone stopped a monster. He stared at the skyline. *A single shot between the eyes at night from a mile away—a professional.*

NINE

"Men like honesty when it favors them."
Anickee Tockukwu Ezekiel

Meeting William T. Marcantonio was the last thing he wanted to do. Next to last was passing a kidney stone.

Eldon Babcock's charcoal pinstripe suit, Burberry velvet-trimmed overcoat, and black Zegna Chelsea boots were out of place in Old Town. It was minutes away from midnight when he parked his white Mercedes on North LaSalle and Clark. Wieland at North Avenue was a ten minute walk. He did not want his car on any video stream around the Ale House, Kanela Breakfast Club, or Zanies Comedy Night Club—known mafia hangouts. His fedora covered just enough of his face to make a positive ID impossible in a courtroom.

He entered the bar disoriented in the thick smoke, dim lighting, and rolling babel. Before he could remove his hat, a large suit and bald head took his arm and whisked him away. Babcock did not resist, even if he could. If he was not taken out back and beaten to a pulp, the aggressive greeting meant he was in the right place.

They snaked through the legion of laughter and bellowing banter, clouds of cigarette and cigar smoke, sloshing beer mugs and rolling eyes. When a door closed behind, the harsh cacophony and sour smells waned.

Without a word, the suit took Babcock through the winding halls and up three dark flights. When the last door opened, he was looking at Marcantonio sitting on a long leather sofa sucking a fat cigar. The other six in the room eyed him with disdain.

"Mr. Babcock. It's been a while. You look like your father forty years ago."

Eldon nodded forcing a smile like a kid swallowing a spoonful of cod liver oil. The large suit with the bald head let go of his arm and disappeared.

"My father said you wanted to meet," Eldon said. Marcantonio's smile immediately left his face. A single nod emptied the room. Before the door closed leaving the two alone, the mafia family patriarch put a sticky glass of brandy in Eldon's hand.

"Sit here," Marcantonio said between cigar puffs as he patted the sofa.

Eldon sat at the far end on the edge as if ready to sprint. After placing his hat between them to mark his space, he swallowed hard. His next words squeaked out, the high pitch even surprised him. "I understand you seek legal services."

Marcantonio flashed a smile and studied the man so different from him. "Yes. That is correct." The room fell silent for a long ten seconds.

Eldon cleared his throat. "There are dozens of capable law firms in the city of Chicago, why Babcock, Boyle & Brayden?" He cradled his sticky glass in his lap like a motion-sensitive bomb. He had no intention of putting anything from the room into his body.

"I like Jennings. He's been good for me."

"I understand. He speaks favorably of you as well. However, I'm not sure we are the best fit today, Mr. Marcantonio."

"Is that right? An interesting comment. Explain yourself, please," he said as he leaned closer and pushed

SERIAL INTENT

Eldon's hat to the side. How would the stiff underling of an old friend manage ratcheted discomfort—Marcantonio was a master at finding a man's limits.

"We are not into criminal law to the extent we were when you engaged my father years ago, sir. We are now a diversified law firm whose primary focus is business, banking, and international trade."

"I am a business. I use banks. I trade internationally. Do you think I only deal in crime? Is that what you're saying, young man?" Marcantonio leaned even closer. He saw the sweat bead grow and emerge from the young Babcock's sideburn. It reminded him of Jennings years ago.

"No sir. I'm not suggesting you only have criminal defense needs. I'm referring to past requirements—your primary focus with my father and our recent legal defense of Mr. Pender. I do not know what you and my father have discussed beyond this history."

Eldon left the droplet of sweat on his jaw hoping Marcantonio missed it. The room was dark enough, there was some distance between them, and Marcantonio was an older man with less than perfect eyesight. Showing weakness would not be the best way to open discussions. The Marcantonio crime family was not the typical client. They were into drug trafficking, tax evasion, gambling, and prostitution. Eldon assumed everything was hidden in the financials of family owned restaurants, clubs, and several car dealerships throughout the state.

Marcantonio pushed out his cigar and picked up his glass of vodka. Swirling the cubes he said with a challenging tone, "Your law firm is about to go under, young man. I am cash heavy and have a problem requiring immediate attention. I also have ongoing needs."

"Depending on your needs, we may or may not be the right law firm."

Marcantonio produced a tattered file from the side of the sofa. He pulled and passed a single page to the pensive attorney and directed, "Read."

Eldon scanned the document. *"This contract entered into by Eldon Michener Babcock (hereinafter referred to as 'the Provider') and William Trent Marcantonio (hereinafter referred to as 'the Client') on this date (left blank) affirms the Client engages the Provider to deliver said services as described herein under 'Scope and Manner of Services'. The Provider hereby agrees to provide the client with said services in exchange for consideration described herein under 'Payment for Services Rendered'."*

"I am quite familiar with a contract for services rendered. The scope and manner of services are undefined. I would need more," Eldon said with growing confidence.

Marcantonio pulled a second page and passed it to the cautious man. He watched as Babcock read and the dollars registered.

With eyes wide, he muttered, "This is a very big number. I cannot imagine any services you could need from our law firm that would justify such a large opening figure and guaranteed minimum annual payments over a ten year relationship."

Marcantonio passed a third document, the confidentiality agreement. "I am sure you are familiar with this legal instrument. Before we can go further, you must sign this. What I am going to share is only for the eyes and ears of my legal representative. Sign this document now or leave as the son of a friend and do not look back."

"But, Mr. Marcantonio, I—"

"After signing this document, and after hearing what I have to say, if you feel you cannot go forward, you are free to leave. However, as you well know, you are bound to maintain complete and total confidentiality on all matters discussed in this room. If you accept the two-million dollar retainer, you are bound to represent me until the initial matter has been concluded to my satisfaction. The money cannot be returned. You cannot change your mind midstream. You cannot disengage without my approval. The annual compensation plan of one-million dollars will adjust with inflation and increase at a twenty-five percent rate each year. There will be performance bonuses. Should you accept this arrangement, you sir become my personal legal representative. You will tend to all my legal needs— only you, not an associate or your father. Do you understand me, Eldon Michener Babcock?"

He stared at the engagement figures and sipped his drink. "Why me?"

"Your father's a good man, but he is unable to keep up. I have watched you over the years. Like it or not, you're very much like Jennings, except you are more practical and a rule person. I've watched you take your father's firm to the top in a very competitive world. You're smart but your weakness is your resistance to cold business realities. I understand the financial complexities facing your law firm. Mr. Babcock, you cannot survive at the level you are accustomed without a serious adjustment in your business strategy. You face more competition every day. You have a meddling father and misplaced power with an over-the-hill founder's board. Those old farts understand one thing— revenue. You need all of these pesky obstacles moved out of your way."

"A lot of what you say is true, but I still don't know why me."

Marcantonio poured more vodka, gulped down half the glass, and crushed an ice cube in his mouth. "The world has changed for people like me. The way I handle problems today must be different. You know this new world. You can help me navigate in a more civilized manner. If that explanation is not good enough for you, know I could put your father away for the rest of his life if my needs are not met."

"Didn't take you long to get there," Eldon chided.

"See. My comment was inappropriate, not necessary.

It's the old way—threats. Instead, I would prefer to enter into a more civilized arrangement, one binding and mutually beneficial."

Eldon smiled. He pulled his Mont Blanc from his pocket and signed the confidentiality agreement. The enormous inflow of new capital would solve his business problems. The annual stipend would take the founder's board out of his life. He would have the board sign over rights based on his commitment to ridiculous growth objectives that now could be reached. The board would not know about the Marcantonio deal until the ink had dried on their new contract with him, the lifelong CEO and new COB for the BB&B law firm.

Marcantonio countersigned. They shook hands, clicked glasses, and finished their drinks staring at each other. Could this deal work, or did Eldon just sign away his life? He had to lay some ground rules.

"I will never do anything illegal, Mr. Marcantonio. And I will advise you not to break the law as well." He held his glass out for more.

Marcantonio poured. "I expect nothing less." He leaned back into his leather cushion and his face hardened. "There are histories and tricky business structures I will protect until they can properly evolve. Those matters will be shared—to a limited degree—so you can participate in the restructure process without being morally or ethically compromised."

"I appreciate that consideration. I do have one other request."

"Please, go ahead."

"Do not ask me to defend another James Pender? That was the single worst experience of my life." He swallowed half his glass and looked at the ceiling in disgust. "That man is evil. He killed innocent people. My defense made a mockery of the justice system. I'm ashamed of the procedural knots I tied." His eyes found Marcantonio. "In the future, you should be very careful around animals like Mr. Pender. They will topple everything important to you."

Marcantonio sighed. "Pender was the son of a man who did something for me many years ago, a man I owed a great debt of gratitude. He asked I help his misguided son one time. I did." Marcantonio puffed his new cigar alive and studied the ash. "James Pender will not be a problem for either of us, Mr. Babcock. Your advice for the future is sound."

He tapped his cigar on the tar-stained onyx ashtray. His voice hardened. He spoke like the powerful mafia boss Eldon had envisioned. "The rest of the paperwork will be delivered to your offices tomorrow by special courier. I ask you execute immediately and return it to me. Upon receipt, I will deposit $2,000,000 in the Babcock, Boyle & Braden bank account."

Eldon nodded. He found Marcantonio easier to work with than he had envisioned. Maybe it could work. "I will return the executed documents as requested. However, may I ask you hold the retainer until I request deposit? I need a few days to make arrangements."

"Certainly, but the terms of our agreement are not altered. Delay in transfer of funds is your preference, no longer a decision point."

"Understood and agreed." The two clicked glasses a second time. "Now, what is the pressing matter requiring my immediate assistance?"

Marcantonio smiled. "I've enjoyed a certain business of mine for three decades. I am referring to the acquisition of various pharmaceutical products and the redistribution of said products on the South Side of our fine city."

"Pharmaceuticals," Eldon said loosening his tie.

"We are the exclusive vendor for a defined region. We have a long-standing arrangement with an independent network of vetted suppliers and dealers. We take our products to market—both small wholesale businesses and consumers. This particular family enterprise is extremely profitable. It generates enough revenue in a week to satisfy our entire arrangement."

"I gather these pharmaceuticals are controlled substances," Eldon said.

"Yes. The best available in the central corridor of the United States."

"Without a need to know specifics, tell me about the problem."

"Interruption in redistribution," Marcantonio shot back.

"I would assume interruption in redistribution is a routine and known risk. I would also assume your operation has safeguards and countermeasures to manage such a risk."

"Your assumptions are accurate to a point. The established safeguards have had no impact on this particular problem. Allow me to share a recent event. It happened in the early morning hours today—2:30 a.m. My people were visiting a new drop site, a trailer parked on a vacant lot. The property belongs to your law firm."

"I think you're mistaken," Eldon chuckled. "I can assure you, we do not own property on the South Side. That part of the city is gangland, not a real estate investment opportunity."

"You wouldn't know about this investment. Not unless you looked in the right place. Your father purchased three lots on 27th Street years ago. Back then the South Side was viewed a sound investment. Unfortunately the area went downhill. A lot of money was lost. Your father ran into financial problems and needed a loan. No bank would work with him. I took the three lots to collateralize my loan to Jennings. I still hold the deeds of trust, although BB&B is still the owner. Should Jennings default on the loan, I would own the property. I never did get paid. I still hold the deeds."

"I see," Eldon said under his breath.

"My men went there early this morning. It was a simple inspection visit. We had parked a trailer on one of the vacant lots and left it there for several weeks."

"Your visit this morning, was it the first after parking the trailer?"

"Yes. Three of my men were attacked."

"Unless I missed something, this sounds like a drug war. This can't be the first time. I'm sure you know your enemies and how to handle such matters. Why do you need my help?"

Marcantonio sat motionless holding his cigar, his thoughts miles away. Eldon waited and watched the anger in his eyes turn into fear. "What's the matter?" Eldon asked.

Marcantonio butted out his cigar and spoke without emotion. "You know why we don't need to worry about James Pender?"

"Why?" Eldon asked. *Tell me that evil man got what he deserved. Tell me another criminal had delivered justice by removing him from the planet.*

"James Pender is dead."

There is a God. "Dead! How?"

"Are you familiar with the Chicago police POD program?"

"I am. Hundreds of cameras around the city."

"Let's just say I have friends in the department." Marcantonio reached for a TV remote and slid a tape into the slot of a dusty video deck. The monitor popped on and lines rolled.

"The CPD and DEA have been watching my operations for years, Mr. Babcock. We've been able to work around them quite well. We knew they had a POD watching our new site on 27th Street. We left it alone for three weeks knowing they typically lose interest after two. End of the third week we visited the site to inspect the trailer for tampering by locals. That's why we were there. And that's when my men were attacked."

"No product on the site?"

"Correct. Just an empty trailer. Regardless of that, two of my men were seriously injured—broken arms and legs and ribs. Pender was killed. This is a copy of a portion of the POD watching our trailer. These thirty seconds cost me $25,000." Marcantonio pressed play.

They watched a large man leap over a chain-linked fence and hide in the brush. He then charged the trailer tackling two men. He hit each with a single blow and threw them across the lot like ragdolls. "My God he's strong," Eldon gasped.

"Is that Pender hiding at the back of trailer?" Eldon asked.

"Yes. Keep your eyes on him. This happens fast." On Marcantonio's last word Pender stepped out of the shadow waving a knife. His head exploded. Pender's lifeless body collapsed and the video went blank.

Eldon covered his mouth to stop the gagging reflex. He looked away. "Do you know the man who charged your men? He had to hurl them thirty or more feet. I don't understand."

Marcantonio stared at the black screen. "The man threw two of my people like they weighed nothing. Someone else shot Pender. It was a high-powered rifle from a long distance. That's why his head exploded. I'm dealing with a sniper and some kind of monster."

"I seriously do not know what to say at the moment."

"Pender is the third on my payroll shot by a sniper. The guy on the video, I don't know who he is, but I don't think he's working with the sniper."

"How do you know?"

"You can see. The man approached Pender on the video. He was just as surprised as me when Pender's head exploded."

"How can I help?" Babcock asked.

"I need your PI resources looking for these people."

"What makes you think my PI people can be any more successful than yours?"

"Mine had six months and got nowhere. I don't like being watched and picked-off by unknown entities. These people are on a mission. I cannot afford interruptions. "

"A mission?" Eldon asked. *Interesting choice of words.* "I will need everything you're investigators have found to date. I want background details on the others you say were executed. I know Pender. I want everything on his kills." His eyes dropped to the video now squeezed in Marcantonio's hand. "And I will take that with me tonight."

With cold eyes, he passed it to his new attorney. "You'll have the rest tomorrow."

The walk back to his Mercedes was not like the walk to the nefarious meeting with a drug lord. Now Eldon Babcock was invested and exposed. He studied the shadows and passing faces, and he looked over his shoulder at each turn. Did he sign the deal of a lifetime, or did he sign his death certificate?

The man Eldon Babcock saw on the video moved unlike any man he had ever seen before—a beast hunting men. The man possessed profound physical strength, astounding agility, and had no fear. On the opposite end of the mystery, the sniper revealed nothing but great skill with a high-powered rifle.

Do these two share a mission, or do they have separate agendas? When I determine that, and how one gets on their list, the trap can be set. Eldon turned his last corner, the wheels in his head spinning. He had clawed his way through Harvard Law and to the top of his profession by applying a superior intellect and employing his honed problem-solving skills. Now he would aim both at taking complete control of his law practice and life.

When he saw his sparkling white Mercedes parked under the south leg trestle in the dirty snow, he had stopped rubbing a nervous finger on the video cartridge deep in his coat pocket. Eldon smiled. The $2,000,000 retainer fee would free him from the meddling grip of his father, and the $1,000,000 annual stipend would neutralize the board. By the end of the week Eldon would have his team of private investigators in place. By the end of the month he would deliver the two unknowns to William Marcantonio. The expeditious completion of his first assignment would warrant a sizeable bonus.

Maybe it's time to trade in the white Mercedes, Eldon thought. On that cold (but triumphant) walk to the car, he did not feel the crosshairs between his eyes, and he did not locate the large shadow under the rusted trestle less than a block away. Eldon did not feel the anger in the eyes of the monster.

TEN

When he opened his eyes, he felt ropes and a gag. Unable to move, his wet head throbbed and one sealed eye seemed to be crusted over. In his dark, cold, and cramped confines he prayed to himself. *Please God, don't let me be buried alive...*

"Where the hell's Hutson?" Landers yelled from behind the stacks of files piled high on his desk. Even though he had been sequestered most of the day, he would be pushing paper into the early morning hours. The CPD could not slow down the runaway homicide rate, but they sure could document the hell out of it.

To make things worse, Landers got the call from the medical examiner—Ramsey took a .50 caliber projectile between the eyes. Experts said it came from a Barrett single-shot bolt-action American sniper rifle with a shooting range of 1.6 miles. Whoever pulled the trigger had to be military trained. That simple reality accounted for three hours of Landers life. He got stuck on the phone with top brass of the Army 197th Infantry Brigade at Fort Benning, Georgia—the home of the U.S. Army Sniper School.

At 10:00 p.m. Landers's detectives were either off-duty or running around the city chasing bad guys. Detective Ben Crowley had just returned from an unplanned day in Algonquin—sucked into Hutson's case, the missing Dr. Sorensen. When Crowley put his foot on the third floor of the precinct headquarters, Commander Landers' rants echoed across the room and bounced off the empty metal desks.

"On my way," Crowley yelled back hanging his coat. The snow had been coming down most of the day. Now he struggled above a glass puddle on warped linoleum wishing he had gone home instead. The smart detective had longevity. He would be the next commander if he didn't screw up.

"First, where the hell's everybody?" Landers boomed as Crowley eased up to the only office with lights burning. "I look up, everyone's gone. There's nothin' on the board, and Miss Higgins is gone." He felt his pocket for a pack of cigarettes and remembered he gave up smoking. "And it just dawned on me, I've not heard from Hutson all day. Is he working the missing person's case, or did he take off another day? He's been taking a lot of time off."

Crowley waited for Landers to stop talking. When he was sure the rant was over, he jumped in. "You told us not to bother you this week, remember? You said you had a pile of paperwork to move out of here—end of month stats."

Crowley leaned against the doorjamb. "As far as where Detective Hutson is at the moment, I do not know. Earlier today he asked for my help on the Sorensen case. I've been in Algonquin all day. Just got back. I don't need to tell you how terrible it is out there. The snow's really coming down.

"I don't need a weather forecast. I can see out the damn window. If you were working a case with Hutson, you gotta have an idea where the man is now."

"I thought he'd be here. I got a text from him around ten this morning. He needed the Algonquin PD to check something. Algonquin is fifty miles outside the city. I guess I didn't plan on spending the whole day up there. You know Joe went to interview Dr. Sorensen's wife in the city. During the interview he sent me a text to get the Algonquin

PD to check the Sorensen cabin. They checked it. They found Dr. Sorensen dead. We think it's a homicide. I went up."

"Hutson sent you to Algonquin to look for a body?" Landers asked.

"He was not thinking a body when he texted me," Crowley said as he scrolled his phone messages. "He told me to contact Algonquin PD. Send car to Jacques Sorensen cabin—a dirt road off Miller Road goin' to Peter Exner Marsh."

Crowley looked up and found Landers' confused stare. "Joe probably thought the old man was at the cabin and the old lady had forgotten about it. I did what Joe asked. When the Algonquin PD got to the cabin, they found Sorensen dead—frozen solid on the floor by the open cabin door. No signs of a break in, but—"

"Then why homicide?" Landers interrupted.

"The medical examiner hasn't done anything with the body yet. They're waiting for Sorensen to thaw out. Conditions inside the cabin lead us to believe someone killed him. The man was on the floor, his body bent in a weird way, his back broken backwards."

"That's odd, but not necessarily a homicide, Crowley. I need more."

"There was one of those old wooden school chairs sittin' in the middle of the room in the cabin. The floor under those fat legs was torn up, fresh scratches and gouges. It was like someone sitting in the chair kept moving. The chair dug into the wood floor."

"I'm still not getting homicide, Crowley."

"There were busted ropes on the floor by that chair. We think someone was tied in that chair. Looks like they busted loose and—"

"Busted ropes?" Landers boomed. "Don't you think you should have started with that?"

Crowley sighed. "Yes sir."

"What else about those ropes?"

"Was peculiar, sir. Was like the person tied in the chair pulled them until they broke, like expanded their chest and shoulders or something. They had to be damn strong to do that."

"Oh, you think so, Crowley?"

"Those ropes were half-inch nylon."

Landers rolled his eyes. "What did Hutson say when you told him?"

"Nothing. I mean, I texted him the APD found Sorensen dead. I asked Joe to call me ASAP. I told him his case looked like a homicide. I never heard back from Joe. I called him a few times and left messages. Then I got busy. I figured he was chasing leads—we were all busy. I thought we'd get together tonight to compare notes."

Landers got up and went to Hutson's desk. He turned on the lamp and found the Sorensen file. "It says here Dr. Jacques Sorensen's a retired psychiatrist. He was reported missing Saturday morning." Landers turned to Crowley blowing into cupped hands at the door. "It's Monday night. Why have we been sitting on this?"

"We got it Sunday night, late. Hutson took it when he got here Monday morning. We're working active homicides. Missing persons' cases drop on the list."

"Wonderful," Landers muttered flipping pages in the Sorensen file. *I can't complain,* he mused. *Nine out of ten missing old people turn up—temporarily lost or misplaced. It's routine to send a squad car. Guess we get it a day or so later after fully vetted."*

"Has anyone gone by the brownstone to tell Mrs. Sorensen her husband's dead?"

"I sent a squad car a few times today. Nobody home. Nobody answers phones. I came in here to check the file for relatives. I also learned that Dr. Sorensen kept an office a few blocks away. I was gonna check that out."

Landers dropped the file on Hutson's desk. "Did you

ever consider Detective Hutson and Mrs. Sorensen could run into the person tied in that chair at the Algonquin cabin?" He started toward the door. "Get your coat, Crowley."

***

What happened to me? Where am I? How long have I been here?

The questions started to flow inside Joe Hutson's blood-encrusted head as the fog and nausea lifted. It was not the first time, but this time his hands were tied to his ankles behind his back like a roped calf.

Hutson rocked and inched his body counter clockwise. As he rotated on his side, with one eye he struggled to make sense of his dark surroundings. No matter how much he tried, he could not open his other eye.

He found a horizontal line of light. Hutson had no sense of distance or dimension. It could be a few inches or several feet away. He would need to move to it to solve the puzzle. When Hutson blinked wet debris from his good eye, two vertical lines of light came into view. They were connected to the ends of the horizontal line. Both shot straight up and disappeared in the dark. He rocked and squirmed. Then his knees touched something. Hutson froze. The soft and spongy obstacle did not move.

Could this be another person? He thought. *Are they alive? God. Are they dead? Or is it a torso or large body part?* Hutson's imagination went wild. His heart beat faster and harder. Desperation washed over him. He had never taken his gun out of its holster. He preferred to avoid uncomfortable and dangerous situations—and he did just that most of his career.

"Calm down, Joe," he whispered. "Think. What do you remember last?" He derived some satisfaction from hearing his voice. It meant he was still alive. Or was he dreaming?

He forced his eyelid, but it did not break free. It seemed to be glued closed.

"What are those smells?" Like his eye had adjusted, his nose started to wake up. *Is it urine and talcum powder and dirty rags? I smell a flowery perfume mixed with mothballs?* "Who uses mothballs anymore?" *Old people use mothballs, and that's old-lady perfume.* Hutson gagged. "It smells like those flowers nobody ever sees—gladiolus I think."

He scooted, avoiding the spongy object. The bottom line of light disappeared. *I'm at the Sorensen's brownstone. I wonder how long? I remember sitting in the living room looking at the fire, the log sinking into the coals.*

The muffled pounding in the distance broke his train of thought. The hard pounds could be imagination. Hutson sucked into a ball. "I am a prisoner," he said under his breath grasping the seriousness of his situation. "I'm in a closet. Those lines, I am looking at the door."

The pounding stopped. Hutson held his breath and started to remember more. *I didn't see your face. In the mirror, I saw the back of your head and your shoulders. You were in the hallway dressed like me, a dark coat. You were listening and waiting. I jumped up reaching for my gun. That was stupid. I've never been a smart cop. You were ready. You hit me one time.*

The creaking floorboards outside Hutson's closet got louder. Someone approached.

Is that you? Hutson wondered. *Did you come back for me? Did you kill that old man? God, did you kill the old lady, too? What's this all about? What did I walk into?* Hutson scooted a few more inches. He saw the bottom line of light. It broke in the middle. Someone stood outside the door. The creaking boards were silent. The knob rattled.

You knocked me unconscious. You put me in here until the time was right. You're back for me. You're going to hurt me now.

SERIAL INTENT

Hutson's heart beat hard. The closet door whined open. Light poured in. The object next to Hutson's knees came into focus. He saw the old lady. Mrs. Sorensen was dead.

ELEVEN

"Ellen purchased the condo across from me six months ago, Mr. Wolfe. She takes her Shih Tzu—Presley—for a walk every morning and night rain or shine." Moving a few strands of hair from her eye, Linda Day smiled and crossed her long legs. She was more than attracted to the handsome detective who had knocked on her door at 9:00 p.m.

She stiffened. Her smile faded. The morbid reason for the visit crept back into her wandering thoughts. "It's been a few days since the terrible tragedy. Do you know more? I just can't believe Ellen is gone."

"I'm sorry. We have many questions to answer, Miss Day."

After Wolfe had studied the crime scene, he followed the blood droplets to the west wall of the Wunders Cemetery. Standing like a statue in the shadows between the seven-foot Nellie Stevens Holly, the killer held a bloody knife ready to kill again. When Wolfe found him, so did a sniper's bullet. Later the dead man would be identified as Frank Pazrro, a serial felon recently released from prison for second degree murder. Wolfe's case had taken another turn. He had two lifelong criminals dead by sniper fire, and both had ties to the Marcantonio family.

"I understand, Detective," Day said with a sobering tone.

Wolfe perused the attractive witness with a discerning eye. He estimated thirty-six, but could be off a few years—

his best guesses were dead people lying on the ground. Walking from the door to the sofa, Wolfe absorbed details of his surroundings that would help define his witness. He noted no signs of pets or plants or anything that needed nurturing and attention. The wall bookcases were lined with softcover mystery/thrillers and erotic romance novels—including the *Fifty Shades of Grey* trilogy. The window seat had stacks of magazines—*People, Time, Newsweek, Glamour, Esquire*—and neatly folded op-ed sections of the *Chicago Tribune.*

In less than a minute, Wolfe concluded Sally Day was an intelligent, independent, self-centered, and sexually adventurous woman. That meant she would be a curious and observant person. He could learn something meaningful if he asked the right questions.

"How long did you know Ellen Dumont?"

"We met two years ago, when I joined the *Tribune.*"

"You both worked at the newspaper?"

She nodded. "We write . . . I mean she wrote . . . I mean we write opinion columns for the paper. I'm sorry. This is very hard for me."

"It's okay. Losing a friend is hard. Just take your time." Wolfe smiled at her for the first time, something she had been trying to get him to do since their eyes first met.

"I told Ellen about the condo the day it went on the market. I knew she'd want to take a look, it being near the cemetery where her parents are buried. They died three years ago on the day Ellen was killed. They were in a horrible automobile accident. Ellen never got over it."

"What can you tell me about Barry Woods?"

"He loved her very much. They were going to get married in the summer. They met after her parent's accident. Barry handled the paperwork—life insurance and settlement of the estate. He's with West Town Legal, probably the smallest law firm in the city. He specializes in wealth management."

"A lawyer, I see. They planned to get married, you said?" Wolfe aimed her.

"Yes. He always says he fell in love with Ellen the day they met. He waited six months before calling her. He said he wanted to give her time—her loss and all. I think Barry needed time to get up the nerve to call her. He worshipped Ellen. I hope he will be okay."

"Do you know how much wealth?" Wolfe probed.

"Ellen told me once. I recall it being around $300,000."

"Good. Did Barry and Ellen live together?" Wolfe knew the answer—testing openness.

"Yes. Three months."

Good. No hesitation. I can—

She reached out and touched Wolfe's hand holding the pen. His eyes lifted from his small leather notepad. "Is Barry going to be all right? I heard he was hurt. He fought the killer."

"Who told you he fought the killer?" Wolfe asked.

She pulled back and sat up unsure. "It was one of the young policemen. He mentioned it to me that night. He was going around looking for witnesses and friends of Ellen and Barry. Please, I don't want to get anyone in trouble. He said it was his opinion—that it didn't mean much."

"He's not in trouble, Miss Day. Do you recall the officer's name?"

"It was Officer Trent, William Trent," she said with a nervous smile as Wolfe wrote.

I need to keep an eye on Officer William Trent. He's the only one who got the crime scene right. "Do you know if Ellen Dumont had enemies, someone bothering her like an old boyfriend or neighbor?"

"No old boyfriends or neighbor issues, Detective. Ellen was a nice person. She stopped dating when her parents were killed. She just went to work, wrote her column, and walked Presley. She went to the Wunders Cemetery every day. I guess the rest of the time she was with Barry or in her condo or at the library doing research for her column."

"What kind of column did she write?" Wolfe asked.

"Local events. Light politics. In the beginning. A few years ago she changed focus. Took on causes—rescue animals, helping the homeless, feeding the hungry, protecting the poor from invasion of human rights—things like that."

Sally Day leaned back on the sofa and adjusted the hem of her skirt with a smile. She was a selective and determined woman. Few men made it inside her condo. Those who did spent the night—one time. She continued to look for the one she wanted to stay.

"Over the last year Ellen wrote about the gross injustices of the legal system."

Wolfe's eyes froze. *This could be important. Did she get on someone's radar? Did she irritate the wrong people?* "What gross injustices?" he asked.

"The most horrific homicides committed by the sickest killers with long felony records. The people caught red-handed."

"Killers caught red-handed," Wolfe said under his breath. "Explain her—"

"Our criminal justice system fails too often. It fails to take real predators off our streets. Ellen called them 'monsters with serial intent'. She said some people are like wild animals, human carnivores. They kill, get caught, get put in jail, and get out for all sorts of crazy reasons. Then they kill again and again. Her column focused on those cases. She did her research and revealed the legal technicalities that tossed vital evidence or minimized eyewitness accounts. She showed how creative defense attorneys tied the legal system into knots. She shined a light on how they made monsters look like misunderstood citizens in the wrong place at the wrong time.

"I save all the op-eds. Her series was entitled—*Serial*

Intent. I can give them to you. She did extensive and detailed research on each case. I'm sure it's in her files at the *Tribune*.

I suspect Frank Pazrro was a recent topic in her columns—that's an easy check, Wolfe thought. *Miss Dumont was stirring a dangerous pot in this town. I wonder if her work can point me to someone on the dark side of the legal community, someone who would engage a sniper, someone with more than a passing interest in Eric Ramsey and James Pender.*

"Did Miss Dumont get threats?" Wolfe asked again.

"Yes. She got threatened all the time. My God, I'm such an idiot. How could I not think of that when you first asked me that question?"

"Sometimes the obvious is not so obvious, when one loses a friend or family member. Our minds can do some crazy things. Tell me about the threats you know about."

"We both get hate mail. I didn't think of it because we never took it seriously. I suppose if we did, we would do nothing but worry. Threatening phone calls, I have no idea how many of those came in each day. The *Tribune* screens everything. I used to think it was a service. We later realized it was probably their way to keep us writing—no distractions."

"We will get with the paper on those calls," Wolfe said. "You've been helpful. I appreciate it." Wolfe got to his feet.

"Would you like a drink? Surely you don't work twenty-four hours a day."

"I would love a drink—" He checked his phone, a text message from Crowley. STUCK IN SNOW OUTSIDE CITY. HUTSON MIA. CHECK SORENSEN BROWNSTONE. SEE ADDRESS. MISSING PERSON NOW HOMICIDE. "—but I have to take care of something." Wolfe pocketed his cell. She walked him to the door.

"Maybe you can come back after you take care of business, Detective."

He turned to her at the door. "I do have one more question, Miss Day," he said.

She smiled and stepped closer. "Sally, please."

"Sally. How did Barry Woods feel about Ellen Dumont's op-ed focus—the deteriorating state of the criminal justice system?"

She leaned inches from his chin and looked up with glassy eyes. "Barry applauded her work. He understood the problems better than most. Barry graduated Harvard Law School, top ten percent of his class."

"Interesting. And he chose a small law firm," Wolfe said as he lost himself in her eyes.

"He said the American criminal justice system is severely flawed for today's world. Even if there was agreement, the fix would take decades—corrective rulings and acts of congress. He said it would be like shoveling sand in a tsunami. Barry co-authored several of Ellen's most recent columns. She even gave him credit in the byline."

He took a cold quiet walk to the car feeling her eyes on him from the only lighted window in the complex. Sally Day had no intention of hiding her interest, but Wolfe had a new set of problems rolling around his head. Maybe both Ellen Dumont and Barry Woods were supposed to die that night. Maybe Frank Pazrro blew it. Maybe that failure put a bullet in his head. The list of potential motives grew.

Wolfe slid into his car and turned on the ignition changing his focus. *Where in the hell are you Hutson?* He wondered. *And where in the hell's Sorensen's brownstone in this snow city?*

He rolled from the curb crushing ice under his tires. He turned an eye to Sally Day still standing in her window. Wolfe smiled. He would be back and she knew it.

***

"What in the hell did you get yourself into now?" He stood at the opened door.

The pile of rags next to Hutson turned out to be an old lady. Wolfe reached down and touched her cheek with the back of his hand. He grabbed Hutson's calf with the other and pulled him from the back of the closet. "What're you doing—hiding?" he teased.

Wolfe pressed two fingers on the old lady's carotid artery. "She's alive," he muttered and turned back to Hutson. "I'll get you in a minute. Looks like just a bump on your head."

He pulled out his cell and tapped 911. "We need an ambulance at—ah—get the location off my phone GPS?" He waited for confirmation.

"Good. Okay, this is Detective Aaron Wolfe, Chicago Homicide. Everyone's alive, but I have an old lady in a catatonic state, a strong pulse and breathing. I've got a CPD detective with a bump on his noggin and a shiner—lucid." He pulled the gag off Hutson's face.

"Wolfe," Hutson gasped. "Wolfe, be careful. He may still be here. The guy who did this may be in the brownstone. I heard sounds."

Wolfe nodded, pocketed his cell, and pulled out his Glock. "Stay here," he whispered. "Don't go anywhere or I might shoot you." He closed the closet door.

A few minutes passed before red lights washed into the living room and hit the wood floor in the hallway. Hutson heard Wolfe talking. He heard him tell the paramedics the place was secured. The closet door swung open. They took care of Mrs. Sorensen first.

Wolfe climbed in the closet, untied Hutson, and sat him up. *Those ropes weren't very tight. He should have been able to get out of 'em.* Wolfe studied the man he knew for ten years. "They need to take a look at you, Joe. Don't try to get up."

"I'm okay. I remember things, Wolfe. I gotta talk." Hutson tried to stand and fell back down. "I gotta talk, Wolfe."

"First, you need to sit your butt down right here and let them check you out, Joe. You're no good to me unconscious. You could have a stroke or heart attack—throw a blood clot. You could die from a concussion—uncontrolled bleeding in your head. Or it could turn you into a vegetable, Joe. Or one of those—"

"Jesus Christ, Wolfe," Hutson boomed. "Fine! I will stay here. I won't move."

Wolfe winked at the paramedics as they surrounded Hutson with their stethoscopes, blood pressure paraphernalia, tape and bandages, and IV starter set. Wolfe knew Hutson had lost some blood. They would hook up an IV and give him normal saline to restore fluids.

After setting the IV and confirming no major injuries, the paramedics backed out and Wolfe went into the closet. "They said we can walk to the ambulance when you're ready, or I can take you to the ER later. We will need a doctor to take a look at you tonight."

"Can I take this thermometer out of my mouth," Hutson mumbled.

"Hell yes. I told them to leave it there to shut you up a while." Joe pulled it out and threw it on the floor. "What happened here? Don't leave anything out. You're on the other side of the investigation, a victim."

Hutson stared at his cell phone. "Damn, I just saw this text from Crowley. They found my missing person—Dr. Jacques Sorensen."

"That's a start," Wolfe said.

"They found him dead in Algonquin. Crowley says it's a homicide."

"I remember the Sorensen case posted this morning—missing person reported Saturday. You took the case. How did Crowley get involved?"

Hutson touched his puffy eyelid and winced. "I must have been unconscious when Ben sent me this. I sent him a text first—needed help. I had asked him to send the Algonquin PD to the Sorensen cabin. I thought the old man could be there. I guess I've been in this closet all day. I've got no sense of time. I don't know when I regained consciousness."

Hutson grabbed Wolfe's arm in desperation. "The old lady—Mrs. Sorensen—is she okay? Is she dead, Wolfe? Tell me the truth. Don't hold back. I can handle it."

"She's alive, Joe. No trauma. Whoever put her in here with you was careful. There was a folded blanket under her. She didn't lie on the hard wood like you, and she was not tied up. They liked her better than you," Wolfe poked.

"I bet she fainted," Hutson muttered. "Probably fell asleep after that like old people do—you know they sleep on and off most of the day?"

From the closet Hutson saw her waking up on the gurney in the living room. "Wolfe, I don't know a lot, but I think I know some things. I gotta tell you now or I could forget it. You know I'm not good at remembering."

"Okay, but slow down. We've got time to talk. When you're ready to move into the living room, I think you will be more comfortable."

"I want to stay here until they leave," Hutson whispered.

"That's fine," Wolfe said.

A paramedic's head leaned in and checked Hutson's IV and pulse. When he finished he gave a thumbs-up and passed a water bottle to Wolfe. "Mrs. Sorensen is doing fine, almost like she just woke up from an afternoon nap. We're gonna run her in and let a doctor check her out. Oh, and she knows her husband's dead."

"I'll get Detective Hutson to the hospital," Wolfe said.

"That will be fine." The paramedic left them alone.

"How does she know her husband's dead?" Wolfe asked. "Paramedics don't tell patients anything. How would she know that, Joe?"

"I don't know," Hutson said. "When we spoke this morning, she seemed not much concerned about it. I was operating under the impression he disappeared on occasion. I was checking off the boxes trying to track him down."

"Who told her he was dead, Joe?" Wolfe turned to the living room and caught the old lady staring in their direction. Surrounded by paramedics, her gaze seemed out of place. The intensity in the eyes did not fit a feeble old woman. She looked away.

"I did not know until I read this text, Wolfe."

"Okay. Just tell me what you remember."

Hutson grabbed the water bottle and unscrewed the cap with a trembling hand. After a few swallows he took a deep breath and blinked like he had just surfaced from a deep dive. "I was in a chair in the living room, my back to the hallway and this closet. I saw something move in the mirror on the mantle—fleeting. I got up and turned. I blacked out."

"Can you describe the man who hit you?" Wolfe asked.

"In the mirror, he looked big like you and me."

"That's it?" Wolfe pressed.

"Dark brown hair like ours. He was angry."

"That's all you got?"

Hutson rubbed his wrist. "A dark face."

"Do you mean poor lighting or a brown-skinned guy?"

"I mean evil," Hutson said.

"Evil? That's a strange description."

"The eyes were scary. He was snarling like an animal."

The paramedics rolled Mrs. Sorensen into the hall and paused at the opened closet door. "We're taking her to the hospital now." Wolfe and Hutson nodded. Mrs. Sorensen raised her hand and patted Hutson's shoulder. The gurney rolled down the hall and out of the brownstone.

Holding up a small tattered leather book, Wolfe turned back to Hutson. Like an old bible, the book was two inches thick with tissue pages. The edges of the pages were stained from age and handling. "Did you see this, Joe?" Wolfe asked as he watched for a reaction.

"No. Looks like a diary," Hutson said.

"Whose diary do you think?" Wolfe asked.

"I have no idea."

"It belongs to your dead man, Joe. Belongs to Dr. Jacques Sorensen."

"Really? I've not seen it."

"It was sitting on the kitchen table under the newspaper. Looks like someone forgot it, Joe. Some pages have folded corners. To be precise—seven. I counted them."

"Anything important?" Joe asked looking at his wrists.

"Come with me." Wolfe picked up Hutson's IV bag and helped him to his feet. They moved to the living room by the dying fire. Wolfe draped the IV bag over the back of Hutson's chair and threw a log on the fire. They both stared waiting for it to ignite. Wolfe watched Hutson struggle with his experience. *What are you not telling me?*

"While the paramedics were checking on you, I called Landers from the kitchen," Wolfe said. "He and Crowley were on their way out here. They were worried about you, Joe. They realized you were missing. They gave up on your dead cell phone. You probably have a dozen messages."

"I was tied up," he mumbled staring at the dancing flame.

"Yeah, tied up." *A kid could have gotten loose.* "Well, FYI they got stuck in the snow. I told 'em you're okay. They're gonna meet us at the hospital, if they can get there. Snow's getting bad. Been coming down steady. They're on the other side of town."

"I've always liked the snow," Hutson said under his

breath.

"Joe, we gotta talk about this diary."

"Okay. I'm listening."

"It's bad, Joe."

"What do you mean, bad?"

Wolfe held it up. "This appears to be Dr. Sorensen's handwriting. We will confirm that later. For now, I believe we are looking at his life as recorded by him. It goes back forty years. I looked at the seven pages with corners folded."

"What did you find?" Hutson asked.

"Dr. Sorensen—in his own words—was not a very nice man, Joe. He talks about how he killed some of his patients."

"This cannot be," Hutson muttered.

What's wrong with you? Wolfe thought. *That's an odd reaction.* "He took the time to chronical selected events in his personal diary. It must have had some kind of therapeutic value, like washing away one's sins. The man puts down names, dates, locations, and how he killed each of these poor people. Of course we will check out all of it.

"Dr. Sorensen says he had no choice but to terminate certain patients he could not help. He rationalized each presented an unacceptable danger to society—homicidal tendencies. He rants on about how he provided an important service, one few could understand."

"How long has he been doing this?" Hutson asked.

"Looks like he killed his first patient forty years ago."

"How?"

"He hypnotized them, or gave them a sedative and made it look like suicide. He talks about hypnotically planting conditioned responses for a specific set of circumstances. When those conditions presented, the patient responded automatically. Through the power of suggestion, Dr. Sorensen put patients in situations where they essentially killed themselves. He also talks about sedating patients and rolling them off a cliff or into a pond. The sedative would dissipate and the death would appear to be an accident or suicide."

"I find all of this hard to believe," Hutson said.

Wolfe ran his finger down the dog-eared pages. "Says here that one of his patients jumped off a balcony. He lived on the twenty-third floor, an apartment building downtown. A glass of red wine and a metal railing triggered the conditioned response to jump."

"I didn't think a hypnotist could get you to hurt yourself."

"Maybe true for the stage acts, but I bet a psychiatrist has a lot more skills and control." Wolfe flipped several more pages to reach the next folded corner. "God! This patient put a shotgun in his mouth. Sorensen says the subconscious triggers were an empty house and the thought to brush teeth before going to bed. Those combined factors led his patient to get his shotgun, load it, put it in his mouth, and pull the trigger."

"This is crazy," Hutson said. "No one can make you do that stuff. I think the diary is no more than the wild rants and crazy imagination of an old and troubled psychiatrist."

Wolfe went to the next folded page. "This patient was instructed to drive her car into a brick wall when she was alone and her speedometer needle touched 60 mph."

"I can't handle hearing this right now," Hutson said. "I'm getting sick."

"Landers said they found Dr. Sorensen dead in the cabin in Algonquin. The good doctor was lying on the floor by the opened door. He was frozen solid. His back had been snapped like a twig, Joe—snapped backward. Whoever did that to him had to be very strong."

"It's possible he slipped on the ice and landed awkwardly," Hutson said.

"There was a chair in the center of the room, Joe. There were broken ropes on the floor next to it." He watched a drop of sweat roll down Hutson's face. The room was cold.

"You think he had a patient with him?" Huston asked.

"It appears that way," Wolfe said. "But this one broke the ropes and killed Sorensen. This one left the broken man to freeze, and to be dragged away by wild animals."

"Maybe Dr. Sorensen had no intention of hurting this patient," Hutson said. "Maybe this patient controlled everything. Maybe he did not intend to hurt the doctor."

That's bizarre rationale, Wolfe thought. *Why would you take the other side? What's the matter with you?*

"They found something else up there," Wolfe said. "They found a syringe on a windowsill. It had a full barrel and was uncapped—the needle ready to go. The syringe was probably filled with a sedative or poison. CSI is looking at it now. We'll know in the morning. If you ask me, looks like Sorensen had plans to kill whoever was tied up in that chair, Joe."

Huston closed his good eye. His head throbbed and arm stung. He wanted to go home.

"We need to find Dario. Maybe that's who you met this morning," Wolfe said.

"Dario? Where did that name come from?"

"He's mentioned in the diary, the page it was opened to on the kitchen table. Maybe he was the one tied to the chair, Joe. Maybe he brought the diary to Mrs. Sorensen. It looks like you came here at the wrong time."

"I don't follow."

"Dario may believe he did the world a great service killing Dr. Sorensen—a serial killer of the worst kind. Dario may have come here to deliver the diary to Mrs. Sorensen. Maybe he felt compelled to reveal the doctor's heinous acts. Maybe that's why she fainted."

"They've been married fifty years. If Dr. Sorensen was the monster you say don't you think Mrs. Sorensen would already know?"

"Can't answer that, Joe," Wolfe said as he closed the diary and slid it into his coat.

"This is my case. I need that diary," Joe said.

"No. You're a victim going to the hospital. I will take care of it."

"This Dario person did not kill us today, Wolfe. Why? It may mean he's not the bad person you paint him to be. Maybe he was defending himself. Maybe he killed the doctor in self-defense. Maybe he didn't kill anyone. This is all supposition."

Hutson's nervous effort to defend a potential killer was odd. Wolfe would give him the benefit of the doubt. It was time to get the shaken detective to a hospital.

"Are you gonna say anything," Joe said grabbing Wolfe's arms.

"This Dario character probably killed Dr. Sorensen, Joe. I think he brought the diary to Mrs. Sorensen for a reason, and you got in the way. It is very likely this sick guy believes he escaped death. He likely believes he killed a very bad man. Dario might be feeling good right now, but we need to find him before he starts feeling bad again."

TWELVE

"The feathered cigar flew through the air like an injured sparrow."

The bent old man with a cane poked along the edges of the tall marble buildings, his dark woolen coat dragging in the snow. Bundled beyond recognition he moved alone at a steady pace down East Washington. When a police car crawled by pushing a new trail in the deep snow, he turned slowly to keep his heavy backpack out of direct view. Through dark sunglasses he watched the cruiser disappear north onto Dearborn and smiled. It was something Norman Levitt rarely did when he was working, but the weather could not have been more perfect for an execution.

He stopped at the edge of the Kimpton Burnham Hotel. Out of view, and after looking both ways, he straightened to his six-two stature. His coat lifted a foot above the snow. Norman collapsed his cane and slid the precision metal pipe in its designated compartment inside his one-of-a-kind coat. He converted his bulky backpack into a squared satchel with handles—another expensive piece designed for certain occasions. Norman left on his sunglasses to deflect the glare off the white snow as he reshaped his hat into a more appropriate cosmo look. He put it on with a tilt and slid the *Wall Street Journal* under an arm. He left his limp outside. With a proper stride and at swift pace, he stared at his watch as he crossed the hotel lobby to the waiting elevator. No one would bother a successful businessman on a timeline.

When the elevator doors closed, Norman pressed fourteen and rubbed his thumb on his programed keycard inside his warm pocket. It pleased him most when the elements of his plans came together, like making sure the southwest corner room was out of service—unavailable to guests and not to be disturbed by management or maintenance personnel. That alone was not enough. Norman had to be certain its availability fit his schedule and that the conditions he created would assure him a twenty-four-hour window of privacy.

Gaining access to the room in advance was not the challenge. Breaking the Italian Verona Marble bathroom sink was. It had to appear the fault of the Verona artisan. The crushing pressure had to be applied in a precise manner to cause an internal fracture along the interface of the rare multi-red onyx and Inca-gold mosaic inlay. The unfortunate imperfection in craftsmanship had to then leak enough water to seep through the ceiling into the room below to insure discovery on Norman's timeline. His due diligence had already confirmed a replacement sink from Verona would not reach the Kimpton Burnham Hotel in less than three days. The corner room on the fourteenth floor was closed. The ideal location with a balcony and access to the roof had been secured. Norman's target would be in his scope at 1900 hours.

The Chase Tower, a sixty-story premier skyscraper and the eleventh tallest building in Chicago, reached for the heavens two blocks southwest of the Burnham Hotel. The meeting room secured by the CEO of the Babcock Boyle & Brayden Law Firm—Eldon Babcock—was more than adequate. Eldon had no intentions of sharing his newest client with the office staff. Holding the meeting at BB&B in the Willis Tower would have generated too many questions and attracted the attention of law enforcement and news media—something Eldon did not need. Fortunately his long-time personal accountant had offered the use of a boardroom at the Chase Tower. Available on Eldon's date, the meeting room met all the requirements—secured enough for a presidential visit, and veiled from building personnel and the general public.

The Cambridge Financial Accounting Firm owned the twelfth floor of the Chase Tower. Their boardroom on the northeast corner was strategically isolated from the accounting offices and had its own elevator. Eldon's list of attendees would be screened by an elite security staff and kept out of view in the underground parking garage. They then would be escorted to the private elevator and depart to the only stop—the boardroom.

Norman Levitt knew every square foot of the Chase Tower; he had obtained proprietary architectural drawings the day he confirmed the meeting had been set and his targets would be present. Norman knew the details of the underground garage, the twelfth floor, and everything in between. He knew the concrete, steel, and design specifications—the labyrinth of crawl spaces and ductwork, and the infinite conduits delivering electricity and security. Although he would only use a tiny percentage of this knowledge, he knew from experience any single piece of information could be pivotal if conditions changed.

Norman also knew the materials used in the construction of the Chase Tower. He took special interest in the walls and windows that surrounded his targets—the shell of protection. He researched composition, thickness, and the angles of installation for each of the enormous panes of window glass. He studied the temperature changes and the wind patterns around the building, usual behavior and ranges of fluctuation. Each variable would affect trajectory of his projectiles. A single millimeter diversion at any point along the half-mile trek from the Burnham Hotel could produce several inches of deviation. Norman was an expert. He never missed. He would have each target in his crosshairs starting at 1900 hours.

***

"Thank you for braving the weather, gentlemen," Babcock said as the last of the three private investigators sat down at the long conference table on the twelfth floor. Each held their favorite alcoholic beverage, a selection they had made upon arrival from the well-stocked bar.

"Where's Marcantonio," Fitz asked, the owner and operator of Fitz & Menara Investigations. His red bulbous cheeks and pursed lips looked to be the result of sucking a lemon for a day. "I thought he'd be here. Based on what I uncovered, I wouldn't miss this get together." Fitz flashed a two-tooth smile like a beaver. His small eyes darted to each at the table, but they ignored the irritating man they had known for years.

"Mr. Marcantonio will be here," Babcock said as eyes around the table found him. "I thought it best the four of us talk first. We need to validate our findings. It's important I have a unified view before making recommendations."

Fitz sipped his vodka and leaned back already bored and hungry. Mark Cranston of Cranston-Peters LLC and Bert Michaels of BLM-Investigations could be brothers. Their lean stature, wispy gray hair, and fake tans nursed drinks like little girls at a cookout. Both nodded at Babcock with no emotion. For them the money was enough to waste a day or two. They were two of the top private investigators in the country with plenty of people working for them. When Babcock called them, and quoted the retainer fee, they both cleared their calendars.

"I've reviewed your reports, gentlemen. Let me begin by thanking you for your participation. I know you had to make adjustments to accommodate my urgent request. I appreciate the speed and quality of your work—I did not expect anything less.

"First, we will talk about the most significant findings, those shared," Babcock said. "Then we can look at the outliers. Each of you will have an opportunity to amplify, correct, and/or to make additional recommendations. We have some time before Mr. Marcantonio and his team arrives. I expect them to step off that elevator at 7:00 p.m. sharp. That gives us twenty-seven minutes, gentlemen."

The sun set on the other side of the Chase Tower with little fanfare—the bland winter sky slowly dimmed above the foot of snow that carpeted the region. From the boardroom of Cambridge Financial, the string of red lights crawled north on Dearborn and white lights crawled west on Madison. Sparse pedestrian traffic dotted the sidewalks twelve stories down. When the office window blowers churned on, Babcock pressed a button on the built-in console at his end of the conference table. The large monitor dropped from the ceiling and the first graphic popped on the screen. The three adjusted their chairs and read in silence.

"I asked you to find out a few things for me. Identify and locate the sniper shooting Mr. Marcantonio's men. Identify the contractor. Identify and locate the man caught on the video I sent you—the vacant lot, 300 block of West 27th, the South Side. My client wishes to stop all threats.

"To identify and locate our shooter, you began with what we know. I provided the names of three sniper victims over the last six months. I saw from your reports that each of you looked into their backgrounds. You found common denominators. Then you launched an investigation. Gentlemen, I don't intend to do all the talking tonight. Here is where each of you can chime in with your findings and thoughts."

"It did not take long to determine Newman, Borden, and Pender were disgusting scumbags," Cranston said.

"The three possessed a laundry list of felony charges and convictions—sexual assault, robbery, drug trafficking, and murder. All three spent time behind bars. They all demonstrated a unique talent for getting out. Each had been charged for murder two or more times. Each had been convicted at least once. And each were back on the streets within three to six years after their down-graded conviction."

Cranston cleared his throat and took a sip of his drink. "The three taken out by a sniper were not your typical bad guys. These people were animals. Regardless of the prosecutorial routes taken to put these people away, they beat the system. I think all of us have concluded these three have killed far more people than is captured in their sick records."

"And this shared success in beating the system is due to one thing—their employer," Bert Michaels said. "Mr. Marcantonio spares no expense getting his people legal representation and manipulating the criminal justice system."

Fitz interrupted. "Marcantonio's reputation for defending his people is why he has survived for decades. His people are long time and loyal. They protect him."

Babcock tapped his finger on the table taking it in. "So you are saying the sniper targets are what you would classify as serial predators, not your run-of-the-mill thugs?"

"Definitely," Cranston said. "And there are several more 'serial predators' walking the streets. Many work for Mr. Marcantonio. What makes his unique is their history of beating the legal system."

"Like the representation James Harvey Pender received," Michaels muttered. The three PIs turned to Babcock to measure his reaction. "How does BB&B fit in this dismal equation?"

"I'm not proud that I represented that man." Babcock took a swallow of scotch. "For this room only, I was forced into it by my father. Jennings had an old debt to close out. He owed Mr. Marcantonio. My representation of Pender was difficult, but my father's debt is now closed."

Cranston smiled. "We understand, Eldon. We're not here to judge—we all have regrets in life. We're working for you. Money makes us all do things."

Babcock nodded. "I must say I was pleased to hear Mr. Pender was terminated at the property on West 27th Street. I sleep better knowing he's not out there. I am not proud of my involvement. The man was born with serial intent."

"We have another sniper victim, one not reported by Marcantonio," Fitz said.

"Eric Ramsey," Babcock said under his breath.

"Yes. Eric Ramsey got himself shot in the home of Lindsey Nolan Fetter," Fitz said. "My people at Chicago PD confirm a headshot, same caliber, and shot from a mile away. The bullet passed through curtains into a dark bedroom on the tenth floor of a building downtown. I found those facts alone to be chilling. Clearly our sniper is gifted."

Eldon rapped his fingers. Heads turned. "The window was not broken. We had another cold winter night when Ramsey got shot in her bedroom. We know Mrs. Fetter lives alone. Someone opened her window in advance. If it was a pre-visit by the sniper, the opened window would have been discovered—the cold night air, the lifting curtains."

"I doubt the sniper did it. Nor did she," Fitz scoffed. "Women don't open big windows, especially on the tenth floor in the wintertime. I was told it was opened a lot— several feet—enough to allow a clear path for a headshot from a mile away."

"The opened window reduced the risk of projectile deflection," Michaels said. The thick glass or metal trim could have caused a miss."

"My ballistics man said it would alter the path of a

bullet," Cranston confirmed.

"Someone connected to the sniper had to be in that bedroom before Ramsey."

"I agree," Fitz said. "The shooting occurred late. Fetter claims she was alone—according to the police report. I don't believe her. She had a visitor or two."

"But how did she know Ramsey was coming that night?" Cranston asked. "I believe she had to take part in setting up the kill. Maybe her visitor knew Ramsey was coming."

"I saw in your report Fetter had a gun," Babcock said. "If that's true, she would have been trained to use it and not need help."

"She did use the gun," Fitz said. "One shot—major miss. I think it's safe to assume she did not know a damn thing about her gun."

Michaels said, "I did some checking on the gun. It was registered to her, but she did not purchase that gun. We located the store where it came from. Turns out it was purchased the day Ramsey was released, purchased by an older man—Charlie Dunn."

"Maybe he loaned her the gun after she found out about Ramsey's release?"

"Don't know. We can't find Charlie Dunn to ask. Apparently he moved the same day."

"How does this connect Fetter to a sniper?" Babcock asked Fitz.

Cranston downed the rest of his drink and went to the bar while Fitz rubbed his forehead looking at his empty glass. "We don't know," Cranston said with his back to the group. He poured and turned with a full glass. "Mrs. Fetter did not appear to control anything at the crime scene except pulling that trigger one time and missing. She's no sleuth, gentlemen. Mrs. Fetter is a victim alone in the world."

"The whole thing had to be managed by a third party," Babcock said.

"We need to get video from around her building," Cranston said. "With some luck we may identify those connected to the sniper."

Babcock walked to the east window of the boardroom and looked north at the city skyline. As he contemplated Cranston's conclusion—one not challenged by his PI brethren—he took in the dark buildings with vertical lines of lighted windows. *A sniper could be anywhere at any time.* Babcock did not feel the crosshairs of Norman Levitt's scope.

He returned to the far end of the table. "I must agree with Mark. I believe the four dead men are connected. At the moment, our route to the sniper's identity is through Lindsey Fetter and Charlie Dunn. Mark, can you get video from around that building?"

"I will have it to everybody in the morning." He sent a text to his people.

"Good. Bert, I want you to make contact with Lindsey Fetter, nobody else. We do not want to shut her down before we get what we're looking for. Use your best methods to connect with Fetter to obtain the relevant information. Find out who was with her the night Eric Ramsey died in her bedroom. I'm looking for a fast turnaround."

"Why Bert Michaels," Fitz complained. "I have people more familiar with that aspect of the case. I obtained the police report and investigated the gun. I think I should meet with the Fetter woman. It will save us time."

"Not your call, Mr. Fitz. I have plans for you. I want you focused on the man in the video on West 27th Street." Babcock changed the graphic on the screen. "We need to speed things up. Mr. Marcantonio is fifteen minutes out."

"What do we want to share about progress on the sniper?" Michaels asked.

"No mention of the Fetter incident. We can talk about everything else."

Cranston got to his feet with his empty glass. "We best make it very clear, Marcantonio needs to disappear. Based on the dots we've connected so far, he and several of his people are on the sniper's kill list."

"I will strongly advise he go into hiding from here. I suspect he knows he's a target." Babcock looked down. *And he knows the sniper and the why.* "Gentlemen, as usual I have a client not sharing all he knows."

"Maybe he believes he can take care of the sniper himself," Cranston said.

"Maybe he wants us to cover all other possibilities," Michaels said.

"Marcantonio has survived a life of crime. Maybe he thinks he's invincible," Fitz scoffed. "The sniper seems to be working up to him."

"Okay. Let's change gears," Babcock said. "Let's talk about the man on West 27th Street. You have the video and the biometrics. This man is frightening."

"Anyone who can do what he did is frightening," Cranston mumbled.

"In a way he is more dangerous than the sniper," Babcock said.

Michaels opened a file. "I have my IT people working on this. They may be able to reconstruct the face from the few data points—advanced software. They only need four topographical points in key areas of the face. The software runs thousands of calculations every square millimeter and builds. I believe we will get a face and can work on identity."

"That's fascinating," Cranston said.

"I wish I could guarantee this will work," Michaels said. "Trouble is the guy is different. He can't even walk down the street during the day without being noticed. His facial deformities are difficult to reconstruct. It's possible that video is the only time his image has been captured."

"I bet he has the same mission as the sniper," Fitz said.

"They both were going after Pender. Maybe the motivation is the justice system that lets animals like that out."

"The system's been broken a long time," Cranston said. "We're all lawyers. We get it. We're part of the problem. We all have represented guilty people and gotten them off."

On Cranston's last word the elevator doors opened into the boardroom. All heads turned—it was 1900 hours. Two large men in dark suits and sunglasses entered the room with hands in their coats and heads scanning the area. One walked the perimeter. The other stood at the elevator door. After nods passed, William T. Marcantonio took a few steps into the room with a wide smile and long cigar. His three-piece black pinstriped suit shined beneath the recessed lighting.

When he saw his reflection in the enormous tinted windows, Marcantonio paused as if for a photo-op on the red carpet. Only a great man could have controlled his complex businesses over five decades. Only a great man could have survived the countless attempts on his life, and the clandestine efforts to take what belonged to him. But no one would ever know what else William Marcantonio saw in the window. Did he see the fracture line in the glass? Did he see the small hole produced by the first bullet? Was he surprised when his bodyguard's head exploded? Or did Marcantonio know it was his time to die?

Babcock froze on his path to greet Marcantonio. The second bullet passed through Babcock's right arm and entered the left eye of the second bodyguard. Both men dropped.

As the private investigators scrambled beneath the conference table, the third bullet pelted the tinted glass creating the third fracture line that had collected the nearby city lights. Instantly, Marcantonio's head exploded, his feathered cigar flew into the air like an injured sparrow. His empty hulk collapsed.

From the floor, Babcock turned to the windows in time to see a large sheet of glass slip away. The cold wind swept through the boardroom like a wild ghost. No one moved. Seconds of aftermath were an eternity, but it was not over.

Bullet number four had no window to penetrate. Its path would be the truest. Eldon heard it penetrate the wall behind him. Then he realized it had creased his scalp down the middle. The well placed projectile took his hair and his skin and left the white boney skull shining under the inset lights. Blood rolled down his forehead and dripped from his eyelids. Eldon would never forget the burn and the pain. Eldon was on the list. The sniper would be back for him.

THIRTEEN

Before Aaron Wolfe got to the Chase Tower, the CPD, DEA, and FBI were already on the ground searching a four block area. The surrounding buildings and projectile trajectory had given them a good starting point, although they had no expectations of finding the shooter.

The balcony sliding-glass door had been left open at the corner room on the fourteenth floor of the Kimpton Burnham Hotel. Staff and guests saw and heard nothing out of the ordinary. The hint of burnt gunpowder hung in room 1424. Remnants of a meal were found on the unmade bed. Furniture had been moved to the walls. Indentations in the carpet by the balcony door matched the tripod footprint of a Barrett .50 caliber sniper rifle. It aligned with the twelfth floor northeast corner of the Chase Tower four blocks away. There were no spent shells.

The FBI found surveillance camera lenses sprayed black on the fourteenth floor and in the back alley of the Burnham Hotel. They would spend hours scouring the grounds for the smallest piece of physical evidence, but would find only boot prints in the snow. The DNA on the food remnants matched the DNA found at prior sites, but still no match when run through the international database. This sniper had eight kills. The time between shoots had narrowed.

When Wolfe walked into the boardroom, the PIs flinched as if they had seen a ghost. When Wolfe stepped into the light, they relaxed—everyone knew the top Chicago homicide detective. "Hello gentlemen," he said with a brisk but troubled tone. The three stood there in silence staring at the detective and somewhat unsure on how they would handle the encounter—their involvement had to remain secret.

Wolfe helped them with their decision. "We can do this the proverbial easy way or hard way." He leaned closer and smiled. "I want all my questions answered tonight, gentlemen."

Fitz had the worst judgement of the three. His anger management issues often got him in trouble. Wolfe was the wrong man to test. "You can't just waltz in here and push us around like a bunch of criminals," he spewed. "I'll remind you we are all lawyers, Mr. Wolfe. We know our rights."

With outstretched arms, Wolfe turned his smile to Fitz and the group. Like an eagle going for a trout with all talons out, he backed them to the edge of the bar. His eyes burned a hole in Fitz's forehead. "I have *you* with a dead drug lord, a Chicago mafia kingpin killed by a sniper at your little meeting. I wonder. Did you set him up? Are you taking over his territory—drug trafficking, gambling, prostitution? Is this a carefully planned power play?"

Fitz turned red. "I never—"

"A smart man stuck in this horrible situation would want me to clear the air as quickly as possible with the media. A smart man would not want *time* to be his worst enemy. He would not want time with no answers to be misunderstood by an underground network of paranoid drug dealers, the mafia, and a sniper on a mission."

"Detective Wolfe," Cranston interrupted with a hand in Fitz's red face. "Of course we will cooperate. We will answer all of your questions."

Wolfe smiled and turned to Michaels. "You on board, Bert?"

Grabbing the Chivas bottle and a few glasses he said, "Yes. And may I suggest we move our discussion to an office without windows?"

In the small side room, Wolfe took a swallow and closed his eyes to relish the Chivas Regal burn. "My questions are simple and few, gentlemen." His next words were abrupt and pointed. "Eldon Babcock works for William Marcantonio. You work for Eldon Babcock. What was your assignment?"

"We were contracted to identify and locate the sniper responsible for killing three of Marcantonio's men over the last six month period," Cranston said.

"Names," Wolfe shot back.

"Borden, Newman, and Pender."

"Are those the only—?"

"We know Eric Ramsey was shot by our sniper," Fitz muttered. "But Ramsey did not work for Marcantonio."

"You know the Fetter homicide details?" Wolfe asked.

"Yes. And the Frank Pazrro homicide—Wunders Cemetery," Cranston said. "Unlike Ramsey, Pazrro had an association with Marcantonio."

Wolfe took another swallow of Chivas. "What else in your contract?"

Michaels looked around as if the room was bugged. "We were to identify and locate a mystery man caught on video. He attacked Marcantonio's people on the South Side. It's a bizarre confrontation on a vacant lot."

Fitz interrupted. "Although the guy is peculiar, finding him is way less important than finding and stopping the sniper, in my humble opinion."

"We will save your mystery man for later," Wolfe said. "What are the common threads connecting the sniper victims?"

"The five dead before tonight, we know about. They're lifelong criminals with records: multiple felony charges and convictions, assaults, murder, and rape. Each served time for murder. Each got out of prison in less than six years."

"That's odd. You're not talking murder one?" Wolfe asked.

"In all cases, charges of first degree murder were pleaded down," Cranston said. "The five were represented by high-priced law firms in Chicago—including Babcock's firm. Eldon represented Pender. The rest were handled by some of the smartest defense attorneys in the country, masters in reducing charges with all the tricks—like lack of intent, lack of knowledge, insanity, tossing evidence, and/or claiming self-defense for God's sake."

"The legal system is unmercifully manipulated," Michaels muttered.

"Give me more," Wolfe pushed remembering the conversation he just had with Lindsey Fetter. Maybe reformation of the justice system was the mission of more than a few vigilantes.

"The legal maneuvers used to free these people were similar," Fitz said. "The defense attorneys did their jobs. Damning evidence against their clients was compromised and often eliminated. Tactics included application of the exclusionary rule, claims of violation of search and seizure rules, challenging the integrity of the chain of evidence, failure to give rights, and accusations of tampering with evidence, witnesses, and juries. In all five cases, the legal knots tied led to plea bargains and reduced sentences. The prosecution was backed into a corner, their cases essentially destroyed before going to trial."

"They all got out of jail early," Cranston said. "The five served less than six years for murder. The reduced sentences were accomplished a number of ways—parole for good behavior, obscure governor pardons, special probation, and various and sundry work-release programs not shared with the public."

Michaels injected, "Pender and Ramsey committed heinous crimes. Their atrocities were covered by the news media. The other four were less prominent. Their crimes were just as frequent, cold-blooded, and vicious."

Fitz poured another scotch. "These five scumbags should have been executed after receiving a fair trial. They finally got what they deserved, a hole in the head."

FOURTEEN

"Escaping an icy winter wonderland would be difficult if not impossible."

He watched the last PI get in a taxi. It pulled away from Chase Tower spitting dirty slush onto the salted sidewalk. Their little chat had gone better than expected—PIs tend to be tight lipped. Most information obtained served only to confirm what Wolfe already knew.

He backed to the curb and looked up at the boarded windows on the twelfth floor. CSI had finished an hour ago. The ME authorized transport of the three in body bags to Cook County morgue—cause of death single gunshot wounds to the head, manner of death homicide. Wolfe did not need to wait for ballistics—.50 caliber, copper jacket, hollow point. He lit a cigarette, raised his collar, and started north on Dearborn.

When he passed the Truven Health complex, he felt eyes on him. When he turned onto West Calhoun by Adler University, he thought he was being followed. When he turned up North State Street he knew someone was closing from behind.

The plows had piled the snow high along the curb. After ten, sparse downtown traffic crawled icy streets and sidewalks. Wolfe turned the corner at Washington and hid in the shadow of the building.

SERIAL INTENT

Could it be the sniper? He wondered. *No—wouldn't make sense. Why hang around after your targets are down? What could you possibly want with the homicide guy investigating more of your kills? You're not gonna risk it. That would interfere with your real agenda. It's gotta be someone else following me.*

Members of the Marcantonio crime family would be working late. Their patriarch had been eliminated. They had questions that could not wait. Someone would pay. The family would reassert its control. For once in their miserable life the CPD would be working for them. They would hunt Marcantonio's killer.

When Wolfe backed into the shadow, it dawned on him he was at the Burnham Hotel. He had parked at the other end of the block. Wolfe leaned back against the cold brick after stepping out his cigarette. The man who rounded the corner did not see him. Wolfe pounced. He pulled his prey into the shadow and crushed him against the wall with a forearm.

"Who the hell are you?" Wolfe asked while pressing the man's neck to the bricks and patting him down for a weapon. "Talk to me," he ordered.

In the scant light Wolfe saw the face. It was disfigured, bruised, cut, and bandaged. Wolfe saw the swollen eyes below the knit cap. Then it registered. He knew his stalker. "Barry Woods." Wolfe released neck pressure. "Why're you here?"

"I needed to find you."

"Why?"

"We gotta talk," he said as he choked beneath Wolfe's forearm.

"We did. The hospital, remember? You had nothing to say." Wolfe dropped his arm, brushed his sleeves, and looked up and down Washington Avenue. He turned back to Woods and lit another cigarette. "You're lucky I didn't bust your stitches."

"Are you closer to identifying the shooter, Detective Wolfe?"

"What are you talking about? What shooter? This investigation's only a few hours old. There's no information out there about a shooter."

Woods swallowed. He was as tall as Wolfe but a hundred pounds lighter, and his muscles were rarely used for anything but mobility. "You don't have to be too smart to figure out what happened here tonight. There's plywood where windows should be on Chase Tower. Three bodies were taken out in black bags. The FBI and DEA vans are parked everywhere, and the Chicago police are all over the place like ants after someone poked their nest."

Wolfe had to agree. They don't hide much even when they try. "What do you want?"

"I know William Marcantonio was executed by a sniper tonight," Woods said, "The same sniper who executed Frank Pazrro and Eric Ramsey."

Wolfe straightened grabbed Woods collar and yanked. "Are you in this, Woods?"

"I'm having second thoughts. I don't know what to do." Wolfe let go like he was dropping a small fish back into the water. Woods said, "It was the right thing to do at the time, but it's gotten out of control. Ellen is dead and it's my fault."

"What are you talking about?" Wolfe stared.

"She was not supposed to get hurt. She was bait. That was the plan." Woods dropped his head. "I failed her."

Wolfe looked up and down the empty street a second time. "Come with me. We're going inside the Burnham Hotel. You're going to tell me everything."

"The place is crawling with FBI and DEA. I don't want to talk to them. I don't—"

Wolfe grabbed his shoulder and spun him up the sidewalk. "They won't bother us. They don't like local homicide boys. We know enough to screw with them." He let go. "Just stay close and don't look so damn guilty."

Two stuffed chairs by the fireplace off the lobby waited. They removed their coats and sat by the popping fire. "Tell me about your *second thoughts* and Miss Dumont's death. Anything you say can and will be used against you in a court of law. You have the right to an attorney. Should you be unable to afford an attorney, one will be—"

"I know all that. Remember, I am an attorney. And it's *could* be used not *can and will* be used. I get it. I could tell you that I killed Ellen and you would not be able to use it unless—"

"Trust me, I'd lie," Wolfe said as he waved for a drink. Woods appeared to be a stronger personality than the one he showed the night he was beaten to a pulp. "Talk to me."

"Ellen writes a column for the *Chicago Tribune*. A few years ago she read about a man who lost his family—a home invasion. His teenage son was beaten to death. His wife was sexually assaulted and then killed. They left the man for dead. He lived. The outcome of the trial caught Ellen's attention. The killer was caught and found guilty, but he only got twelve years and served six."

"There are always extenuating circumstances. Not everything is as it seems."

"Legal tricks got him out, Detective Wolfe. The prints and DNA—the important physical evidence—were thrown out based on trumped-up accusations and creative legal maneuvers. The sole survivor, the husband, had his testimony discredited. The defense convinced the jury the poor man was biased."

"Probably supported by a team of doctors," Wolfe muttered.

"Yes. Their professional opinion suggested he manufactured the events while in a six month coma. The prosecution was forced to plea bargain or risk setting the guy free. First degree murder became second degree with extenuating circumstances."

"You say this case caught Miss Dumont's attention. So what?"

"In 2014 there were 419 murders in Chicago, 1,479 criminal assaults, 11,823 robberies, 6,341 aggravated battery, 15,557 thefts, 12,615 motor vehicle thefts, and 2,084 shooting incidents. Sorry, I have a photographic memory," Woods said.

"Good for you. Welcome to my world," Wolfe scoffed.

"It shocked Ellen to see the level of crime in this city. Like so many, she did not know the extent. She felt she had to do something. Ellen decided to focus on the crime of murder. From 1991 to date the murder rate in this city stayed above 450 a year. That's when I got interested in the statistics and joined her research. We discovered almost 87 percent of the killers had extensive prior arrest records and awful felony histories."

"Is this going anywhere soon?"

"The criminal justice system knows all about these bad people before they kill."

"Get to the point, Woods."

"But it's important to—"

Wolfe turned to the waiter. "Two scotch on rocks." The waiter disappeared.

"I don't drink alcohol," Woods said.

"I didn't get anything for you." Wolfe lit a cigarette and tossed the match in the fireplace.

"Maybe a Coke—"

"Ellen Dumont wrote for the *Tribune*," Wolfe said. "One day she finds out about the big nasty city she lives in and decides to make it her cause. She is gonna clean up the rat hole, home of 2.7 million people and a law enforcement agency with small brains. She is so smart she knows we can't figure out the obvious. Cut to the chase. Tell me how all this got her killed and got you responsible."

They paused as two scotches were put on the small

table between them. Wolfe slid both to his side. The waiter left them alone again. "Ellen started writing about this, the failures of the criminal justice system," Woods said. "Her column was entitled—*Serial Intent*. Each month she focused on one case. As you know, there are plenty to choose from. I started helping with legal research. I could explain the law—like justifiable homicide, first and second degree murder, felony murder rules, the role of prosecution and defense, rights of the accused, jury selection, and plea bargaining—"

Wolfe crushed a cube between his molars and glared. "You're killing me. Do you always use so many words to say the obvious? I understand. You're an attorney, a Harvard man. You know the law. You know the courtroom. You supported your girlfriend by teaching her all that stuff as she wrote her column and got even more pissed off. Now, get on with it."

Woods leaned back in the chair and stared at the fire as he spoke. "She got hate mail all the time. She got terrible phone calls at the *Tribune*. It was routine, mostly from the sick friends of the convicted. It got bad when she wrote about the Janice Franklyn case."

Wolfe knew about Franklyn, the young school teacher followed home by a monster. She lived alone in a quiet neighborhood, had her whole life ahead of her. Wolfe was the first homicide detective on the scene—it was a bloodbath. The medical examiner did not find all of Franklyn's body parts. She had been butchered. Like hiding Easter Eggs, the pieces were all over the house. They did find enough to prove rape and that Frank Pazrro wielded the knife. Like so many, Wolfe had lost track of the human refuse. There were too many active homicides in the city of Chicago to investigate.

"Frank Pazrro called Ellen at her home," Woods muttered. "We called the police, but they couldn't do anything until he did something. Using the phone was not a crime, and the threats were his word against ours. We could not believe the guy was out of prison after six years—good behavior qualified him for some experimental work-release program."

"Continue," Wolfe pushed.

"We got a call one night, anonymous, an elderly man. He asked if we needed help with Pazrro. He said he was a member of a private organization that protected people from monsters. There was no charge for their services."

"Sounds too good to be true," Wolfe sighed.

"It did to us, too. We rejected the offer," Woods said. "Pazrro kept calling. He took great pleasure in describing how he would have his way with Ellen. He said that once she had satisfied all his sexual needs, he would dismember her—remove parts of her body in a way that would keep her alive as long as possible. He wanted Ellen to experience what Franklyn experienced."

Woods face turned white as he sunk into the chair. "We found dead animals around the house. First birds, their heads cut off. Then mutilated cats and rabbits. The police came. A report was filed. They talked to Pazrro. He claimed he did not know Ellen Dumont. He said he had no idea why she would say he did such terrible things. He said she was trying to sell newspapers. The police could do nothing."

"Another scotch, and add a Coke," Wolfe said to the waiter standing behind Woods. "Okay, continue counselor."

"The man I told you about, the one who offered to help us, he called again. They knew everything Pazrro was doing. They knew the police could do nothing. It happens all the time. He explained the hands of law enforcement were tied—it was not their fault. More often than not they were blocked from protecting and serving the innocent like they wanted. The man on the phone offered a solution. He proposed a meeting. We agreed to listen. We met in an abandoned building on the corner of 64th Street and Green, an old Masonic Lodge building."

"When did you meet with the guy?"

"Midnight, August 27. It was a foggy night in the city—spooky. We almost didn't go because of the weather. We met in the old crumbling building. Never saw him, though."

"How'd he manage that?" Wolfe asked.

"He stayed in another room. It was dark in there. We understood his desire to hide his identity. We didn't need to see him. The man spoke through a hole in the wall. He said their anonymity was a requirement. He said he belonged to a secret organization of shepherds for justice. He said they had operations in three cities—Detroit, Memphis, and here."

"Wonderful. Do they have a name?" Wolfe asked.

"The Dario Group, I had never heard of them before."

Dario! Wolfe took a swallow of scotch. *A possible connection.*

"He said they weren't listed anywhere. Unlike most people frustrated with the judicial system, the Dario Group has a singular mission. They represent victims and protect survivors. They talk about serial intent—those people who intend to kill often."

"Interesting," Wolfe said. "That's the same mission of law enforcement and our judicial system minus the subjective judgement of vigilantes."

"They don't believe you guys have done a very good job with the real monsters."

"Real monsters—you've used that a few times. What's their definition?" Wolfe asked.

"I said they are known serial killers that the criminal justice system cannot or will not keep out of society. The Dario Group is done waiting."

"Nice," Wolfe muttered. "I assume Frank Pazrro is one with serial intent."

"Yes. He qualified. The Dario Group does their research. Pazrro killed five times. His legal representation got him off two times on legal technicalities, and two times witnesses disappeared. The fifth time their representatives pleaded down to second degree—six years."

"The Dario Group has their own legal experts."

"Yes they do. And they are not encumbered by a fledgling legal process hell bent on eliminating proof to insure the most horrific serial killers get a fair trial at the cost of justice."

"Enough on philosophy, tell me about the process," Wolfe pushed.

"First, we had a planning meeting to decide the best way to handle Mr. Pazrro and his death threats. We agreed it best to terminate Pazrro. He would never change."

"There's a surprise," Wolfe said under his breath.

"We would lure Pazrro to a designated location—the Wunders Cemetery. Once there, it was my responsibility to kill him."

"Really, I didn't see that coming."

"They were very clear on that procedural point. The Dario Group was not in the business of killing people. They were researchers, organizers, coordinators, and protectors. If the victim was unwilling to kill their monster, the project was unworthy of their time."

"So this Dario Group gets you all fired up with a plan, then they put you out there alone? And you didn't walk away?"

"We did walk away. I couldn't kill anyone. But Pazrro didn't walk away. He increased his harassment, his relentless threats. I became convinced he would hurt Ellen. She was too exposed. So, we reconnected with the Dario Group."

"You agreed you would stop Frank Pazrro, a hideous serial killer? No offense Woods, but I've had more fight from girls than I had pinning you to the wall."

"I am not a fighter. I had to prepare."

"I would think so," Wolfe said. "Guess you stopped working out."

"I was given instructions. The knife you found at the crime scene belonged to me."

"This is not going to help you."

"Ellen was to let it be known she walks her dog in the cemetery every night alone. Each night for weeks I went first, entered the cemetery from the back. I hid behind a large grave marker with my knife. I waited for him.

"Then it happened. Yes. Pazrro was more than I could handle. He knocked me out."

Woods dropped his head. "I regained consciousness and saw him on top of Ellen." Woods looked up at Wolfe. "Pazrro was raping her. She was not moving." Woods squeezed the arms of his chair. "I went crazy. We fought a long time. He was about to kill me. Headlights moved through the cemetery, someone going by I guess. He kicked me in the head and ran off. I called 911 and passed out." Woods sunk deeper into his chair.

Wolfe casually surveyed the lobby. He saw DEA activity, but they were leaving them alone. "You're a smart guy, a Harvard grad. I don't get it. How did you convince yourself you had a chance against a killing machine like Pazrro?"

"I knew I couldn't stop him," Woods said. "But the Dario Group said I had to try. For Ellen's sake, I had to show we were willing. They would cover my back. They didn't tell me how, but I believed they would be there for us if necessary."

That explains the sniper, Wolfe thought.

"I lost Ellen. They were late. They shot him in the head too late," Woods mumbled.

That information has not been released. "How do you know this?" Wolfe asked.

"A phone call at the hospital."

"Tell me more."

"Don't worry. I know the information is not out there," Woods said.

"I'm not worried. Tell me what you know and how," Wolfe pushed.

"The phone call came in the middle of the night. I was lightly sedated in a private room. I heard the phone. No one picked up. The lady on the phone said she was sorry about Ellen, but the monster is dead—a bullet in his head. He would hurt no one else."

"What lady?"

"I don't know. I didn't go to any meeting, Ellen did. This lady did not identify herself except to say she represented the Dario Group. She was old. She said I would never hear from them again. And she reminded me of our agreement."

"What agreement? You didn't say anything about an agreement."

"It wasn't much. Ellen and I had to agree we would never implicate the Dario Group. I guess I agreed not to do what I'm doing right now."

"Interesting request," Wolfe said staring at the fire.

"They would see it as an act of aggression. They could not allow anyone to put them in more danger than they already were. Their mission was too important to be jeopardized. They would protect their members, the victims, and the survivors. That was the deal."

"I'm sure you're familiar with the Serious Crime Act of 2007," Wolfe said.

"Yes, I am. The offence of encouraging or assisting a crime is an inchoate offence. I encouraged and assisted in the act of murder."

"In your case you and the Dario Group are complicit in the deaths of at least two people, Ellen Dumont and Frank Pazrro. You participated in the planning and implementation of cold and calculated murder. As an attorney you know better than most our legal system does not differentiate between good and evil. Our justice is based on the premise no one should be killed by another."

Wolfe flicked his cigarette into the fire and put a wad of bills on the table for the drinks. "You leave me no room here, Mr. Woods. I gotta take you in. It's my job."

"I understand and really don't care. If the legal system was not screwed up, Ellen would be alive today and Pazrro would have been executed the first time he killed. Unfortunately our society seems to be okay with a monster killing five innocent people, destroying five families, and punishing the one meaningless person left standing."

"I agree with everything you said, but my job is enforcing the law. Someone else convicts and punishes. Right now you're my ticket to the next dance."

"If people like you and I allow this craziness to continue, there's going be a lot more death and despair in the world, Mr. Wolfe. We're graduating 45,000 lawyers a year. When I got out of law school in 2011, there were 1.2 million licensed attorneys. If they don't deliver results, they're on the streets and replaced. In criminal law, that means find a way to get your client off. The judicial system is being gamed everyday like a two dollar blackjack table in Vegas."

Wolfe got to his feet. "We need to go. You can educate smarter people than me on this Dario Group. If those people are for real, we've got a much bigger problem than I thought."

The two stepped outside onto East Washington into a frigid blast of air whipping between the buildings. The plowed streets of Chicago were now covered with black ice, and the curbs were buried beneath glassy three-foot piles.

"My car is parked on Dearborn," Wolfe said turning west. He had no need to handcuff Barry Woods, a broken man going nowhere. Wolfe wanted to let him go, but he had no choice. The Dumont case connected to seven other unsolved homicides. Now Wolfe knew the sniper who killed Pazrro worked for the Dario Group. Careful dissection of Wood's meetings and conversations with other CPD members could shed new light. Woods cooperation would be why the city prosecutor would offer a plea deal and send the broken man home.

When they reached the alley, the crack of lightning rolled down East Washington. Wolfe knew instantly what he should have known at the fireplace in the Burnham—Barry Woods is a target. Wolfe instinctively tackled Woods. At the edge of the hotel, the second blast caught up to the exploding bricks inches above Wolfe's flying and outstretched body shielding Woods. When the chunks of brick and mortar stopped raining down on the black ice, and when Wolfe and Woods stopped sliding across the alley into a mound of snow, the echo faded and sounds of winter crept back into the city.

Wolfe was covered in blood—not his. Woods had been hit, most of his face gone. Wolfe rolled to his feet and sprinted east on Washington. The sniper had to be on foot—the shots fired at street level and close. Escaping the icy winter wonderland would be difficult, and the sniper had to hide a weapon. Wolfe had a chance.

FIFTEEN

"His existence was far less significant than a wisp of wind on the farthest edge of the smallest storm."

What did I just do? Where have I been? Joe Hutson's car steamed in the garage. He got out of the shower and threw on a robe—it was time to end it all. Standing in the kitchen he looked at his reflection on the sharp edge of the turkey carving knife. *Go ahead. You gotta do this now. There are no more excuses for your miserable existence. You gotta stop—*

The knock at the door in the middle of the night came as a surprise. Joe dropped the knife in the sink. He had expected no one at three o'clock in the morning. He was released from the hospital six hours ago. His orders were to go home and go to bed. They gave him enough pain meds to choke a Clydesdale. Taking all of them at once had never dawned on him.

When he opened the door, he saw his boss. Commander Landers stood under the light in the snow with two bags of groceries. "I knew you'd be up." He walked by Hutson like he lived there. "Close that thing before you lose all the damn heat."

Landers set down the bags in the kitchen and started unpacking. He had stopped at an all-night deli and got sliced turkey, ham, beef, two cheeses, and three breads—

French, rye, and Brioche. He picked up a head of lettuce, tomato, red onion, and handful of sprouts. "I'm assuming you got mayo, vinegar and oil, and mustard," Landers said eyeing the knife in the sink—it looked out of place. Why would a clean shiny knife be sitting in an empty sink with nothing in the dish drainer and no signs of food prep?

Hutson leaned on the edge of the counter in his wet robe with his head down.

"Just get out of the shower?" Landers asked.

Hutson nodded. "What are you doing here?"

Landers draped his coat on a kitchen chair, pushed his gray shaggy hair off his lined forehead, and approached the detective he had watched grow over a decade. Landers put a hand on Hutson's shoulder and shook him back into the world. When their eyes met, he spoke with the smile of a proud elder, "You're not killing yourself today, Joe."

They ate most of the food and talked until the sun came up. Landers ignored his pager—the bee on the coffee table in the other room. Whatever it was could be handled by someone else or wait until he got to the office—the city never slept.

Hutson needed someone now more than ever. He struggled over a day and night of total confusion. He had too much time in the dark closet to think about his lackluster career and pitiful life. Both were boring, unremarkable, and now unbearable. He had convinced himself his existence was far less significant than a wisp of wind on the farthest edge of the smallest storm. In the closet at the Sorensen's brownstone, Hutson had concluded his life made no difference. His end would go unnoticed. His memory would be forgotten faster than a bag of garbage tossed on a pile of swarming flies in a city dump. He had to accept the truth. He did not really know what happened at the Sorensen's place.

"We all have fears, Hutson," Landers said. "Personally, I can't stand to be alone. Don't know why.

Probably goes back to something as a kid. But I've never had a problem taking on responsibility or being held accountable. I've never been afraid of anything I do in my job on a day-to-day basis. Did you hear me? I'm afraid of being alone, Joe."

"I heard you," Hutson muttered. "I go around all day afraid I'm gonna screw somethin' up, and others counting on me are going to pay the price for my mistakes."

"Okay. Then that's your thing. Doesn't mean it's any more important or any more real than any other thing tugging at a man. It's something you know exists. Next thing you do is manage it so it doesn't drive you crazy."

"I don't get that part—managing it."

"When I'm alone and my sick feeling creeps in, I get up and walk around. I distract myself. Before I know it, I've forgotten I was feeling alone. I work through it by not giving it all my attention. I discovered that works for me."

"So you're saying when I feel inept and incapable, I should accept it as a feeling not as reality, and then I'm supposed to distract myself somehow?"

"Exactly. It's a feeling, Hutson. You're not inept. You're not incapable. If you were, you would not have lasted as a CPD homicide detective. That feeling is not a true measure of reality. Find a way to give it as little of your time as possible. Instead, focus on the problem that gave rise to that feeling. Take the Sorensen case. When did you feel you were in over your head? Let's identify what triggered your worst fear? Did it happen the moment you took on the case?"

"Not until I got to the brownstone and started asking the lady questions," Hutson said.

"Okay. What triggered the negative feelings?" Landers asked.

"The way she answered my questions, like she already knew me."

"Good. Now develop that thought."

Hutson put his coffee cup down. "I got the sense she was being dishonest. I believed her husband was missing. She acted like she did not have great concern, but I felt she was holding back. She was sharper—more aware—than she wanted me to know. That's when I felt like I was going to screw things up."

"First time for the feeling?" Landers asked.

"I think so. Yes. It was."

"Let's focus on that event. Something triggered your most negative personal feelings. You say you got a sense Mrs. Sorensen was hiding something. She was manipulating you."

"Yes. That's when I started to—"

Landers cut him off. "What made you think that, Joe?"

Hutson took a long swallow of coffee looking out the kitchen window at the snow covered trees—Mrs. Sorensen appeared. "Her eyes, I read something in her eyes."

"Good. Go with that," Landers pushed.

"Her eyes darted around after she delivered each piece of information—she seemed to analyze her performance. Her eyes were intense, not tired and empty like old people. Each time I looked at her she looked away. She didn't want me to read her. But I knew she knew something important. Mrs. Sorensen pretended to be old and feeble. I caught her studying me. It was as if she was waiting for me to do something or remember something."

"What else did you find out?" Landers asked. "Go back in your mind. You questioned her. You observed her. You saw a man in the hall. You had a confrontation. You were injured, tied up, and stuffed in a closet. You experienced more than you're letting yourself remember. Instead of dealing with the reality of the moment, you've spent the last twenty-four hours distracted, drowning in your fears of inadequacy. It's time to be a homicide detective."

He leaned back in the kitchen chair rubbing his neck

like he was awakening from a coma. The commander's words made perfect sense. Hutson started to let the details of his investigation flow for the first time. After six hours of talking to Landers, he stood at a crossroad. Either he changes his life, or he buries the turkey knife in his chest after Landers leaves.

"She knew Dario was there," Hutson said.

"Mrs. Sorensen knew what?" Landers asked with a slight smile. He could see him evolving—stepping past his fears. Joe's focus had moved to the right place.

"Dario, the name Wolfe mentioned. She knew he was in the house and she was not afraid. She knew her husband was dead and that was okay."

"Keep going."

"Why did she go into the kitchen? Why did she make sure I stayed in the den by the fire? Maybe she went in there to hide her husband's diary. She couldn't remove it from the kitchen without me seeing, so she covered it with a newspaper. Maybe Dario was cornered somewhere. I should have walked through the residence the moment I arrived."

"You're talking about the diary Wolfe brought to the station?"

"Yes. That's Dr. Sorensen's diary. It may be helpful. Someone needs to read all of it."

"Do you remember hearing anything while you were in the closet?" Landers asked.

Hutson got to his feet and walked to the kitchen window. The sun was up. A squad car pulled into his driveway. "I heard something about more monsters to kill."

"Okay. Good. Do you know who tied you up?" Landers asked.

"No. When I regained consciousness, I was tied up. Mrs. Sorensen was in there with me. I was cold. She was warm. I thought maybe she was put in there later."

The knock at the door startled Landers. "Who the

hell's that?" He jumped up and ran to the door. Hutson poured more coffee and waited. Over the last hour he had not thought once about his personal inadequacies. He had focused on the case and it felt good.

"Sir. There's been another shooting downtown," the officer said with urgent eyes.

"I've been fully briefed on the Chase Tower shooting. Detective Wolfe is handling the case. You need to find him for questions and developments. I'm busy here."

The officer caught his breath as he waited for Landers to finish. "No sir. I'm talking about the shooting after the Chase Tower."

Landers straightened. "Another shooting?" Hutson stepped into the entry.

"Detective Wolfe left Chase Tower and met Barry Woods at the Burnham Hotel. Woods is the boyfriend of Ellen Dumont, a homicide victim. Wolfe and Woods left the Burnham Hotel around midnight. The sniper returned, sir. Mr. Woods is dead. Shot outside the hotel. Detective Wolfe pursued the shooter on foot. Well sir, it's not good."

SIXTEEN

"The thing about the truth is, not a lot of people can handle it."
Conor McGregor

"Are we sure *John Doe* wasn't hit by a car," Dr. Provost said tongue-in-cheek as he adjusted the new LED light over the body. "Never thought I would actually see it," he muttered. His team assembled in the autopsy room.

"See what, doctor?" The field agent leaned in lowering his fat clipboard.

Provost's eyes continued to peruse the corpse like no one else in the room could, and they all knew it. "Someone with virtually every bone in their body broken."

Like androids the two gowned and masked dieners stood in the light on the other side of the naked body. With stocked carts on their sides, the histologist and toxicologist waited at the dead man's feet. When the medical examiner completed his external examination, and the medical photographer's last flash dissipated, Dr. Provost put a hand over his mic and said, "Okay people, let's get started. They're lining up on the runway." And as always he added, "These people want to talk to us."

The ME always made the first cuts. In this case, he went further. Provost opened the chest and inspected the crushed rib cage with a magnifying glass. While shaking his head, he spewed Latin into his headset, and then waved his dieners into action.

The first diener focused on the chest. With the skill of a surgeon, he moved his scalpel deep in the thoracic cavity isolating organs in the gathering blood pool. The second diener began work on the head. He dragged his razor on a course from one ear to the other across the back of the head. The single pass cut a perfect incision down to the skull bone. With a long curved spatula he probed the depths of the wound he had created. He sent the sharp metal tool in all directions separating the periosteum (underside of the scalp soft tissue) from the skull bone. He then grabbed the loose scalp flap. Like taking off a rubber Halloween mask from the back, he pulled the scalp forward folding it up and over the top of the head until the back hairline rested on the nose of the deceased.

The medical examiner studied the surface of the bloody skull. Every square inch revealed micro fractures radiating from the lateral aspect of the cranium and merging medially. Provost spoke into his headset as he dabbed at the bloody bone.

"The macro examination of the external cranium reveals an intricate network of micro fractures emanating from the left and right temporal regions. The fracture network moves from a 0.1 millimeter matrix size to a 0.4 millimeter matrix at the crown. It appears an external force applied sufficient pressure equally and at the same time to both temporal regions crushing the skull inward. Severe damage to the brain and underlying soft tissues is expected."

Provost nodded to the diener with the bone saw. The circumferential skull cut path followed the largest head diameter on a line above the ears. The ME inserted the skull breaker instrument and hammered in various locations until the skull cap released. After removing the dura sheath he spoke into his headset again. "Consistent with the observations on the CT scans, the external aspect of the deceased's brain tissue is severely bruised with more than a dozen subdural hematomas and micro tears homogenous on the right and left cerebral hemispheres. The Rolandic fissures are compressed and ruptured."

The Office of the Medical Examiner for Cook County was established in 1976. It is responsible for handling all unexplained and traumatic deaths occurring in an area representing half the Illinois population. Unlike the old coroner system it replaced, a medical examiner is an appointed position. The candidate must possess a medical license and be certified by the American Board of Pathology in anatomic and forensic pathology. Dr. Leonard Holt Provost had the credentials and experience. Sought by most major cities, the top-five forensic mind in the country chose to go home. With graying temples and a natural tan, Provost led the sweeping changes that transformed the Cook County ME Office into one of the top forensic facilities in the country. Today it efficiently processes several hundred unexplained and traumatic deaths from their region each month—all homicides, suicides, accidental deaths, and questionable deaths that may (or may not) be found to be due to natural causes.

The dieners passed organs to the ME for inspection. After the external examination and weighing, he carved each like a Christmas turkey and selected a representative tissue sample for microscopic examination to take place later in the day. Each sample was preserved in a labeled jar of formalin for processing in the forensic histology lab. This time Dr. Provost demanded his slides be ready by noon. He had to eliminate disease process from the list of possibilities rolling around his head. Although this *John Doe* was a healthy male in his thirties, well nourished, athletic, and normal in all ways, the ME had never seen the extent and nature of the injuries produced by hand-to-hand combat as described by the CPD.

"I don't need to tell you they're waiting," Winston Foster said from the edge of the light by the head of the deceased. His words were meant for Provost.

With his nose in the empty cranial cavity, the ME held up one finger.

The only people talking during a Provost inquest were the medical examiner and the field agent who handled the case, unless Provost asked a question of a member of his medical team. Winston Foster was brought to Chicago by Provost on the day Provost accepted the position of Chief Medical Examiner for Cook County. Winston was the best forensic investigator Provost had ever encountered in his thirty years.

The introverted man trapped in a boy's body—a sinewy stature, long unkempt wavy hair, long narrow face, and small nose supporting oversized round glasses—looked more like the quiet neighborhood nerd employed by a major fast food franchise. Winston looked like he could screw up an order of cheese fries. Instead, he was a forensic investigation genius often the most pivotal contributor in Provost's rulings on his most complex cases. Without Winston's field expertise, the ME could miss too much on the autopsy table.

Provost backed out of the cranial cavity wiping his bloody gloves on another towel. The two stared at *John Doe* under the LED lights. They had another difficult one. "The CPD is always waiting. I can't rush these things. You know that."

"Yes. I know that, but they don't." Winston breathed.

Provost turned the deceased's head on its side and examined the hole pushed into the temple. It was the size of a thumb. From the corner of his eyes he saw Winston push his glasses up the bridge of his nose and step back. Provost knew it was time he listened. "Talk to me Winston. What's going on in that mind of yours," he said as he hovered over the body.

"The person who killed *John Doe* is not your average strong guy with martial arts expertise. The crime scene—the damage in that parking garage off East Washington—is epic."

"Epic!" Provost said snapping his other glove. "That's a word I don't believe I've ever heard you use," he said with a turn of the head and curious smile under his paper mask.

"The cement column near the body was missing a significant chunk of concrete."

"I see. But, what do we really know about it, Winston? It could have been damaged by a car prior to the killing. People are running into those things all the time. I need more."

"It's not old. And it's not mechanically induced. CSI is taking samples for closer examination. We are checking for prints and DNA."

"Fingerprints? DNA?" Provost rose up from the corpse and turned to his field agent. "Why would you go to such great lengths with random rubble? What does it have to do with the killing? Where are you going with this?"

Winston kept staring at the head without a brain. "I think the killer removed a chunk of cement from the pillar. I think he did it with his hand."

"It must be an old pillar."

"We have seen a lot of strange things. This is important because whoever did that is still out there, the person who killed *John Doe*. He has incredible strength and rage. I think this guy got beaten to death by someone who is very angry and not done."

"I'm seeing the rage," Provost muttered. "The bruising all over the body. I believe the killer held him by his ankles and swung him like a ragdoll into the ground a dozen times."

"There was blood spray twenty feet from the body. The floor of the parking garage looked like the floor of a slaughter house. I never saw so much blood from one victim."

"This is not good," Provost said as he looked at the deceased's hands for defensive wounds—there were none. "Wrists are broken."

"There was a rifle at the crime scene—the Barrett .50 caliber sniper rifle."

"I heard. I understand ballistics has it now. I'm sure we'll find it connects to the other sniper kills that night." Provost looked over at the chalkboard on the wall, the list of pending cases. "Mr. Marcantonio, his two bodyguards, and a man by the name of Barry Woods. All head wounds. Sniper fire."

Winston checked his notes. "Eric Ramsey, James Pender, Jake Newman, Charles Bordon, and Frank Pazrro are the other .50 caliber GSWs to the head in the city over the last six months."

"Commander Landers wants to get with me later this afternoon to compare notes. I would like you there, Winston."

"Yes, sir."

"If *John Doe* is the sniper, we should see an end to the exploding heads around here. That would be lovely," Provost said under his breath as he considered the next case.

"Have you seen the Barrett rifle?" Winston asked.

"No. I came here from the airport. These homicides are priority." Provost accepted the bloody heart from a diener. He rinsed it off and studied the tissue and structures under the brightest light—each ventricle, atria, and coronary artery. "Pink. Pliable. Perfect. The poor guy could have lived to a hundred. Probably a runner. Too bad."

"What about the rifle, Winston?"

"The condition of the rifle is another reason why I'm asking for a closer look at the cement pillar," Winston said. "The barrel was bent 180 degrees in the middle. The rifle was hung on an antenna, a random car parked next to the body. The killer is sending us a message, sir."

Provost passed the heart to the histologist and turned to his field agent. Resting his bloody hands on his bloody scrubs above his protruding stomach, he smiled. "Sometimes you wait far too long for me to catch up, Winston. We've talked about this before."

"Yes, sir."

"Are you saying the sniper in Chicago is John Doe? Are you saying although he's a heinous killer, you believe he is far less dangerous than the man who killed him?"

"Yes, sir."

"And you are saying this unusually strong and angry person will likely wreak more havoc upon our city, more than anyone can imagine at the moment?"

"Yes, sir."

"You are urging me and the CPD to not mess around. We must examine each and every clue to identify and locate this man post haste."

"They found Detective Aaron Wolfe in the parking garage one row over. He is still unconscious. The CPD believe after Barry Woods was shot, Wolfe pursued the sniper. They say it appears Wolfe got to the parking garage while the fight was underway. Wolfe's blood and prints were all over. He was a participant in the fight. The CPD was surprised Wolfe found the strength to call 911 before he collapsed. He is in ICU."

Provost's eyes narrowed. "Detective Wolfe—ICU?"

"Yes, sir. But there's something more you should know," Winston whispered.

Provost turned. "What more?" Then he saw Winston's face, the look that said empty the room. *Oh God . . .*

"Ladies and gentlemen, I must ask you to leave us alone. You may leave your things where they are. We need about fifteen, please. Thank you."

The two waited in silence over the body until the last

door muffled closed. They listened to the laminar airflow fans another minute.

"Okay. We're good now. What is it, Winston?" Provost asked.

"It's peculiar, sir. I'm not sure what it means, or if it means anything."

"I can appreciate that. Go ahead. We will sort it out together," Provost reassured.

"The blood and DNA found at the death scene—"

"Yes. What about it?"

"—although we're still waiting for finalization of the DNA analysis, the preliminary results are confusing. The only matches we are getting are John Doe and Detective Wolfe."

"That's impossible," Provost said.

"Is it?" Winston muttered.

SEVENTEEN

"Someone killed Levitt! I did not see that one coming. The guy's a professional."

People living in the Miller Beach area east of Gary want privacy more than anything else. Outsiders are rare. There are only two reasons to turn off North Lake east onto Birch, either you are lost or you are a member of a secret organization—the Dario Group.

In 1975 the Sorensens purchased the house at the dead end on Birch. Ten years later they purchased the one across the street. They wanted complete privacy, and they had money to burn. Jacques Sorensen's booming psychiatric practice needed tax shelters. Although poor liquidity, real estate offered the best opportunity to hide money for extended periods. The cabin in Algonquin belonged to Jacques. The two worn down houses on Birch belonged to Margaret. To maintain secrecy, they were deeded to her dead stepmother.

"Is anybody gonna say something?" Charlie Dunn prodded the group.

Robert Mason looked around the dismal living room in the tired house. The pitiful fire across from him produced cartoon shadows on the walls and little heat. Amidst the backdrop of torn sagging curtains and peeling wallpaper, all heads hung except Margaret's. "I think Charlie's right," Mason said. "We need to talk. No one signed up for this. There's a dangerous man out there. Mr. Levitt was a professional and now he's dead. We're out of business, and I think we're being hunted."

"There's a good chance that psycho killed your husband, Mrs. Sorensen," Dunn added.

"The newspaper said you and a Chicago homicide detective were found tied up in a closet," Mason said. "Although the police are not saying it, they think the person who killed your husband came for a visit. You need to tell us. Who came to see you? What did he want? Why did he put you in the closet?"

Margaret stared out the window as if she could see through the snow-filled stick woods all the way to Calumet Lagoon. Years ago she and Jacques hiked the rabbit trails and had picnics on the beach. They talked for hours. Back then they had big dreams. Now it was different. Now everything was dead or dying.

"Jacques knew the risks," she whispered. "He took on a patient, one he should have referred. He couldn't help himself. The case was so very different and special, a unique combination of psychiatric and physical manifestations completely new to medical science. Jacques tried to make progress, but he failed. He was tired. He made a decision to transfer his patient to younger more capable doctors. He reluctantly had to step away from what would have been his greatest contribution to psychiatric medicine."

Margaret sipped her steaming tea and cradled the warm cup in her lap. "This patient proved to be far more than he could handle at the end." *Far more than either of us could handle in a lifetime,* she thought with eyes on the fire.

"Who is he? What is he?" Mason asked. "And is he coming for us?"

"I don't have all the answers," Mrs. Sorensen said.

"How can a doctor take care of a patient with no identity?" Dunn pushed.

"I cannot speak for my husband. I can only tell you this patient can change from very weak to very strong, from gentle to angry, and from subdued to dangerous. Jacques explained the changes as being beyond known science."

"This situation is inexcusable," Dunn said.

"Do you see why the people in this room believe we are being hunted?" Mason asked.

Margaret continued to stare into the fire. "Jacques said when he was with this patient he felt exposed—like standing in a tiger's cage with a raw steak hanging around his neck."

"Then why'd he do it?" Dunn barked.

"He was a psychiatrist. He had to know why a man was a tiger," she said.

"The patient has a name," Mason said.

"He calls himself Dario."

"My God in heaven," Dunn gasped. "Have mercy upon our souls. We are all going to die horrible deaths."

"He read Jacques's diary," Margaret said. "He came to the brownstone to give it to me. We did not talk. We started to, but he changed before my eyes. I fainted."

"And you and a homicide detective end up in a closet," Mason said. "I read that in the newspaper, but nothing about Dario."

"Dario is a confused man," she said. "I believe he has adopted our mission—to kill all the monsters. I'm afraid I do not know his definition of monster."

"It appears he has defined your husband and our sniper as monsters," Mason said.

"We're screwed," Dunn gasped. "We are associated with both."

"You should take comfort in knowing he did not kill me or the detective," Margaret said. "We were left alive in my closet."

"That is true," Mason said.

"Our mission has not changed," Mrs. Sorensen said

turning to the group. "There is no turning back. We have had many successes, all in accordance with our bylaws. Some of the most heinous killers in our city have been eliminated. We should hold our heads high. The Dario Group is protecting and serving survivors of great tragedies. We are doing what our criminal justice system has failed to do."

The room fell quiet as they digested the words that had brought them there—personal loss, pain, and a commitment to find justice denied.

Charlie Dunn broke the silence. "I never really understood the genesis of our name—Dario Group. Now it's tied to a psycho. We should come up with another."

"Our name is in honor of the Dario child taken in 1980. The boy was mutilated. They caught the killer. He was convicted and sentenced to life in prison, but he got out on good behavior. That monster found and killed the grieving family. On that day Jacques and I decided we would fix a broken criminal justice system. The Dario Group was born in 1987."

"If your husband had not made mistakes, we would not be sitting here worried about our survival," Mason said looking around the room at troubled faces. "I can't speak for anyone but me. Mr. Peters, say something. Mrs. Johnston, what do you think about this? Mr. Crothers, Mrs. Fetter, Miss Day, someone please speak up."

Peters cleared his throat. Heads turned to the old Texan wearing the brown flannel shirt and black Stetson. "I share your frustration Mason, but I don't see how anything's changed 'round here. We still have terrible people out there to put in the ground."

"I know our mission," Mason replied. "The problem is Dario. He is going to do more bad things. He's unpredictable and wild."

"He seems to operate on his own," Sally Day said. "I agree with Mr. Dunn and Mr. Mason. We could be in danger. This man named Dario could be hunting us."

"This Dario character adds a major wrinkle," Dunn said. "I think he killed Dr. Sorensen. We know he killed our expensive sniper. What we don't know is his thinking. Without a sniper on the payroll we can't take care of business and we can't stop him."

"Dario went after our sniper because he shot Barry Woods, an innocent man," Mason said. "When Levitt was shooting serial killers, this Dario guy left him alone."

"But Barry Woods talked to a Chicago homicide detective about our group. He knew better," Peters said. "It's stated very clearly in our bylaws. It's in the contract we all signed. We are not permitted to talk to law enforcement about the existence of the Dario Group."

"I'm sorry but we can't start killing innocent people," Mason said. "The boy lost his girlfriend. He had been beaten up bad. If he had not screwed things up, Ellen Dumont would be alive today. I'm sure he wished he had died at the cemetery, not the girl he loved. The man was in shock, heartbroken. So what if he talks to the police? He should not have been executed."

Lindsey Fetter got to her feet after being quiet long enough. "I talked to a homicide detective, too. Are you going to execute me?"

"No dear," Mrs. Sorensen said. "You had to talk to the detective. Your case is still being investigated and the police are doing their jobs. You did not go to the police."

"I asked a detective to come to my place to talk. All of this is hard for me. I told him two men came to me the night Ramsey was shot. I explained they gave me a gun and told me I had a choice to kill Ramsey or to leave Chicago. I told the detective there was a group that could no longer live with our inadequate justice system."

"Nothing Miss Fetter said can help the police find us," Mason said. "So what if there are people in the world keeping track of released criminals and helping victims?

There's no law against it. There's no reason to do anything to Miss Fetter."

Margaret Sorensen took a deep breath. "Why did you call the detective, Lindsey?"

She sat down on the tattered sofa. "I know him. He's like me. He hates the failures of the legal system. His life is about putting dangerous people in jail. He sees too many of them beating the system, and he sees too many innocent people dying. I thought he would understand. I thought he would want to help us."

"Did he understand?" Sorensen asked.

"Yes."

"Does he want to help?" Sorensen asked.

Lindsey swallowed hard. "I don't know. He had to leave. He is thinking about it."

"Who are we talking about," Dunn asked.

"Detective Aaron Wolfe," Fetter said.

Mason got up and poured a drink. "That's just great. Aaron Wolfe happens to be the top homicide guy in the city. He's a very smart man."

"Are you suggesting we need to find a way to stop him?" Peters asked.

"No. Well, I don't know," Mason replied. "I didn't get that far."

Peters chuckled. "We're focusing on small stuff. Wolfe is not near the problem Dario is for us as individuals and an organization. It's one thing to want to cover our butts. It's another thing to protect our mission."

Mrs. Sorensen held up a hand. The room turned to her. Her age had no impact on her intellect or energy. Hiding both from the world was a challenging task. "We need to make some decisions—how do we want to proceed? There are several actionable items on the table requiring a vote. I think a show of hands on each will suffice."

"We are going to vote so all can see?" Mason asked.

Margaret controlled the room. "Yes. There is no reason

to hide our views—the majority rules here. For future matters, it will be helpful to know positions on these delicate matters." She looked at her notes. "Should Lindsey Fetter be terminated for violating rule twenty-seven, discussing Dario Group secrets and mission with law enforcement? All in favor raise your hand." She waited. "Okay, all opposed. Thank you Mr. Peters for the one vote to terminate Mrs. Fetter. However, the majority wants no action taken. The matter is closed.

"Next, I believe we should decide if we wish to eliminate rule twenty-seven. All in favor of keeping the rule raise your hand."

All hands went up, except Lindsey Fetter's.

"Okay. Rule twenty-seven stays. However, I will amend it to allow for an 'approval of action' meeting with all members prior to enforcement. Possibly Mr. Woods would have received the same generous consideration as Mrs. Fetter."

"I can't believe that young man is dead," Mason sighed. "A terrible mistake."

"We have lost our sniper," Mrs. Sorensen pushed onward. "I propose we put our pending clients on hold until we refill the position. I will contact our people in Detroit."

"We should employ three," Dunn said.

"That is an expensive and risky proposition," Mrs. Sorensen said. "Why three?"

"Our immediate focus must be to eliminate Dario. Although the CPD are hunting this man, the addition of three snipers with special skills could bring this dangerous period to a close much faster."

"I agree with Dunn," Peters said.

"I agree with Charlie," Mason said. "We don't know Dario."

"May I see a show of hands from those members who agree with Mr. Peters, Mr. Dunn, and Mr. Mason?" Sorensen asked.

All hands went up except Fetter's and Day's.

"We have a majority. I will hire three snipers," she said without referencing Dario as the reason for the additions. "Ladies, may I ask why you did not vote in favor of this action?"

Lindsey Fetter looked at Sally Day and then Margaret. "We don't know if Dario killed your husband. If he did, we don't know why. I'm sorry. We are not suggesting Dr. Sorensen deserved to die. We just do not know any of the facts surrounding his death or Dario's actions. It would be wrong to order the termination of a life with no facts.

"Regarding Norman Levitt, he was terminated after killing Barry Woods, a man who never hurt anyone. It is possible Dario did us a service. Maybe Mr. Levitt is the only monster."

Mrs. Sorensen would keep her *Dario secrets* for another time. The fire popped in the quiet room. Heads hung except for the one outside. He stood in the snow looking in the window. He always knew about the houses on Birch.

EIGHTEEN

"That man's going to die out there."

Commander Landers stormed out of the private room off ICU and marched up to the front desk. Ben Crowley and Joe Hutson followed at a safe distance. "Who the hell said Detective Aaron Wolfe could leave this facility? I want to talk to that doctor right now."

The floor nurse in charge was not impressed. She got yelled at everyday by the best. She had no plans to take orders from anyone who could not affect her pay scale. "Back off, mister. I don't know who you are or what you're talking about. If you want my help, I'd start over and take it down a few notches."

Crowley stepped between Landers and the floor nurse. He read the plastic nameplate in a flash. "Nurse Pamela Rooster—"

"It's Pamela ROUTSER, mister—R O U T S E R. And it is head nurse."

"Of course. Excuse me. Head Nurse Miss Routser," Crowley said ignoring nudges and pokes in the back from Landers. "Please ma'am, we are with the Chicago PD. We were expecting to find Detective Aaron Wolfe in room 432. We left there an hour ago. He was in an unconscious state. We went down for a bite and returned. His bed's empty. The IV line is hanging from a full bag of something dripping on the floor, and all his things are missing. Was he taken somewhere like x-ray or for tests? We must know if

Mr. Wolfe is somewhere else in the hospital, or if he has left on his own account."

Routser looked at her clipboard and flipped a few pages. "Nope. He is still assigned to room 432. Mr. Wolfe should not be moved. His next examination is scheduled for 7:00 a.m. tomorrow morning. That assumes he makes it through the night with no events."

"Then where is he? Has he been misplaced? Did he leave?" Crowley asked.

"This is not a prison, mister. We don't have guards walkin' the halls."

The three turned and headed for the elevator. Landers huffed, "This is not good."

"You know Wolfe. He hates hospitals and rules," Hutson said. "I'll bet he woke up, got dressed, and headed home. He does not trust doctors."

When the elevator doors opened on the ground level, they walked in silence outside the hospital. The commander put on the brakes. He waved for Hutson and Crowley to follow him off the sidewalk into the snow. They moved into the shadows and out of earshot of hospital pedestrians. "I gotta talk to someone about this," he muttered.

"What is it, Commander?"

"It's looking like Wolfe killed our sniper."

Crowley jerked upright like he had just taken a sharp jab in the back. "What're you talkin' about? Wolfe would never kill unless there was no other way, someone's life in jeopardy. The ME said the sniper was beaten to death, his skull crushed by barehands. You realize what kind of strength that takes? Wolfe couldn't do that. He called 911 and collapsed."

"Yeah," Hutson said. "Whoever killed the sniper also attacked Wolfe and left him there to die. It took all Wolfe had to make the 911 call."

Landers grabbed each coat by the lapel and pulled the two detectives to him. With a look on his face they had never seen before, Landers said, "I met with the ME today. The DNA from the crime scene belongs to the sniper and Wolfe. Nobody else was there."

"Then the third guy didn't bleed," Hutson said under his breath.

Landers yanked his coat again. "I find that hard to swallow after seeing the devastation in that garage." He let go of both and looked up at the black sky for answers. "It had to be one hell of a battle. No blood, no DNA, except the sniper and Wolfe. I don't see how it—"

"You're telling us you think Wolfe's a killer?" Crowley kicked the snow and turned a full circle. Half way he remembered he was talking to the boss. "Okay, sir. You know Wolfe. I've known him my entire life. He moved into my home when he was twelve. His parents died in that apartment fire. He's had it rough from the start, but Wolfe's no killer. You know better."

"I'm not sayin' he did it, but we do know he can be a little strange at times," Hutson said. "You gotta admit he's an internal guy. I'm just sayin' if Wolfe killed him, then he's way stronger than I ever imagined. I saw the crime scene. A cement pillar was missing a chunk like someone pulled it off with their hand. The car parked next to the sniper looked like a bulldozer had run into its side. And how many people can bend a rifle barrel like that?"

"The sniper got pulverized," Crowley said. "Beaten to death with wild rage."

Landers blew into his cupped hands. "All good points, but consider the whole picture. Wolfe spent that evening working a triple-homicide, three guys dead from sniper fire. He just worked two other homicides, both dead by sniper fire. That makes five. Then he's interviewing a witness, Barry Woods."

"The boyfriend of the girl killed and raped at Wunders Cemetery," Hutson said.

Landers nods. "Right. Woods and Wolfe are leaving

the Burnham Hotel together. Bam! Woods takes a bullet in the head. Wolfe tackles Woods. They fly into the alley. Wolfe is trying to pull his witness to safety and discovers the man's face is gone.

"Hell yeah, Wolfe is mad," Landers said. "He sees red. He is not himself. Wolfe went after the shooter he knows killed six people. What would you do if you found that man? Would you cuff him or would you beat the living hell out of him?"

"I guess I might be judge, jury, and executioner," Hutson muttered.

"No way," Crowley said. "You're talking about the top homicide investigator in the city for the last ten years. Wolfe may keep things to himself, but he has it together more than most."

"Are you sure? Does he have it together?" Landers asked. "We know he went off the deep end five years ago. You're his friends. You're Wolfe's family. He lost it at Lincoln Park."

"The Webster House," Crowley whispered. "We all had a bad day, commander. It was bad. Everyone died. It put all of us into counseling."

"It never should have happened. The bastard would not let them go," Hutson said.

Landers squeezed his eyelids tight trying to block the memory. He spoke as if he stood alone in the snow a hundred miles away. "Joseph Durbin wanted a million dollars and a city bus. He demanded Stockton Drive be cleared north ten miles. He wanted a helicopter waiting. He said if he saw one police car he would use his MP5 on the Tinsley family—the children first, and then the mother. The father was already dead in their apartment."

"We did everything humanly possible," Crowley said.

Landers shook his head. "Wolfe was there. He volunteered. He hid on the bus. We all knew it was a death sentence. His chances of saving anybody were small, but we knew Durbin would kill everyone before he got on the chopper. He would kill the pilot. Durbin could fly."

"I remember like it was yesterday," Crowley said.

Landers blinked his way back into the present. "They all died that day, except Wolfe. He couldn't deal with it. He felt like he failed and should not have lived."

"None of us would have been able to deal with that, commander," Crowley said. "Wolfe saw everything. Nobody could have saved the children or the mother."

Landers nodded. "Wolfe got one shot off—a head shot—but it didn't kill the bastard right away. Durbin had time to spray the inside of that bus with his MP5."

Hutson said, "It was bad but Wolfe got help. He went to all those sessions for two years. I know because we took turns making sure he went."

"You're right," Crowley said. "He stopped after two years. It's been three since. He is a different person. I think we all are."

"We've all seen the change," Landers said. "I'm concerned because he's been shutting out the world. He is a loner more than ever."

"I say we assume Wolfe is innocent until proven guilty," Crowley huffed. "Let's give him the benefit of the doubt. Let's focus on how the real killer got away without leaving behind DNA, prints, or any other telltale physical evidence."

Hutson shivered and coughed as he fumbled with his top button. "The killer we're lookin' for is a lot stronger than the Aaron Wolfe I know."

"Wait a minute," Crowley said. "What about the PODs? There's gotta be some eyes on this. We need to get with the POD people and check video streams around the time of the shootings—Chase Tower, Burnham Hotel, and the parking garage on Washington at Clark."

"It is standard operating procedure following all homicides," Landers said. "After filing the police report, the POD command is notified. They are to assess active video feeds in the area of the homicide."

"I'm sure they're behind like everyone else," Hutson said.

Landers started walking out of the snow. The other two followed. "Sergeant Irwin is over the POD program," Landers said. "We go way back. I'll get him out of bed if I gotta. This is our priority, gentlemen. We gotta see who went into and came out of that parking garage. If we are lucky, the video will tell us everything we need to know."

NINETEEN

The walk down the snow-covered driveway onto Birch was long, cold, and quiet. The members of the Dario Group were not friends. They shared an unimaginable world filled with tragedy and pain. All carried emotional baggage, but some held dark secrets with different agendas.

Frank Peters took his time. He wanted to be at the back of the crowd when they all left Margaret Sorensen's house that night. He wanted to follow Sally Day, the newest member. He had his eye on her ever since the meeting with Woods and Dumont, the young couple harassed by Frank Pazrro. Peters was twenty years older than Sally Day. She stirred the emotions deep inside that he could not control. Now that Dumont and Woods were gone, Day would be alone.

As cars started, and red lights turned off Birch onto North Lake, Peters followed Sally Day to her Chevy Malibu. Because she was the first to arrive, she was parked deepest on the dead end and at the edge of the woods. He appeared at her car door grabbing her handle.

"Oh. Hello, Mr. Peters. I didn't see you," Day said catching her breath.

"Miss Day," he said. "I'm sorry about your friends. It's a terrible set of circumstances." He pushed his Stetson up with one finger and looked down at the beautiful thing he wanted to take home with him.

"Thank you for that Mr. Peters, but we've all lost

friends or family. That's why we are here. We believe there's a better way to stop evil in the world. I only wish I could have been more help to Ellen and Barry. They were very dear friends. I can't believe they're gone."

"It's unfortunate the Dario Group allowed Mr. Woods to be terminated. I don't think it was right in his case, although he could have jeopardized the group. I guess if we are going to change somethin' big in the world—like the justice system—we gotta have some rules."

As the last set of taillights left Birch, Sally cringed. Standing alone by the woods with a man she did not know felt unsafe. He had only recently joined the group. "I suppose so," she said. "Well, I need to go. Thank you again for your concern."

"Would it help to talk more, Miss Day? I hate to see you go home alone after all this bad news. It's a dangerous world. A pretty lady like you has men watchin' your every move. Some are just waitin' for an opportunity to have their way with you, Miss Day. You know they hurt pretty women like you all the time. I'd be pleased to follow you home and make sure you're safe until things settle down 'round here."

Oh my God. What is he talking about? Is he threatening me or trying to be helpful? I got to get away from him. "I don't think that will be necessary, Mr. Peters. Thank you for the consideration." She looked down at the door handle. "I need to go."

Frank Peters held onto the handle a few uncomfortable seconds beyond normal. When he opened the door, interior lights popped on and captured his blank stare. Sally forced a smile as she slid onto the seat reaching to close the door behind her. Again Peters controlled the door long enough to send shivers up her spine. The old gentleman with the Stetson, who sat in the stuffed chair by the fire moments before, had transformed into a mysterious entity, one with hollow eyes, a chilling presence, and questionable motives.

He stood by the woods like a scarecrow.

When she started the car, the doors locked. She nodded and pulled away watching him in her rearview mirror. He did not move all the way to North Lake. She spun her wheels off Birch and disappeared.

Peters spit in the snow and lumbered up to his Chevy Tahoe. He stood at the grill staring at the only light in Margaret Sorensen's window, the old lady still sitting by the fire. This time she was not knitting. Sorensen was on the phone setting up a meeting with Detroit.

The drive to Day's condo took thirty minutes. The Tahoe caught up to the Malibu in ten. She never knew Peters was behind her. *You're like all the others,* he thought. *You don't think to look around. You never see us. We're always watching you pretty things. I remember my first, a most beautiful lady, and a real fighter. I didn't want to kill her. I just wanted to have some fun. The drinking got out of hand. The sex wasn't even that good. Come to think, none of it was worth doin' the first time. I should have cut her loose and left town. Maybe my life would have been different. What made me decide to kill that first time?*

The Malibu exited the main highway and Peters followed. He stayed two cars back. There were a lot of black SUVs in the city. He blended.

"Why did you kill that girl, Heather Palmer, summer of 1989?" Peters asked himself in his bold voice.

"Because she said she was tellin' the cops," he answered himself. *This is crazy. I have this same conversation with you every single day.*

"Then why didn't you stop after that? Why did you keep hunting ladies, raping ladies, and killing ladies?" He asked this time in the voice of his judge.

"Well judge, I don't got no answers. I just like doin' it. I feel bad sometimes. But most the time I want to do it."

"You're one lousy son of a bitch," the judge bellowed. "I sentence you to death for the crimes you've committed against humanity. You will be tortured first and burned at the stake."

Sally Day turned onto West Irving Parkway. Peters knew her address. He would park at the north end of Kenmore. He would have a view of her bedroom window. It was a short walk. Peters had been to Day's place several times. He walked the different routes to her condo and chose the best for this night. He even had a favorite tree. It was a big one, off the road, the perfect distance away, and surrounded by thick bushes. With his binoculars he could blend even during the day. Peters knew where Day kept her spare key. He borrowed it one day when she was at work. He made a duplicate at the corner hardware store and returned it to her secret hiding place. He went in the condo three times. He knew the layout and her panties drawer by heart.

From the Tahoe, he watched Sally park her Malibu. He savored her walk to the condo. Just the thought of what he would do to her in three hours made his wait even more erotic. It was an important part of his thrill—the imagery.

He waited for her to go to bed—the last light out. She had to be asleep when he let himself in. No alarm system and no pets meant he could go early. He preferred to sit in his girls' living rooms in the dark. He could revel in his heightened fantasy—the violation and the smells. Sometimes he would take off his clothes. He always took time to select the perfect knife from the kitchen—the strongest blade and wood handle. And he would layout the six-foot clothesline. There were four, one for each ankle and wrist.

Everything was perfect. Frank Peters knew perfect. He had done it many times before. He had come to Chicago to disappear, and for a new hunting ground. He could hide in a high crime-rate area with ease. He left a dozen dead women behind in four southern states. The time to move on had arrived. The noose was tightening. No one would look for him in Illinois in the winter.

Police had his DNA and fingerprints, but they did not have his identity. Frank Peters had never been arrested—there was no record. When Frank got to Chicago, he met Mason and Dunn at the area CVT meeting. He knew the grieving group would be the perfect place to hide and to find women alone in the world.

The time had come. Sally Day's bedroom lights were out, two hours had passed. Frank turned off his car and country music. His heart beat a little faster, he was aroused. Frank reached for his hat and the door handle. "You are mine Sally Day," he crowed in the quiet interior of his warm Tahoe.

"No she's not."

The words hung in the dark. Peters lifted his head and stared straight ahead. He let go of the handle and the hat and swallowed hard. Was it happening? Was he finally going insane? Was Sally Day the one who would push him over the edge? Is thirteen the magic number?

Peters had been talking to himself for so long that he did not know which of his invented characters had just spoken to him. Was it the judge? Was it the wise ass? Or was it him being the man who once was good, the one who always lost the argument?

"You're done, asshole." The words hung in the Tahoe.

Peters straightened in his seat—now he knew he was not alone. He kept his eyes straight ahead. He had to think. This was new. He was at a disadvantage.

I was so busy thinking about what I was going to do to Sally Day that I did not tend to the basics. I forgot to look in the backseat. Peters had a passenger all the way from Birch—but who? The back and side windows of the Tahoe were tinted—Peters had them prepared for daytime abductions. Now that prep worked against him.

His eyes searched the rearview mirror. He could not find his passenger. He had to position him based on sound.

He had to have a conversation. That would work. That would distract his passenger, too. "What do you want?" Peters asked as his fingers slid off his hat.

"You're a sick man." The words floated, but from where? Peters needed more. He had to know exactly where his mystery passenger sat in the dark backseat.

"I'm not sick," Peters said. "I have dedicated my life to stopping killers. That's why I'm here tonight. I'm watching over another delicate flower, a young woman in danger—she lost her friends to monsters. She asked me to protect her tonight. Why do you think I'm parked here? I'm watching to make sure she's safe."

His fingers touched the cold steel barrel of his .38 caliber Glock. Peters had one second to get off one shot. He had to work it up into his hand, and get his finger on the trigger.

"Heather Palmer . . . Beverly Martin . . . Carole Bergeson . . . Mary Grambling . . . Susan Stringer . . . need I go on, you pathetic animal?"

On his last word Peters had had enough. He raised his gun and shot into the back of his Tahoe. Burnt gunpowder filled the air and the explosion muted the world.

Peters had made another mistake. His calculations were off. His passenger sat in the dark in the most impossible position to reach. Before a single second ticked off, the clenched fist dropped like an anvil and Peters slumped over. The serial killer would not be visiting Sally Day.

Morning came three hours later. The prints in the snow leaving the Tahoe were gone. Three days later they discovered the man behind the wheel and dark tinted windows. The freezing temperatures had slowed decomposition, but could not forever hide the smell of death. The Chicago police were called. At the death scene, untrained observers thought the dead man had committed suicide. Bystanders watched the morgue clerks slide the body into the crash bag. They saw the bloody head and watched CSI remove the Glock from the front seat with a stick in its barrel. Not until later would the facts begin to trickle out. Dr. Provost would confirm what Winston had hypothesized at the crime scene.

The cause of death had nothing to do with the gun. The man identified as Frank Peters died from head trauma recently observed with other victims. The microscopic examination of the crushed cranium and ruptured brain tissue revealed a single blow to the parietal bones (top of the skull) rendered the man unconscious. It was the opposing bilateral pressure applied to the temporal regions that caused death. Winston did not use the medical jargon in his report. He described a human vice grip—hands pressing the sides of the head together. The holes on the back of the skull were from thumbs pushing through occipital bone.

It was standard operating procedure to submit Frank Peters' DNA to CODIS—the combined DNA indexing system containing DNA profiles from the federal and state level. In the routine effort the medical examiner learned more about the dead man lying in his freezer. Frank Peters was a serial killer wanted in four states.

TWENTY

They would have to be as high as me to get me in their crosshairs.

Eldon Babcock came out of hiding only after he heard the sniper that killed three at the Chase Tower had been found dead a few blocks away—homicide. Standing at the edge of his office on the 97th floor of the Willis Tower, he still felt unsafe. His creasing head wound took more than a hundred stitches and three days for the swelling to go down and oozing to stop. Now with a bulky head dressing and unbearable itch, he peered out the edge of his ten-foot windows and wondered if he was still a target. Who sent him the message the night Marcantonio was killed? There were four head shots in the room that night. Why was his not fatal?

He pressed the button and waited for the mechanical drapes to close the eastern and northern exposures of his corner office. He avoided his desk—too obvious. Instead, he sat at the small conference table in the alcove. His OCD had made him thorough. Regardless of the assignment, he was a stickler for details and a methodical development process for an organized plan. At the moment his life was on the line. His world was in total disarray.

Scanning each page in the files stacked before him, Eldon absorbed the PI reports a third time. He had studied them prior to the Marcantonio shooting and again during recovery. Still looking for answers, he set up another meeting with the three investigators. Fitz, Cranston, and Michaels were reluctant to come out of hiding. The Chase Tower shooting put their lives at risk. The *Chicago Tribune* told the world they were working for the Marcantonio crime family. In an instant they were the topic of rival families, the CPD, and the FBI.

Eldon Babcock saw no reason to correct the *Tribune*. They did not need to know he was the one employed by William T. Marcantonio and the PIs worked for him. Eldon's lucrative arrangement ended when Marcantonio's head exploded. Fortunately the two million dollar retaining fee had been deposited into his personal bank account days earlier. Now Eldon's focus had turned to more personal matters—his survival.

To secure his future, he had to find out who had Marcantonio and his five henchmen killed. In addition, Eldon had to find out who killed the sniper. Dropping dominos held the secrets that could set him free. The bootlegged POD video had grown in importance. The mystery visitor on 27th Street could be on a shared mission.

"I don't like this any more than you," Eldon said stirring his coffee. "The good news is we're alive and the sniper's dead."

Leaning back in his chair Fitz twiddled his thumbs on top of his belly. With a smirk on his pudgy face, and eying Babcock's bandage, he said, "Do you know why you got a new part?"

Eldon straightened a stack of files a third time. "I don't find that amusing, Bill. I will remind you that you work for me. That can change."

"Seems to me your benefactor lost his head and you lost your contract," Fitz barbed as the others looked at their shoes.

"Although the family could request a continuation of my legal services, I have not heard from them. I assume they are quite busy with funeral arrangements and other important personal matters."

Cranston huffed. "Come now, Eldon. You know better. Marcantonio ran illegal operations for fifty years. The man has a lot of enemies eager to take control of his now unattended assets. I would not be surprised to see the family wiped out."

"I'm not holding my breath for a phone call, Mark. My business arrangement may be over, but that has no bearing on why we're here. Everyone is smart enough to know it is in our best interest to figure out who is killing who and why. Only then can we manage our exposure."

"Seems to me the man with the new part in his hair is the one exposed," Fitz said. "I don't see how the three of us have any reason to be here."

The blowers cut off. The room fell silent. Fitz had made a startling point. Eldon Babcock's next words would decide everything. "The Marcantonio family has several dangerous enemies," Eldon said. "Someone tried to disrupt their operations. Someone wanted the kingpin dead. They killed the most guarded man in the state. It seems to me the *Chicago Tribune* named you three gentlemen as employees of this mafia kingpin. That can't be good for your business. Someone's work may not be done yet, gentlemen. Fortunately I have not been named. I am a victim visiting my accountant—wrong place at the wrong time. My arrangement is stealth, gentlemen. You three survived a meeting where three men died. Seems to me you have two problems. You are targets of the Marcantonio family, and you are the targets of their enemies."

"Wait a damn minute," Fitz bellowed. "We can tell the *Tribune* to print a retraction."

"Why would the *Chicago Tribune* print a retraction on something they could not corroborate? I'm certainly not putting that gun in my mouth, gentlemen."

"I should shoot you myself," Fitz spewed.

Cranston held up his hand to shut down Fitz and to

calm a squirming Michaels. "Eldon makes a good point. None of us would do what Fitz told Eldon to do—go to the newspaper. Look. Eldon's right. It's the way things are. To add insult to injury, if we were to attempt a retraction we would only increase our exposure, and no one's gonna believe it. Face it, Bill. We're screwed."

Eldon set down his coffee cup with a flat smile. "I have no intention of leaving you holding the bag. I'm only pointing out one of many reasons why we need a concerted effort to solve this puzzle. It benefits all of us."

Michaels nodded. "I'm on board."

"Me too," Cranston said.

Fitz glared at Babcock. "I don't know when or how, but one day I will get you back."

"Let it go, Bill," Cranston snapped. "Let's get to work. I have some conclusions and thoughts on all this. How do you want to go forward, Eldon?"

"I've been going through each investigation report looking for common threads. Our focus has been on people and events prior to the Chase Tower shooting. That's good because we need to understand what led to it. Only then can we get our hands around the total picture."

"An unknown entity systematically terminated Marcantonio henchmen," Fitz said.

"What connects those killed?" Babcock asked.

"I looked into the backgrounds of the three I had—Bordon, Newman, and Pazrro. These guys were animals," Cranston said. "They all had records a mile long—robbery, rape, theft, assault, and murder. They had at least two charges for murder. They were acquitted or found guilty to a lesser charge. They served short sentences, less than six years. Their criminal records are terrible. They got away with a lifetime of terror."

"I looked at sniper-fire deaths in the city over the last six months," Michaels said. "I came across two more—Eric Ramsey and James Pender. These guys fit the mold. They had long criminal records and served minimal sentences for murder. They had top legal help."

Fitz crumpled paper in a ball and threw it at Cranston. "You guys got nothing. Of course people who work for Marcantonio are scumbags—what a surprise, please."

Eldon flipped through a few files and pulled out a page. "This is a profile done on thirty of Marcantonio's top people—more henchmen. The five killed by a sniper are different from the thirty on this page. The majority of the thugs working for Marcantonio had felonies—robbery and assault. They did not have charges for rape or murder. Their jail time fit their crimes."

"What's your point?" Fitz squawked.

"We're onto something," Cranston said. "Someone is targeting the serial offenders who beat the legal system. Their records say they'd do it again. They were real monsters."

Michaels left the table to pour more coffee. He paused and turned to the group. "Is it possible we have a vigilante going after Marcantonio's worst people? I don't think they care about his illegal businesses. They are hunting the monsters."

"Two of the five killed by a sniper were not employed by Marcantonio but had similar criminal histories."

"How many vigilantes hire a sniper?" Cranston asked.

"How many vigilantes are snipers?" Fitz said.

"We can conclude this vigilante group—for lack of a better descriptor—is behind these linked shootings. I do not believe it is a rival organization," Michaels said. "If it were, the kills would be more random and portions of the Marcantonio operations would be taken over."

"They're targeting in the city of Chicago, shooting the worst of the worst," Eldon said.

"People who have killed and beat the criminal justice system," Fitz muttered.

"Serial predators," Eldon added.

"They have an agenda and rules of engagement. They have the necessary unsavory connections to contract quality snipers," Cranston injected.

Fitz smiled. "It explains why they marked Eldon. He is part of the judicial problem. He defended a monster, James Harvey Pender."

Although he loathed Fitz for what he happily shared, Eldon had reached the same unfortunate conclusion. In Eldon's defense, Cranston yelled, "You are an irritating fool, Fitz. I've had enough of your arrogant, self-serving narratives. I suggest you close your mouth or I will come around this table and beat the hell out of you."

"Fitz has always been a royal pain in the butt," Eldon said. "Unfortunately, he is right. I defended James Pender. My wound is likely due to that fact. Someone is clearly unhappy with the legal process. They are well on their way toward fixing it."

Fitz sunk in his chair and stared at the group without uttering another word. Cranston could beat him senseless if there was a second event and Babcock allowed it.

"We agree there is a vigilante group out there killing what I call serial predators," Michaels said. "That's still all we know. I'm afraid we are still at square one."

"Maybe not," Eldon said. "Their operations have been interrupted—their sniper is down. There have been no shootings since the Chase Tower and Burnham Hotel incidents."

"Where would one go if they wanted to hire a sniper?" Cranston asked.

Fitz sat up with a sinister smile. "The best snipers are in Detroit."

"That's it," Babcock said. "We need to connect with Detroit. When they get the call from Chicago, we find the vigilante group. It will cost us, but it's our only way. We pass the information to the Marcantonio family."

"And our lives go back to normal," Cranston said

under his breath.

"I have some connections in Detroit. I will need a lot of money to buy that kind of information," Fitz said. "I'm thinking $100,000."

Babcock nodded. "Good. Make contact tonight. I will arrange for the money."

"I'm still not satisfied working only one avenue," Cranston said. "Eldon's assessment was accurate, we are exposed. Time is not on our side. One of us could be taken out tonight by one of many enemy factions out there, or a rogue member of the Marcantonio family who wonders why we were not killed along with their patriarch. "

"We don't have a lot more options," Fitz grumbled.

"What about the POD video?" Eldon asked.

"That's what I had in mind," Cranston said. "We have at least one case where someone other than a sniper targeted Marcantonio's people. We've all seen the video, the mystery man on the vacant lot on the South Side. That man—with unique physical characteristics—seemed to be there for Mr. Pender, the one shot by the sniper. I submit he and the sniper had similar agendas but not a coordinated effort. They both acted independent of the other."

Michaels opened his briefcase and pulled out a half-dozen still shots. He studied the first and passed it around. "I have a talented friend in the IT field—computerized enhancements. He takes a photograph and loads it into a special program. There are thousands of calculations made to optimize grain densities, variations between pixels, color balance, contrast, and a lot of other things I cannot pronounce. It builds what he calls 'logical bridges' between existing pixels."

"Wait a minute," Cranston said. "What's a pixel?"

"A pixel is the smallest picture element in an image."

"So his software takes one frame from a video and enhances the undefined space between the well-defined pixels? I suppose it is like bringing into focus a portion of an image there but not visible to the camera lens."

"Yes. The software fills the undefined gaps between the defined pixels employing the most logical information gathered. That means it creates and adds to the knowns."

"This is not rocket science," Fitz said. "FBI and CIA have had this stuff a long time. They use it in satellite-intel and with drones. Their optics can read a license plate from space. Their computerized enhancement programs can find a fingerprint on the license plate."

"That's impressive. What do you have here, Bert?"

"I've got biometrics on this mystery guy. Look at the first few pictures. We now know he is six-three and weighs 235. He is quite muscular, probably a body builder or professional athlete. If you saw him walking down the street, you'd notice. His biometric profile makes him stand out. He is enormous from all angles. Why is that important? Because it tells us he travels at night or the world would know about him by now."

"Is there more to those muscles than size?" Fitz asked.

"Yes. The guy's very strong, Fitz. They estimate strength in the order and magnitude of five men. One hit from this guy, you probably die. And he is agile. We have video of him jumping a six-foot chain linked fence with two feet of coiled barbed wire across the top."

"He had to jump eight feet up and three feet out to clear that barrier," Eldon said.

"And he did it from a crouched position," Michaels said rubbing his forehead.

"Okay. What else do we have?" Babcock asked.

"We have minimal facials." Michaels passed more pictures around. "His face is abnormal and somewhat shocking. Again, if you saw him you'd never forget it—an overhanging brow, a hideous scowl, bulging facial muscles, and a thick neck. He has shaggy black hair and a wild mustache. He looks hideous. Only his mother could love him."

After the soft chuckles, Cranston said, "I'm afraid this information is not as helpful as I thought it could be. We are still no closer to identifying this man than we were the first time we looked at the video."

"We need only confirm he is a problem for our vigilante group," Eldon said. "If so he becomes another viable avenue of investigation. Remember, our focus is to identify the group that killed Marcantonio and his people."

"That beast was not happy when the sniper shot Pender on that vacant lot," Fitz said.

"And now we have a dead sniper found in a parking garage on Washington Avenue," Michaels said.

"Although they don't identify the dead man as a sniper, inside information says his head was crushed by barehands," Cranston said.

"Sounds like our guy," Michaels said.

Eldon shuffled some papers. "We need to confirm it. Can you get a hold of POD video on Washington Avenue? I want to see who went in and came out of that garage."

"I can get it," Michaels said.

"If we can confirm the man on the South Side is the one who killed the sniper on Washington Avenue, then I am sure our vigilante group would be interested in obtaining that detailed information. They will want to protect their sniper investment in the future." Eldon leaned back comfortable with the strategy they had backed into.

"Access to that information should smoke them out," Cranston said.

"I'll make a call to my contact at CPD," Fitz said. "If the POD video exists, I'll have it by tomorrow and get it to Michaels."

"Good. We have an action plan, gentlemen," Eldon said closing his file.

On the other side of town, Sally Day put down her cell phone with her heart beating faster. Margaret Sorensen just told her the Chicago police had found Frank Peters. He was dead in his Tahoe parked on her street.

When Sally looked out her kitchen window thinking about her odd encounter on Birch, she saw Detective Wolfe walking her way in the snow.

TWENTY-ONE

"The problem isn't the statutes," Landers said. "It's the maneuvering of high-priced defense attorneys. If you got the bucks you can get murder one reduced to murder two—killers are back on the streets under six years. That's the argument. Our criminal justice system was never intended to handle the deluge of creative and overly ambitious lawyers, or new technology."

"It is a dog eat dog world," Crowley said.

The Citizens for Criminal Law Reform (CCLR) held the annual meeting at the Congress Plaza Hotel in downtown Chicago. The hotel offered rooms discounted to $110 and provided free meeting facilities and complimentary catering services.

"The CCLR is not to be confused with the ACLU," Landers said. "They do not seek an end to harsh policies from policing to sentencing. CCLR members are the survivors of murder victims. They believe the justice system failed miserably."

Crowley walked into the Congress Plaza Hotel behind the commander. "I suppose all these people witnessed first-hand the legal maneuvers that buried damning physical evidence and discredited eyewitnesses. I bet the system stomped all over their rights."

"The courts transformed their truth into something perverted. They saw facts twisted or omitted. They experienced a system that set aside the inexcusable."

"I don't think I could handle it if someone killed one of my family members and the legal system let 'em go," Crowley said.

Three days after the shootings at the Chase Tower, Burnham Hotel, and parking garage on Washington Avenue, members of the CCLR trickled into the city. Their agenda was packed. Six months earlier Commander Landers volunteered Detective Wolfe to speak on crime prevention. It was Wolfe's turn to represent the homicide department. Landers saw the outing as part of Wolfe's ongoing therapy. He needed him to engage with the community in more ways than standing over dead bodies and chasing killers.

"You think Wolfe will show up?" Crowley asked.

"Don't know," Landers said while surveying the bustling lobby. "I got a text from him early Friday morning, a response to my inquiry on his status. He said he was fine, reminded me he was off duty, and suggested I leave him alone."

Crowley chuckled. "I guess I can understand that. He's been through a lot. I was surprised he walked out of the hospital the other night. I left him there out cold with IVs."

Without a word, Landers walked to the registration counter and returned with a CCLR program packet. In the small alcove on the edge of the flow, he scanned each document and passed them to Crowley. "I don't know about this group," he muttered. "These people are way too emotional and definitely on a mission that could get them in trouble. Vigilantism has no place in the modern world," Landers said. "Taking the law into one's own hands to get justice according to one's own understanding of right and wrong is a roadmap to failure. History has shown us the way. Our system has problems, but it's still the best way to get to the truth."

"Our justice system is based on one premise—people are innocent until proven guilty," Crowley said. "Today that premise no longer holds. A lot of people are guilty and use the system to get away with a crime. They use all those rights to beat the system. They got nothing to lose."

"You think so?" Landers sighed.

"Today, we have people committing crimes on video. We have DNA putting them at a crime scene," Crowley said. "We have the best investigational processes in the history of the world—CSI, forensic pathologists, advanced technology. In spite of all that, we let too many guilty people go because of an outdated legal process and crazy technicalities. Today when some people walk into a courtroom we are one-hundred-percent certain they are guilty. They laugh in our faces. They can tie us up in knots. They can cost county and state governments millions."

"I can't disagree with much of that," Landers said. "But I don't like rapid change. I got a bad feeling about what's going on here. One day you will have more respect for the work that came before you. A lot of good people put their heart and soul into this legal system."

"Did you hear from Sergeant Irwin?" Crowley asked.

"POD program? Not yet," Landers said still surveying the lobby for anything irregular. "He's got people on it. He'll call when he has something." He grabbed Crowley's arm. "I think I just saw the Sorensen lady." He pulled him behind the pillar. "We need to watch her."

"I never met the lady," Crowley whispered. "I thought she was in the hospital after spending the day in that closet with Hutson."

"That was Tuesday. It's Saturday." Landers leaned out. "Well, she was crossing the lobby at a pretty good clip. Nice recovery," he muttered. *Where the hell are you now?*

"Hello, Commander Landers." The soft voice came from behind them.

Shit! "Ah . . . Mrs. Sorenson, I thought you were in the hospital." Landers pinched his tie. Crowley stepped back. "How are you feeling?"

"Thank you for asking. I feel much better. My husband's funeral is now behind me. I had to get out of the house. I don't think I will be able to stay there, Mr. Landers. I don't feel safe."

"I see." Landers eyes moved to her CCLR badge. "So, you are a guest speaker."

"Do you support the CCLR?" Mrs. Sorensen asked. "Jacques and I have been members for many years. They asked for our support. So many here have lost loved ones and still have no justice. That is a terrible situation, Mr. Landers."

"I spend every day of my life trying to right those wrongs, Mrs. Sorensen."

"Oh my! I just realized now I am one of them." Sorensen's busy eyes found Detective Crowley watching from the fireplace. She looked down, removed a handkerchief from her black pearl purse, and dabbed her dry eyes.

"Have you had contact with Dario?" Landers asked watching for a reaction.

"The Dario in my husband's diary?" she asked looking away.

"Yes, the Dario who killed your husband and brought his diary of secrets to you."

"I hope you do not judge Jacques too harshly, Mr. Landers. I seriously doubt the authenticity of that old book. I believe it is my husband's wild imagination. I think he was writing a book. If I'm wrong, I am saddened because I never knew he was troubled. I suppose psychiatrists are masters at hiding emotions."

"I believe the diary is authentic," Landers said looking down at the old lady. "There are several people named, Mrs. Sorensen. We will investigate each one. I know you want to know the truth. We will have answers soon."

"I hope so," she said stuffing her handkerchief back in her purse.

"You didn't answer my question, Mrs. Sorenson. Have you had any contact with Dario?"

"I don't know the man. I never saw him." Her eye twitched.

Landers pushed. "You didn't see him when he delivered your husband's diary?"

"No. And I don't know that he did."

"That's what has us scratching our heads, Mrs. Sorensen. We don't know how that diary got all the way from you husband's cabin in Algonquin to your kitchen table in Chicago and you not know it."

"Maybe Jacques kept it at the brownstone," she said. "This is the first time I've talked to anyone at the Chicago police department about the matter. No one has asked my opinion."

"I'm sorry. I thought you were interviewed at the hospital."

"I was, but it was very brief. My attorney is an old family friend. He was concerned my medical condition was deteriorating. He stopped the interview."

"I apologize for the question," Landers said as he continued to study her every word and body language. He was no longer surprised by people who believed they could outsmart everyone. Landers knew truth and facts always stuck together, and lies always fell apart—eventually.

"I guess when you were interviewed we did not have the physical evidence in place that moves your husband's diary from Algonquin to your kitchen table."

"I can't imagine anything that would prove such a thing," she said.

"Oh yes, that and the timing. I don't know much about the science. I do understand fingerprints and DNA. And God knows we had plenty of that all over the cabin—your husband, your kitchen, Detective Hutson, and even the ropes used to tie him up."

"I don't see how that—"

"Seems we caught a break, Mrs. Sorenson. Our CSI people are very talented. They found something. They found *chlamydomonas nivalis*—microscopic algae. Turns out that stuff is all over the Peter Exner Marsh and your cabin. It is a snow algae—a derivative of that polar ice algae you hear about on the *National Geographic* channel. They call it watermelon algae. It turns pink and smells like watermelons. We don't see it much in the city."

"I don't see how this algae you have helps—"

Landers leaned over Mrs. Sorensen. "It is in Dario's fingerprints on the diary."

"I see," she mumbled. "But how does that put this Dario person in my kitchen? I suppose the algae and his fingerprints prove he handled the diary, but we still don't know when."

"Did I forget to tell you *chlamydomonas nivalis* does not like warmth?"

"You did not mention that."

"It dies when the temperature goes above freezing. It's a colony of cells. The cells closest to the warmth die first. Layers of cells beneath die later. Amazing, isn't it? We can determine timing based on the death of layers of algae cells." He leaned closer. "That diary was brought into your kitchen Tuesday morning around the time Detective Hutson arrived."

"I don't know why that is important. I did not see it or the man."

"I wonder why Dario would bring that diary to your home after killing your husband."

"I don't know if Dario killed Jacques," she said.

"And why was that diary found under a stack of newspapers?"

"I'm sure you will figure all that out one day, Sergeant Landers."

"Commander," he corrected her. "May I ask, are you meeting someone here?"

"I know a few—" Her eyes widened. Her mask of deceit dropped away as she stared into the crowd behind Landers.

Seconds later a large hand gripped Louie Landers' shoulder. He turned to find Aaron Wolfe. "Hello sir," Wolfe said with eyes locked on the old lady.

"Detective Wolfe," Landers said. We were just talking about you. I mean Detective Crowley and me." Landers spun around searching the alcove knowing Crowley had backed away on purpose. "Never mind, he's around here somewhere."

"Detective Wolfe," Mrs. Sorensen said. "Yes. I met you that day. You were so kind as to release us from that dark closet. I'm sorry. You startled me. I could not place you, but then I remembered. I was groggy that day. The doctor said I had an attack of some kind."

"You seem better now," Wolfe said with curious eyes.

"Yes, much better, thank you," she said with an awkward pause. "Well then, I will leave you two gentlemen to discuss police things. Thank you again for your help. Goodbye."

They watched her melt into the crowded lobby that was moving into the main hallway and meeting rooms. Landers pulled Wolfe closer. In a harsh whisper he asked, "Where the hell have you been? Three days, Wolfe. I need to know from you what happened on Washington Street and in that parking garage."

Wolfe towered over Landers. He was not intimidated in the least. He had expected an even more colorful greeting from the man he had known for two decades. Wolfe reached into his coat and pulled out a fat sealed envelope. "These are my reports, hand written, and detailed," he said. "All of your questions are answered here."

Landers eyes dropped to the envelope and returned to the only man he did not understand and could not control.

"That does not tell me where the hell you've been." He grabbed it.

"You don't need to know where I've been. I have my time. I was off the clock."

"You keep that up and you'll be off the clock for good, Wolfe."

"Any time you want my badge, you tell me. I have enough history with you and the CPD to be left alone when I want to be left alone. I work for you. That's it."

Although he did not like it, Landers could not argue. Wolfe had a right to privacy. "Fine. What was that thing with Mrs. Sorenson? Why'd she freeze up like that when she saw you?"

Wolfe panned the lobby more out of habit than purpose. "I'm not sure. I think she knows I'm watching her. Maybe she thinks I know more than I do."

"What the hell does that mean?"

"It's in my report," he breathed. "The Sorenson's were up to something. There's a reason the old man was killed in the cabin in Algonquin. Hutson showing up at the brownstone when he did, it may have messed up someone's plans. Mistakes were made."

"What mistakes?"

"Hutson saw something. Not enough to kill him. Killing a homicide detective puts everything under the microscope—they didn't want that. Maybe it was best to knock him out, tie him up, and buy time. Along the way someone forgot to take the old man's diary. The contents of that little book are sick and incriminating. It could be a map to something bigger."

"And how does that implicate Mrs. Sorenson?" Landers asked as Crowley walked up.

Wolfe acknowledged Crowley with a slight nod and turned back to Landers. "How does someone live with a serial killer for fifty years and not know they are sick? How long was Mrs. Sorenson in that closet with Hutson? Why wasn't she tied up? Why wasn't she injured?

"I saw her that day. She knew her husband was dead, and it did not bother her in the least. She played the role of frail little old lady at the brownstone. Now watch her. She's gallivanting around this hotel like a middle-aged woman. She's a guest speaker at a meeting for people who want to take the law into their own hands. That should tell us something."

Crowley leaned into the conversation. "Where have you been, Wolfe?"

"Shut up, Crowley," Landers boomed. "We'll talk about that more, later. Tell me what happened in that parking garage on Washington, your words."

"It's in my report," Wolfe said, still looking around the busy lobby.

"I don't want to read it now. I want to hear it from your lips."

Wolfe rolled his eyes. "When I got there the sniper was dead. I saw movement on the ramp going up to the next level. I went to check it out. Next thing I know I'm on a gurney in the back of an ambulance. You should have more information than me." He turned away and continued to eye the undulating crowd.

"Your DNA was all over the place. You sure you don't want to change your story?"

Wolfe turned back to Landers with calm eyes. "I don't know why my DNA was all over the place. I told you what I remember. I'll get back to you if I remember more."

"How'd you hurt your hand?" Landers asked. Crowley peered over to see.

Wolfe folded his fist and studied it, the dark bruise on the outer edge of his clenched hand. "I don't know."

TWENTY-TWO

"Whispers crawled through the room like butterflies crossing a field."

"I'm Aaron Wolfe, homicide detective, Chicago PD." He looked from one end of the theater-like room to the other and up to the balcony. Nobody moved. There were more than five-hundred staring at the man who once represented hope in their world of monsters. Wolfe knew exactly why Commander Landers had volunteered him.

"I was asked to talk to you about murder in our city and what we're doing about it."

Landers stood in the left aisle, the back of the room. Before the door closed and the rectangle of light swallowed, Wolfe recognized him. He saw Crowley enter the right aisle. Both would take a seat on the back row.

Where's Hutson? Wolfe thought.

The break-out sessions scheduled during Wolfe's presentation were unattended. The CCLR members had one chance to hear the city's top homicide detective speak. Although they had issues with the criminal justice system from investigation to incarceration, Wolfe was still a main event. The other speakers of interest included a law professor from Harvard, a retired judge from Texas, and a sociologist from Stanford University. Wolfe was closest to the real monsters.

The audience was made up of mostly females of all ages and few men. The males attending were primarily in their fifties and sixties. Everyone had dressed for a funeral. Wolfe assumed they saw the annual CCLR conference as a religious occasion. All had lost loved ones to heinous crimes. The system had failed them. They needed much more.

"The Chicago Police Department has a mission."

Wolfe had labored over the right opening words for days. Now, looking into the bright lights, he thought the whole approach was stupid.

"We are empowered by you—the community." *I hate the word empowered.*

"We are committed to protecting the lives, property, and the rights of all the people of Chicago." *This is so lame. Why am I doing this?*

Wolfe scanned the audience. *Are you people dead? Is life that bad for you that you cannot move on? Why are you here? Why feed the beast that is tearing you apart? The world is not fair. Bad things happen all the time. We will never stop it all. Get over it!*

He took a long swallow of water from the pitifully small glass and returned it to the shelf under his notes. Looking back down at his scribbles he wished he had remained unconscious in the hospital bed long enough to give the stupid gig to Crowley. *Next time I tell Landers to stuff it.*

He moved his finger to the next paragraph and squinted into the lights. "The Bureau of Detectives is responsible for the investigation of crime and the apprehension of offenders." *I should say responsible for running around hell hunting the demons that haunt us all.* "We handle felonies, some misdemeanors, missing persons, and unidentified deceased." *Yeah. There's no one here representing those poor bastards, those who die alone and nobody gives a damn.*

"We process all offenders." *And that includes the juvenile thugs, whores, basic drugies, and the losers who are in development for future crime waves.* "Our department provides protective services for witnesses." *And we don't do a good job. We wonder why people don't come forward. Hell, I wouldn't.* "We investigate bomb and arson incidents." *And that's another climbing stat in hell.* "And our CSI unit processes forensic evidence." *Thank God for science bringing some form of objectivity to our subjective world.*

Wolfe paused and eyed the quiet audience again. He could see the faces on the first two rows. *Are you that interested in death and despair that you get here early enough for those seats?* After another swallow of water, he cleared his throat. "Although the Detective Bureau does all these things, I do just one. I am a homicide investigator.

"Homicide is when a person kills another. Most of the time, the action violates criminal laws. Some of the time, the action does not—like justified self-defense. I investigate all. It is up to the courts to determine if a law has been violated. They determine guilt or innocence, and then they impose punishment."

The rectangles of light reappeared at the end of the aisles. Wolfe watched more people enter. "In 2014 the Chicago Police Department handled over 57,000 criminal complaints. That number includes robbery, aggravated assault and battery, theft, burglary, shooting and stabbing incidents, and murder."

From the depths of the audience a voice called out, "Talk about murder!"

"In 1991 we had 928 murders in Chicago, and then there was a steady decline. By 1999 that number had dropped to 650. By 2011 it dropped to 450 murders a year. Although the population has continued to increase and the numbers are going down, we have more to do. The experts tell us education and jobs are the long term solutions. In the short term we must increase police on the streets and raise public awareness, living defensively."

The same voice yelled out, "We know people are being killed."

Wolfe squinted into the lights trying to see the one speaking. It was impossible. "When I talk about public awareness, I am talking about what each of us can do to protect ourselves and our families. There are motives for murder—money, narcotics, sex, anger. For a murder to occur there must be an opportunity. If the motives are known and the opportunities are removed, we have a better chance to not become a victim."

A hand shot up on the front row. "Can you illustrate what you just said?"

"If I drive an expensive car and park in an unknown neighborhood at night, I provide an opportunity to someone looking for money. If they are desperate for drugs, I can fill their need. They will kill me for money so they can get their fix. By not parking my car there, I remove the opportunity for a heinous act.

"90% of the killings are by men. 87% are by people with long arrest records. Although 60% of the killings in our city are gang related (drugs, territories, control, retaliation, money), that leaves 40% that are not."

Another hand shot up. "How many of the 450 killers do you catch?"

Wolfe patted his notes. He actually preferred going off script. He knew his audience was full of desperate, emotional, and broken people that despised the legal system. If he was going to help any of them, he had to choose his words and aim them to what was real.

"We make an arrest in more than 90% of the homicides we handle."

"How many of those are charged and convicted?"

"Most are charged, and most charged are convicted."

"And some get out of jail early."

"That is true on both accounts. We do not arrest and convict on all cases. Some cases need more investigation. Some are held in abeyance until new evidence becomes available."

"*In abeyance* means *cold case*. Isn't that right, Detective Wolfe? It means you failed. A killer is still out there. Justice did not prevail. Society is not safe."

Wolfe looked down at his notes but did not see them. "That's right."

The heckler persisted. "When we don't do our jobs, we get fired. What happens to you? Do you get fired? Are you punished for letting down society?"

"Yes, we get fired," Wolfe said as whispers crawled through the room like butterflies crossing a field. "I'm not sure how this helps anyone," Wolfe said. "Maybe some of you need someone to blame. I suppose you wouldn't be here today if you were satisfied with the outcome of your case, the terrible experience that stole your loved one and changed your life.

"I get it. I'm fine with that. Blame people like me if it helps. But if you are seeking more, seeking something that will heal, I suggest you avoid the hopeless trap of blaming the people in this with you, the people working every day for you and people like you. We get a lot right. We will always strive to do better.

"Some think they could do my job better than me." Wolfe smiled, and then his face hardened as he leaned into the microphone and leveled his eyes on the audience. "I'm here to tell you no one in this room could do my job better than me." His words dripped from his lips like fresh blood from a butcher knife.

"After you walk a thousand miles on a thousand dark roads, and after you look in the eyes of a thousand victims and put a thousand monsters behind bars, maybe then."

The room went silent. Wolfe straightened at the podium. *Where are you people now—where are your* heads? Are you hearing anything I'm saying? Do you get it—life sucks? No. It's something else you despise. What is it? It's gotta be the courts. Go there.*

"Maybe it's the courtroom that lets us down. Maybe that's where change needs to happen to make things better, to right the wrongs."

Wolfe pulled the mic from the stand and left the podium. "Do you think you can be more just than the judge who invested a lifetime on the bench? Do you think the jury of your peers is the problem? Do they let us down? Maybe we could weigh the evidence better? Maybe some believe we could do a better job searching for truth and protecting rights of the innocent?"

No one is moving. I can't read their faces. Am I wasting my time? Am I trying to help those unwilling to be helped? Wolfe walked to the side of the podium and rested an arm. *I should have stayed with my notes. Winging it is not working.* He glanced over and saw the bold print, *"KILLING IS A CRIME AGAINST US ALL."*

"The killing of a human being is a crime committed against us all," Wolfe said. "Finding and convicting the monsters responsible is the common goal of good people. Yes, the process is flawed. It is flawed because we are a nation governed by the rule of law, not a nation ruled by the arbitrary decisions of individuals. It is flawed because our first commitment is to the innocent. To insure we protect the innocent, some of the monsters get away."

Wolfe watched an obese man on the front row struggle to get to his feet. *Oh God. Here we go again,* he thought. *Be patient. Don't show anger.* With a hand holding his coat over his belly, the man raised the other and waited to be recognized. "Yes. A question," Wolfe said.

The man lowered his hand and his smile vanished. "No question here, an obvious observation. *Your* justice system failed everyone in this room, Detective Aaron Wolfe. I'm sure I speak for everyone here when I say to you that we

SERIAL INTENT

don't need a lecture from you. We need, no, we demand justice." Wolfe studied him. The man looked familiar.

Oh God. That guy has no idea who he's talking to, Landers thought as he squirmed in his seat on the back row. *Come on Wolfe. You've been doing a good job holding your temper. Granted you've gone off script a few times and thrown out some unnecessary challenges. Do not lose it now. You are representing the CPD. News media's all over the place. I don't need you on the front page of the Tribune lambasting victims of crime.*

"Do I know you?" Wolfe asked from the side of the podium.

The obese man flashed an insincere smile. "I think you're trying to forget me. I am Paul Timberman." On the last word Timberman pulled a revolver from his coat and began shooting.

The cries and screams rose above the popping in the front of the grand auditorium. Like children's firecrackers going off in the street, the shooting launched people from their seats. They broke to the aisles and became a part of a coagulated morass of human flesh, gasping wails in black satin. Landers and Crowley struggled to get to Wolfe, but they were blocked behind the human tidal wave. Their urgent efforts were muted. Then side exits broke open and the sun poured in. Streams of people flowed out to the white snow.

"He's reloading!" The frantic words rose above the chaos. Landers climbed bodies to reach the center of the auditorium. He pulled his gun. Crowley ran into the lobby and up the stairs. The balcony would be his only opportunity to help.

More shots poured from Timberman's gun. Then there was one more. It was louder and carefully aimed. Then another came from the stage curtains.

Only a few saw Timberman flop to the floor. No one saw him tremble in his own blood and his eyes roll into his head. And no one saw under the cloud of burnt gunpowder, the .22 caliber Smith & Wesson spinning on the floor.

Crowley reached the edge of the balcony—he had to get down. Landers reached the center of the back row—he had to get to the stage. On his way, he thought he saw Margaret Sorensen's head poking out the stage curtains.

Landers had counted fourteen.

TWENTY-THREE

The gun smoke settled above heads. The long flat cloud reached across the theater, poison fingers seemed to search for more. Like hurdles at a track meet Landers jumped rows of empty seats moving toward the stage with his gun up and eyes hunting. The screaming and pushing masses stampeded the exits desperate to escape the surrealistic world closing in on them. Death floated in the air and triggered painful memories for the masses.

Crowley hung from the balcony railing, his only chance to get to the stage through the mob. He dangled five feet above calling for help, but nobody cared. He took his chances and let go. Swallowed by the swarm his fall was broken. The few climbed out from under him and continued their march out of the meeting hall. Crowley pushed his way upstream. When he got to the front and the blood and Landers leaning on the stage behind the podium, Crowley asked, "Is he hit? Is Wolfe okay . . . ?"

Landers stood quiet and still as Crowley stepped over the body on the theater floor and grabbed his arm. Then Crowley saw the blood on the stage. His boss turned to him with a blank stare. "Call this in. The guy on the floor is dead. Wolfe went back stage or was taken back stage. I don't know which. Wait here for Hutson. The guy's always late or missing. I gotta find Wolfe."

"Backup and ambulances are on the way," Crowley said.

"Wolfe's been hit," Landers said as he leaped onto the stage with his gun out. "I've got a blood trail." He disappeared behind the curtains.

Hotel security had already manned the exits and moved people into a secured lobby now converted into a holding area. Surrounded by red-velvet rope lines and locked doors, each CCLR member would be vetted by the CPD. Crowley checked the dead man's pulse as routine. The man had a single gunshot wound between the eyes. Wolfe only needed one. It was a .45 caliber.

"What happened?" The words came from behind Crowley.

Crowley spun around and saw the size, the build, and the hair. "Wolfe! You're okay." The man stepped into the light. "Hutson," Crowley barked. "Damn, I thought you were Wolfe. You guys look too much alike. I guess I was hoping . . . never mind. Where have you been? All hell has broken out."

"Sorry. The place is crazy," Hutson said. "I was late for Wolfe's speech, and then got stuck in the crowd. What'd I miss? Where's Wolfe? Where's the commander?"

Crowley pushed the .22 caliber revolver away from the deceased. He got up from his knees and into Hutson's face. "Do you ever know what's going on, Joseph?" Crowley's eyes scanned the diminishing crowd and balcony for anyone watching them. There was no one.

"Sorry Ben. I'm not even supposed to be driving. I'm supposed to be home in bed."

Crowley noticed Hutson's hands. "What happen? I don't remember those bruises."

Hutson pulled each coat cuff over his hands and turned away. "It's from the Sorensen case. The doctors said bruises can show up days later."

"Right—you were knocked out and spent a day in a closet." Crowley sighed. "You're here now, so I need help. Stay with the body. This guy emptied his gun two times on

Wolfe. The blood on the stage means Wolfe got hit." *It would be damn near impossible to dodge a dozen bullets from this short distance.*

"Most hit the podium. I counted nine," Hutson said pointing a penlight. "Not a very tight pattern. The guy was clearly not trained with a gun."

"Thank you, Sherlock. Look, I gotta go. Wolfe and Landers are back stage—God knows what's happening. I remember taking a look at the hotel schematics after agreeing to speak at this convention. There's a network of halls, dressing rooms, and stairs that go up two levels and down one, access to the basement under the hotel. There's gotta be a half-dozen exits and a hundred places to hide. Get SWAT here. I don't know what I'm gonna run into. Wolfe is hurt and Landers is looking for him."

Hutson pulled out his cell. "Go."

"Landers is ahead of me by three minutes. You're in charge of this crime scene, Hutson." Crowley disappeared behind the curtains.

Back stage the blood trail crossed the musicians' room and led into a dimly lit hallway. Crowley looked in each door window and checked the knobs: the conductor's quarters, company manager's office, instrument storage room, and dressing areas. The blood drops lead him down the hall. He reached the iron stairwell in the schematic. It was open and gothic. He saw blood on the steps going down. Wolfe had gone to the basement. Landers probably followed.

When Crowley reached the cold darkness under the hotel, a hollow explosion rang out, a single gunshot. He moved toward the sound running his hand along the wall. He found the circuit box, but the fuses were gone. The smell of gunpowder got stronger. The wet sticky substance on the floor had to be blood. Crowley had decided early not to use his flashlight. As backup to Landers, he thought it best he kept his presence stealth as long as possible—that way he would not walk into the trap set for Wolfe or Landers. He listened and inched his way forward in the dark underbelly of the hotel ready to shoot.

Wolfe and Landers would not be quiet if either one had fired the single shot. The silent passage of time increased the likelihood of a grim outcome. When Crowley reached the end of his wall and another hallway, he heard the whisper; "You will not stop—"

Who is talking, Crowley wondered. *That's not Landers. It is not Wolfe. Stop what? Stop, like leave something or someone alone? Or stop, like bring something to an end?*

Another explosion!

This one was closer. Crowley dropped to the wet floor, his world muted. Now he was blind and deaf. He looked back from where he came. It was a black hole. *Where is my help?*

Light poured into the hall around the bend. It vanished with a metallic thud. But the light lingered long enough for Crowley to see the body. He crawled. *Is that Wolfe?* Crowley reached a boot. He pulled out his penlight and moved the small beam up the blood soaked pant leg to the torso and shirt sleeve. He recognized the bars.

Oh God! "Commander, it's me. Crowley, sir. I'm here. We're gonna get you help." He pressed fingers to Landers neck.

***

The relentless beeping and flashing lights would bother anyone conscious. It did not bother Landers. In the secured wing of ICU, the CPD Homicide Commander was strapped in the bed and surrounded by monitors, pumps, and IV bags. Outside his private room and at each floor exit, armed guards waited for an opportunity to blow somebody away.

He had a gunshot wound to the head. Commander

Landers' condition was critical; his vitals were unstable and future unknown.

"Doc said he had a chance," Hutson muttered.

"A small chance," Crowley breathed.

Wolfe stared at the monitors rubbing his bandaged leg. His arm had stopped hurting.

"I can't believe that Timberman guy," Hutson said. "And I can't believe you didn't recognize him, Wolfe. He was on the front row. How could you forget a nut like that?"

"You always know exactly what not to say," Crowley scoffed.

"Leave 'em alone," Wolfe said. "He's right. I should have recognized Timberman."

Crowley blinked back wet tired eyes as he stared at Landers' white corpse-like body—his leader had fallen. The smell of alcohol swabs piled deep in the nearby trash can, and the smell of hospital-clean sheets on the bed made him vomitus.

"I hate fucking hospitals," Crowley said. "I hate everything about them." He turned to Wolfe. "It's been seven years since you saw Timberman. I must have worked a couple hundred homicides since then—you, probably more. There's no way you could remember everyone associated with every homicide case, Wolfe."

"I should have remembered Timberman. He told me he was going to kill me if I didn't find the guy who sexually assaulted and killed his wife."

"I guess a lot of people make threats," Hutson said trying to get back into Crowley's good graces. "I read somewhere it is part of the grieving process for some. They gotta blame. For most the day comes when they realize they can't blame the world for what one sick bastard did."

Looking at Landers, Crowley asked, "You think we'll catch the shooter?"

"Yes. I promise we will," Wolfe said. "And we are

going to know everything, if it's the last thing I do."

"'We're gonna know everything', what's that mean," Hutson asked.

Crowley shook his head and leaned out from the wall so he could see Hutson's face. "I'm about to lose it with you, Joseph. We do not have time for you to be so dense."

"I guess I missed something," Hutson said.

"Let me catch you up. We've got a string of sniper executions in the city. We got an odd connection with the Sorensen family. Dr. Sorensen may be a serial killer, and some guy named Dario is runnin' around with a diary and killin' people. Old lady Sorensen is a member of the fucking CCLR. And now we have two of our people shot by an unknown assailant."

"There were a lot of people at the Congress Plaza Hotel that don't like the criminal justice system," Hutson said.

Crowley leaned back shaking his head and checking his watch. "I think Wolfe nailed it. We are seeing only the tip of the iceberg and the CPD is the Titanic."

"After Timberman shot you, why'd you go back stage?" Hutson asked.

"They pulled a .38 caliber slug out of me," Wolfe said. "It went through my arm and buried in my leg. Timberman had a .22 caliber."

"Someone backstage shot you. Did you see them?" Hutson asked.

"When Timberman shot the last of his first round, I found my gun. When he shot the last of his second round, I got my shot off and saw him look backstage before he dropped. I turned and got hit. I saw a gun pull back into the curtains. I must have moved just enough to avoid—"

"—getting it in the head," Crowley said. "Landers and I got up there after Wolfe went backstage. Landers followed Wolfe's blood trail. You arrived later, Hutson. That made it possible for me to go look for both of them."

"Landers and I were shot with a .38 caliber gun," Wolfe said. "I was bleeding. Got lost in the dark. Passed out."

"I followed your blood trail to where Landers got shot," Crowley said. "When the paramedics got there, I continued on the blood trail and found you out cold—blood loss. I got a couple of tourniquets on you and called paramedics. We got the lights down there turned on. I checked basement exits and found the .38 revolver stuck between ceiling pipes. It had been shot three times. No prints or DNA. We don't know who shot you guys."

"I get Timberman," Hutson said. "I don't get why anybody would take the chance to shoot you and the commander at a public event."

"I took a look at Glendora Timberman's homicide case file last night," Wolfe said.

"Damn Wolfe, don't you ever give yourself time to heal?" Crowley scoffed.

"I know my limits," he said rubbing his leg. "Paul Timberman's wife was raped and killed in front of him seven years ago. The poor man had a photographic memory—bad in so many ways. Although beaten unconscious, he remembered everything, including the killer."

"That had to help," Hutson said.

"He picked the guy out of a lineup—100% positive ID. Timberman had previously filled out the paperwork. The guy who killed his wife had a scar below his left ear. He had a gold star earring with a red stone—a fake ruby—and he walked with a limp. Later Timberman picked him out of a lineup."

"What about biometrics?" Crowley asked.

"Even biometrics. We had them from Timberman months before the lineup—height, weight, age, hair color, complexion, and build. The guy had a leg shorter than the other."

"So, you caught him," Crowley said. "I don't get why Timberman had a beef with you."

"Jack Noway. He pronounced it—no way," Wolfe said. "The guy was a real clown. He had top legal representation. Belonged to the Marcantonio crime family. Noway had an airtight alibi on the night of the killing. His attorneys got the DNA thrown out. They successfully challenged the integrity of the chain of evidence. They built a case around police tampering and got Paul Timberman's testimony as an eyewitness thrown out—delusional. Prosecution was forced into a corner."

"Happens too much," Hutson said. "Forced to plea bargain to get them off the streets."

"Pleaded down to manslaughter," Wolfe said. "The bastard was out on parole in five years, another one of those early-release programs."

"So Timberman watched Noway have sex with his wife and then kill her," Crowley said. "The courts screw them again, and the monster gets back on the streets to do it again."

Wolfe got up and walked to the only window in the room. He lifted the slat and squinted at the sun on the white snow. *I'm not going to tell you about my private chat with Lindsey—her story about the two visitors and their organization that seeks justice denied.*

And I'm not going to bring up the Dario Group mentioned by Barry Woods. I don't need more people on a list. Sure as hell Crowley and Hudson would blabber and get a bullet.

And they don't need to know the identity of the person who shot me and probably shot Landers. I'll find them alone, but I could use help connecting the dots with the Sorensens.

"Back when I was working the Timberman homicide, something said at the time did not mean anything to me then," Wolfe said.

"What didn't mean anything to you," Hutson asked.

"Paul Timberman had anger management issues. He was under the care of a doctor."

Crowley got a text from Sergeant Irwin, the POD program. He stared at the short message in all caps— LANDERS INSTRUCTED I CONTACT YOU IF HE OUT. WE FOUND SOMETHING AT GARAGE ON WASHINGTON. DO NOT DISCUSS WITH TEAM. COME SEE ME ASAP.

Crowley pocketed his cell and joined Wolfe at the window. Looking down at Landers and all the tubes, he swallowed hard. The words on his cell added to his nausea. Was it actually possible Wolfe killed that sniper with his bare hands? Is he capable of such a thing?

"I don't see how anger management issues seven years ago matter today," Crowley said. "After losing a wife and getting screwed by the legal system, it seems normal to go nuts. Granted, few people would actually follow through with a plan to kill somebody."

Hutson cut in. "Shooting a CPD Homicide Detective in front of 500 witnesses is suicide, Wolfe. That guy wanted to get even with society and have someone put him out of his misery."

"It's not that," Wolfe said. He dropped the slat and turned to Crowley and Hutson. "Paul Timberman had $100,000 deposited into his personal account days earlier."

"That adds a wrinkle," Hutson said.

"Who would want you dead?" Crowley asked.

"I don't know."

"What did you find in Timberman's file that means something today?"

"Paul Timberman was a patient of Dr. Jacques Sorensen."

TWENTY-FOUR

Why is he coming here? What does he want? If they see him, it could be misinterpreted. They could think I'm breaking rule number twenty-seven.

"Mr. Wolfe," Sandy Day said opening the front door. Her alluring persona from the first visit had curiously morphed into an irritating sneer and impatient demeanor.

"Miss Day. May I come in?" Wolfe asked

"No. It's not a good time. I'm leaving."

Wolfe gently pushed the door open with little resistance and walked inside. "I won't keep you long. Thank you."

"Okay, a few minutes, only. I have an appointment, an interview for my column." She peered up and down her street and closed the door.

Wolfe missed nothing. He sat in the same spot he had for the interview following the Dumont killing in the Wunders Cemetery. "Did you know Frank Peters, Miss Day?" he asked. He watched her lose her balance and sit on the edge of the sofa. She then pulled her hem down over her knees, an action opposite her behavior the first time she had met the handsome detective. *That answers that question. Now how and where?*

"I don't know, Mr. Wolfe. Why do you ask?"

"So, you may know Frank Peters," he pushed.

"I said I don't know," she snapped. "I'm sorry. I've been on edge lately."

"Did your phone call from Mrs. Sorensen put you on edge?" Wolfe asked

"Excuse me. How would you know I got a call from a Mrs. Sorensen? Are you bugging my phone? If you are, I will press charges for invasion of privacy. I know the law."

Wolfe smiled. "Do you? That's always a good thing. Do you think I would know if I had not taken the necessary steps to satisfy a circuit court judge? I don't think you want to make any waves, Miss Day. Actually, I like you. I hope you do not get any deeper into this mess than you already are."

She stiffened. "I don't know what you could possibly be talking about."

"Did Mrs. Sorensen tell you Frank Peters had been watching you?" Wolfe asked

"If you bugged my calls, you would know the answer to that." *She never said a word.*

"Actually, I doubt if she did warn you," Wolfe said leaning back in the stuffed chair and studying the attractive woman with a major problem, possibly the largest problem in her life.

"Frank Peters is dead," Wolfe said. "He died in his Tahoe parked in front of your condo. Did you know Frank was a serial rapist-killer, a real sicko?" He watched her take the news like a hit on the jaw. "The pervert left twelve women dead in four states. We never would have figured that out, but his odd death put him on the medical examiner's autopsy table. Frank Peters died waiting for you to go to sleep, Miss Day."

"There are a lot of people living in this complex. What makes you so sure it was me this man was watching?"

"That is a very good question," he said as she straightened and raised her chin of defiance. "Funny thing, he had a key to your condo." She sank. "He must have found where you hide your spare. Please tell me you don't put it under the front mat."

"I do," she mumbled. "I'm not feeling so well right now. I think you should go."

"You didn't ask me how Frank died, Miss Day. Aren't you the slightest bit curious?"

"How did he die?" She asked.

"Someone out there is watching out for you, Miss Day. Someone stopped Frank Peters from tying you to your bed, raping you for hours, and then butchering you. Seems Frank liked to carve up his victims and hide body parts around the house."

"That is horrible," she muttered.

"We never would have known about him. Turns out Frank had been a busy boy for several decades, but he had no record. Standard operating procedure, the ME submitted his DNA to CODES and got a match. Frank Peters' DNA connected him to a dozen dead ladies in the south." Wolfe leaned toward her. "You were number thirteen."

"I can't talk to you," she whispered.

"Is it because you will be executed like Barry Woods?" Wolfe shot back.

Her eyes widened. "How do you know?"

"I was with him. He told me everything. He told me about the Dario Group. Is that where you met Frank Peters? You need to talk to me. This thing has gotten out of control. More people are going to die. You could be next."

She slid back on the sofa and nodded. "But he was a kind old man, I thought." Nervous, she got up and went to the window. "He did act strange the last time I saw him. We were leaving a meeting. He walked me to my car. He offered to follow me home, concerned about my safety. I felt uncomfortable. I declined. I thought that was it."

"He followed you home. The meeting, was it the Dario Group?"

"Yes."

"What were you meeting about?"

"They had a contracted sniper who backs up our

members. The sniper was killed. They were very concerned about how he was killed. They also needed a replacement."

"Who killed the sniper? Do they know?" Wolfe asked.

"Yes. Dario killed the sniper."

"Who is Dario?"

She opened the curtain and wondered where Frank Peters parked his Tahoe and why she had not noticed him out there. She always looked outside for unusual things. After Ellen was killed, she had no idea what would happen next. She had never wanted to join the group.

"Dario is a sick person. We don't know much about him. He was being treated by Dr. Sorensen. Dario took on the name and mission of the Dario Group, but no one knows who or why he kills. Now that Dr. Sorensen is dead, Dario may be out of control."

"Who runs the Dario Group, who are the members, and where do you meet?"

On Wolfe's last word the glass exploded and Sally Day flew back against the sofa and fell to the floor. Wolfe dove from the chair and dragged her into the kitchen and out of the line of fire. Three more bullets pelted the interior of the condo. Glass window panes exploded.

Wolfe yanked a dish towel from the edge of the counter and pressed it against her shoulder wound. *Must be the new guy—he missed*, Wolfe thought.

"This is Wolfe. I'm at the Kelly Park Condominiums on North Kenmore south of Byron. Don't have the street address. Triangulate my cell. Get SWAT to cordon off a two block area, West Byron Street, North Wilton Avenue, West Grace, and North Kenmore. We've got an active sniper. I am under fire. Get an ambulance out here now— use the alley west of Kenmore. I have a wounded female. She's losing blood fast. Bring blood for transfusion or we'll lose her."

The next two bullets shattered the kitchen window.

You can't see me. You're guessing. I will find you.

TWENTY-FIVE

"I heard Louie is gonna die," Sergeant Irwin said so only Crowley could hear him in the busy coffee shop. They hid in a corner beyond the glare of the sun beating down on the melting snow.

"It doesn't look good. But the docs told us the bullet lodged in his brain where it is possible he could be okay. They just don't know much about the brain. He could die all of a sudden, or wake up like nothin' happened. The good news is the swelling's down. That was the first hurdle. Avoiding infection and throwing a clot are the next worries."

"I don't know the details about how he got shot, but I did get a look at the confidential report that goes to top brass—the highlights. It said the commander was in pursuit of a shooter at the Congress Plaza Hotel."

"Right. One of our detectives was speaking at the CCLR conference. A guy on the front row had a problem with the CPD. Some time ago he lost his wife—killed. They caught the guy. The killer was in and out of jail in no time."

"It seems the scum of the earth are getting away with murder more and more."

"We thought it was that simple here—thought the guy snapped and wanted to take it out on the homicide detective that worked his wife's case. We later find the guy made a deposit for $100,000 earlier. We're not sure it's connected, but it looks that way." Crowley waved for a coffee refill. "We are at square one on this thing. We have no idea why anybody would pay that kind of money to kill a CPD homicide detective."

"Did he shoot Landers?" Irwin asked.

"No. He emptied his gun twice on Aaron Wolfe, the speaker. Commander Landers was shot backstage trying to find Detective Wolfe."

"I don't follow. Wolfe is shot at and Landers gets the bullet in the head?"

"Sorry. I guess your brief doesn't go into much detail. After Wolfe was shot at twelve times, he killed the shooter in the audience. Someone behind the curtain shot Wolfe. The bullet just missed his head. It passed through his arm and buried in his leg. Wolfe went backstage to find the second shooter. Commander Landers went backstage to help Wolfe. Somehow Landers ran into the second shooter and took a bullet in the leg and head."

"I see," Irwin muttered with a questioning look. He leaned closer to Detective Crowley. "Louie told me if anything happened to him I was to speak to you only. He was adamant on that point. He did not want his request to get out until he or you said it could get out."

Crowley nodded. "Okay, I think. If that's what Commander Landers said, then it must be important."

"Louie was suspicious, or maybe concerned is a better descriptive word. He was concerned about the death in the parking garage on Washington, the one after the shootings at the Chase Tower and Burnham Hotel. It must have been a busy night for you boys."

"Yes, it was." Crowley hid his knee-jerk anger at the glib comment—people died.

"He asked I personally look into the matter. He wanted me to review the POD video in the area an hour preceding the Burnham shooting and hour following the parking garage death."

They both leaned back as the server poured and set down a fresh pot of coffee. Crowley studied the man across from him. He did not know Sergeant Irwin. He had never spoken to the man on the phone or seen his name in a report. *Why would Landers do it this way,* Crowley thought? *He could have prepared me for this but didn't. Something smells, or I'm being stupid. Irwin may be ready to drop a bomb that would even scare the hell out of the commander.*

"Louie shared the medical examiner report on the dead sniper pulled out of the parking garage. Clearly the man was beaten to a pulp, every bone crushed. I've been a cop thirty-eight years. I've never seen anything like it. The poor bastard could have fallen in a gorilla cage and come out looking better."

Crowley resisted rolling his eyes. Irwin was starting to piss him off. *Just get to it, please.* "Right. It was pretty bad."

"After hearing about the shooting at the Congress Plaza, the stealth treatment of my findings made more sense. I see why Louie wanted to keep the circle small."

"I'm sorry Sergeant Irwin, but I don't have a clue what you're talking about." Crowley pushed away from the table finding it near impossible to cope with the arrogant sideliner mentality that saw police work as some sort of game to be played.

Irwin smiled like the Grinch who stole Christmas. The whole experience had added color to his mundane black-and-white life of staring at screens searching for needles in haystacks. "I will get to the point. You see, we did capture important images on two of our PODs aimed at the parking garage on Washington the night of all the upheaval. Turns out we know who went in and came out of the garage."

"That is good news, I suppose," Crowley said still not knowing what the strange sergeant was trying to set up. "Please continue."

"The sniper entered the parking garage precisely twenty-four minutes before Barry Woods was shot in front of the Burnham Hotel. The sniper entered on foot carrying a suitcase one would typically use to transport a saxophone or similar musical instrument. Because the parking garage is a self-service, there were no attendants present. His entry was unremarkable and swift."

"What was the length of time you examined POD video aimed at that garage?"

"Two hours."

"Did anyone else go in or out of the garage prior to the shooting at the Burnham?"

"Three couples entered the garage prior to the shooting. Three cars departed within minutes. Close ups on the vehicles exiting confirms the same three couples who entered did in fact depart without event."

"After the shooting on Burnham, what did you see?" Crowley asked.

"We saw Mr. Wolfe enter," Irwin said with a smirk.

"What's the smile about?" Crowley asked. He would not let the sergeant get away with continued wise-ass behavior. "This is a serious matter."

Irwin stopped smiling. "I'm sorry. I know what's coming."

"Just tell me what you came here to tell me. I have things to do."

"That's right. You are taking over for Louie, the interim commander. Congratulations, Mr. Crowley." Irwin opened a file of black-and-white pictures. "This is a picture of Detective Wolfe entering. If you look closely, you can see he is being extremely careful." Irwin flipped to the next. "Here is a close-up. Note how he is dressed. He is wearing dark slacks, a dark shirt, and a dark coat. He is also wearing a dark fedora."

"I get it—dark," Crowley growled. "So what?"

"It is important later," Irwin said ignoring Crowley's

ire. "Nobody entered the parking garage after Detective Wolfe for the next twenty-three minutes. We were very lucky to have PODs operating in the area that had excellent views of three sides of the garage. The fourth side is walled up to the third level. I don't believe anyone could survive the drop if they attempted to leave that route."

Crowley started to get a sense of where Irwin was headed. "I understand."

Irwin fought back a smile. "No one left the garage, Detective Crowley. According to these visual documents, only two men were unaccounted for in that parking garage—the dead sniper and the unconscious Detective Aaron Wolfe. One was a bag of broken bones transported to the county morgue and the other was a bruised and unconscious CPD detective taken to the hospital.

"This is not good, Detective Crowley. I believe this is what Louie was worried about. It appears one of his own has killed someone. This cannot be easily explained away. Video does not lie. Not only did Detective Wolfe kill the sniper in that parking garage, he did it with his bare hands and in a way that is almost superhuman. I'm afraid Wolfe will face murder charges."

"I don't think so, Irwin," Crowley shot back. He watched the joy drain from the eyes of the monitor-watching sergeant searching for a life. "You don't have much here."

"Are you nuts?" Irwin said. "I've got Wolfe by his gonads. The boy killed the sniper."

"No. You have a half-ass video of eight people going in a parking garage on three sides. You don't have video of the forth side or the three exits that connect with buildings in the area. I guess you forgot to check those."

Irwin opened his file and fanned through an inch of papers. "You are wrong."

"No, you are so busy creating mystery fiction in your spare time that you've failed to do the most basic investigational work—called research. The whole world's not captured in your PODs, Irwin. You see slices of a world in slices of time. Not only do your PODs not see the entirety of the target area, you limited it to a two-hour window. The person who killed the sniper could have been there long before the sniper arrived, and could have left in the trunk or backseat of anyone driving out of that place. Did you find out if anyone parking there disappeared? No. I don't think so. All you do is look at video and jump to conclusions."

"You're just spewing smoke, Mr. Crowley. Even Louie suspected something terrible."

"I'm not concerned about your assessment of my investigational skills or objectives. Out of courtesy to my commander, I will give you the benefit of the doubt and some advice." Crowley finished his coffee and leaned over the table. "The person who turned the sniper into a bag of broken bones is a monster. He should be easy to find, easy to distinguish from normal men. You need to study your videos. Maybe you can find this creature. Going after a CPD detective who also got clobbered is pitiful. For your career sake, I suggest you forget this meeting."

Crowley started to stand. Irwin reached over and stopped him. With a troubled look he said, "Wait. I think I have seen the *creature* you described."

Crowley sat down. Although he argued for Wolfe, he was leaving with more questions than answers. Even he was not 100% sure about what happened in that parking garage or on those videos. Crowley was using logic more than listening to gut. Clearly Landers was struggling with something, and Wolfe had been acting strange lately.

"What do you mean?" Crowley asked with a dipping brow. *Could he believe anything Irwin had to say?* Landers trusted him, so maybe Crowley could learn something.

"We have video of such a man, although creature may be the better word. I've never seen anything like it. We were covering a drug drop site on the South Side, a routine surveillance. We had a POD watching the location two weeks. We were about to pull the plug."

"Get to it. I invested too much time in this," Crowley said.

"You need to see the video to believe what I'm going to tell you. Three men show up at the property. They were attacked by a fourth man. He jumps a six-foot chain linked fence with a two-foot barbed wire coil on top. He cleared eight feet from a squatting position."

"Is this a joke?" Crowley scoffed. "I really don't have time for—"

"No. This is no joke. It is unexplainable. A very big man attacked three men with guns. He had no fear. He moved so fast it didn't matter. We have him on video picking up one and throwing him into the side of a car fifteen yards away. He threw the next guy over the top of a damn semi-truck trailer. We could only stare at the monitor in shock."

Crowley watched Irwin relive the terror, his hands trembled. His eyes were wide and darting around. "Did someone watch with you the night this happened?"

"Officer Stahl. He was there. He was the coordinating officer on duty. I was not even supposed to be there that night." He took a breath. "I was putting new PODs in service, and then this happened. The drug drop site was visited for the first time in two weeks, a truck trailer parked in a vacant lot on the South Side. It was a frightening experience. I never saw anything like it in all my years running the POD program from the CPD."

Maybe Irwin did see something, Crowley thought. "What about the third man? Did this creature go after him?"

Irwin swallowed and spoke as if the movie started running again. He looked up and closed his eyes. "We think he was there to get the third guy. He got the other two out of the way. When he turned to number three and started to approach, a sniper killed the guy."

"Sniper," Crowley gasped. "Are you sure about that? Did you get that to Landers?"

"Positive. That night Louie got everything we had."

"Wait," Crowley said scratching his head. "Was that the Pender shooting?" *That's gotta be it—our sniper shooting on the South Side. But no one said anything about—*

"James Harvey Pender," Irwin recited. "Just paroled the week before. Like you guys, we're notified when those animals get put back into the general population."

"The Pender case, it was handled by Wolfe years ago. *Landers must have passed the file to Wolfe without saying anything.* Did anyone request this POD video?" Crowley asked.

Irwin flipped a few pages in his dog-eared file. "Sure did. Signed out by Aaron Wolfe."

Why didn't Wolfe say something to me or Hutson? This bizarre hellion has the strength and anger to tie him to John Doe's and Frank Peters' homicides. Landers had to know about this. No excuses Wolfe. It's time for a come-to-Jesus meeting.

"I'm gonna keep these photographs," Crowley said as he got to his feet.

"You want video from the PODs watching that garage on Washington?"

"I want six hours on both sides of the kill," Crowley said as he turned to the sun pouring in the window. "And for now, let's keep this between me and you."

"It will be on your desk this afternoon," Irwin said.

Crowley left the café biting his lower lip.

TWENTY-SIX

I'm surrounded by demons. They're even growing inside me, eating my guts. I gotta get all of them. I'm on a mission.

He slid down, his back pressed against the cold brick wall. He sat in the only beam of sunlight that somehow found a way into the maze of the Masonic lodge ruins.

I thought I could control you, he mused while ignoring his screaming wounds and pounding head. *Jocko controlled all of you, but now he's gone. He had to go. He was a demon.* Dario dropped his chin to his chest and let his hair cover his eyes. In minutes, he was asleep.

When he opened his eyes, his confusion replaced the sunlight. He felt his way through the dark building and climbed out a boarded window. In the quiet, he brushed his pants and shirtsleeves, combed his hair, and walked south on the sidewalk without streetlights. He thought it odd that he knew the graffiti and every broken slab. And he knew where to find his car. When he slid onto the cold seat and saw himself in the mirror, he knew who gave Paul Timberman $100,000 and why.

***

"The new sniper is not very good," Jennings Babcock whispered over his scotch. His boney fingers, snaked with blue veins and painted with rainbow splotches, gripped the small crystal goblet like it was a delicate hundred-year-old egg.

"I have another bottle of Bowmore, Jenn."

He sipped, savored, and smiled. Only she called him Jenn. "1957?"

"Of course."

"There were only twelve bottles released that year. It spent forty-three years in a sherry cask and eleven in a bourbon cask," he—the sophisticated wine connoisseur—spouted.

"Still trying to impress me."

Jennings let it sink in—she was right. He took another sip and rested his arthritic hand on the plaid blanket tucked over his knees. They both looked out the window from the 97th floor of the Willis Tower taking in the city and touching the memories.

"Are we losing control of things?" he muttered.

"Very possible," she said as she looked over her shoulder and down the dimly lit hall. "Are we safe up here? I would prefer not to run into your son. He's always been such a snoop."

They chuckled. The moment wouldn't last.

"It's late. The only people we need to worry about are the janitor and night watchman. Both know me well. Give 'em a Christmas turkey. They'll forget they ever saw us." He winked.

"You're such a thoughtful man." She carefully opened the box on her lap. "May I light your gift?" she asked. "I've not had a Cohiba Behike in years. Last I heard they were going for $18,000 a box, when you could find them."

"Of course you may have one now. If I had known you were bringing the Bowmore, I would have brought my last two Double Corona Regius cigars. Was saving them for a special occasion. It would have gone well with the 1957 scotch at $165,000 a bottle."

"We've had a good life," she said between sucks of the

flame into her Cohiba.

"In retrospect, I wish we had thought things through better," Jennings said. "Maybe we would not have embarked on our little mission the way we did."

"At the time it seemed the right thing to do. There had to be a way to kill all the monsters that you lawyers were setting free. If your profession had not required such exorbitant fees for services rendered, and if society had not needed a way to—"

"—survive," Jennings politely inserted.

"Yes, survive. Then our little mission would have been unnecessary."

"Nobody planned it this way," Jennings said. "The criminal justice system was never built to handle what was coming its way. It was not prepared for the onslaught of intellectuals pouring out of law schools all over the country. It could not handle the tidal wave of brilliance. These people creatively and legally used the vast array of legal tools before them."

"And they bastardized the legal system by using those legal tools to achieve the outcome they desired in a courtroom. It was never about searching for the truth. Innocent until proven guilty changed into innocent regardless of guilt with the right representation"

"Conscience is the chamber of justice," he muttered. "I don't know who said that, but it is a pure truth. Our conscience reveals that one point in space and time defining humanity."

"Yeah, well the bastardization of the criminal justice system put the hole in the dam that protected society, and you were part of that evil force. You did it all for money, Jenn."

"I did. You are right. But I also led the mission to find a way to close that hole in the dam. Reforming the laws and modifying the legal process would take decades. Only modest change could be achieved in my lifetime. But more smart lawyers would come and get around those changes too. No. We need something like the Dario Group. It does what the criminal justice system was intended to do but could never do. It focuses on 'pure guilt' regardless of process or legal tricks. The Dario Group focuses on one thing—killing real monsters."

"I know. That's why we joined the effort. Who can argue the simple truth? Every logical person knows the difference between a questionable killer and a killing machine. The Dario Group only goes after the hungry Bengal tiger walking down the street at dinner time."

"Serial intent, I could not put it more succinctly my dear."

She sucked the cigar like a man. Through the smoke she watched Jennings sip his scotch. He was dying. She had to push for answers. "I've gone into hiding."

"I know."

"How do you know?"

"You're having trouble with your snipers, dear. I know because my son was employed by Mr. Marcantonio a few weeks before the termination order. I understand the dissatisfaction over the violation. I don't agree with the grazing of my son's scalp to show displeasure."

"Did you know Marcantonio's name got on the Dario List?" she asked.

"I did." Jennings stared out the window like a blind man facing a wall.

"Your son chose to represent a monster you knew had been scheduled for termination. Your son's involvement jeopardized our mission. It got our sniper killed. The meeting site and security measures presented too many variables, and then Barry Woods showed up."

"That is what caused the problem, not my son or Chase Tower. A decision to address Mr. Woods's bylaw infraction the same night of the execution of a major drug lord was the error."

"We had no choice. Mr. Woods was talking to Aaron Wolfe. You know very well that Wolfe is a special problem. I'm sorry Jenn. Your son became an unacceptable variable."

"The only reason Eldon took the assignment was because I forced him. Our firm was navigating very choppy financial waters. We were facing bankruptcy. William Marcantonio offered me a way out, a lucrative deal that righted our ship. I had to take it.

"As an officer on the board of the Dario Group, I thought I would get some consideration after all these years. My hope was the Marcantonio execution could be delayed to the summer. I would have handled it myself, but my health prevents me from doing many things. I sent Eldon."

"We've always had an understanding. Once a name is voted onto the Dario List, they are off limits. That means they are no longer a viable source of revenue. Your decision to engage Marcantonio was a conflict of interest. You know better, Jenn."

He sipped his scotch. He knew she was right. "My son is busy, you know."

"Busy with what?"

"He's frightened, convinced he and his private investigators are exposed."

"Please tell me more."

"Sometimes Eldon's not as smart as I had hoped. To this day he has never considered the possibility his office is bugged." Jennings held out his glass for more. She poured. "Eldon met with his PIs late Friday."

"I thought the three private investigators quit that night at Chase Tower."

He sipped with a shaking hand. "They concluded that a vigilante group is out there."

Finally! You're getting to the reason I'm here, she thought.

"Friday they constructed a plan to find it."

"Why?"

"They believe the vigilante group intends to terminate each of them because of their association with the Marcantonio crime family—they connected the sniper dots. They see what connects the targets."

"Serial killers who have beaten the criminal justice system," she said.

"They believe competitors of the Marcantonio crime family will hunt them down over the territorial reorganization period. They want knowledge and then they will take my son and the PIs for a walk on the ice. They also believe the Marcantonio family will hunt them because the new guys probably had something to do with the execution of their patriarch."

"A paranoid group to say the least," she said.

"Their only chance to survive is to locate and expose the vigilante group."

She puffed her cigar and squinted in a cloud of smoke. "Their paranoia has painted them into a corner," she said.

"They spent a good deal of time planning. Their methods to locate the vigilante group include accessing our Detroit-based sniper source and searching for Dario."

She sat up. The ash broke from her cigar, hit the floor, and exploded. "They know about Dario?"

"They don't know Dario. They know about a unique individual, his memorable appearances on the South Side and at the parking garage. They have POD video. Unlike the CPD, these guys are employing the most advanced technology available to enhance Dario's image. They have his face—which won't help much."

Looking across the city she pushed out her cigar in her empty glass. "This is the price we pay when we step away from the bylaws. Now we have Fitz, Cranston, Michaels, your son, and God knows who else involved in hunting the Dario Group."

Jennings knew with the first sip of scotch—still, he enjoyed delivering the bad news even when his stomach began to cramp. "The $100,000 you put in Paul Timberman's account for the Detroit sniper is creating unintended consequences, my dear. Not only are the people in Detroit unhappy with the Dario Group, the Chicago police discovered the sizeable deposit and believe someone paid Mr. Timberman to shoot Detective Wolfe."

"Timberman went rouge on us. We had to salvage what we could"

Jennings turned to her for the first time. Images began to blur more than usual, but he did not let on. "Who shot Detective Aaron Wolfe and Commander Louie Landers? It seems to me you've lost your way."

She smiled—they had been talking almost an hour. Jennings finished his second glass of tainted scotch. He was supposed to think the abdominal pain was dinner related—a bad piece of meat. And most days he felt nauseous—this would be no different. She thought the blurred vision, labored breathing, salivation, and perspiration would go unnoticed until the end. Her only regret was the possibility she had missed something important before Jennings's heart stopped.

"You've had an amazing life, Jennings. You accomplished so much. You have much to be proud of." She wetted a napkin and picked up the lone cigar ash off the tile. Struggling to keep his eyes open, Jennings found her below his wheelchair doing her clean up. With her gloved hand she reached up and took the empty glass from his gnarled fist.

He smiled. "What is it—*Clitocybe rivulosa*?"

"Yes, Jenn. The best."

"You are so thoughtful to use the muscarine toxin, a most gentle route. You knew my heart could not handle—"

She closed his eyes and kissed his head. *Jacques would be proud* . . .

SERIAL INTENT

TWENTY-SEVEN

The money never arrived in Detroit, and they were not interested in excuses—they had a reputation to keep. The four deployed were uneducated specialists, trained in the streets. In their world, rank was not bars or stars; it was age and scars. The oldest wounded knew best how to kill and disappear, but no one had ever met a man like Dario before.

***

The security of the Dario Group (and their bastion) depended on the security of the second floor of Northwestern Memorial Hospital. There, Sally Day lay in a bed down the hall from Commander Louie Landers surrounded by CPD guards—someone wanted both of them dead and Wolfe had no more time to spare.

On the elevator ride down from the ICU, his phone rang. There had been a death at the Willis Tower building. Normally Wolfe would release an old man found dead in a wheelchair with no trauma, but this one caught his interest. The name Jennings Babcock rang a bell—an owner of property on West 27th Street. It was the place where Pender got a sniper's bullet between the eyes and Dario made his debut. The Babcocks got on Wolfe's list. In route, he left instructions no one moves the body until he gets a look.

Crowley got the POD video from Sergeant Irwin as promised. He took a sick-day to get out of the office and away from the phone. Six hours on each side of the parking garage incident meant a lot of tape to watch. He was convinced the video held the keys to solving the string of homicides in his city. He also believed the man called Dario was at the center of the carnage. Crowley had to find the connection between the Sorensens, Marcantonio crime family, and members of the CCLR. And if he got lucky, he would uncover the explanation for targeting Wolfe and shooting Landers.

"Mr. Babcock, we meet again," Wolfe said.

"This is not a good time for me, Detective. My father died. I need to make arrangements. Can we meet at a later date?"

"I'm sorry. Did you think this was about something other than your father's homicide?" Wolfe studied the lawyer and immediately saw the shock in his eyes. It was as if Eldon Babcock just realized there was a possibility his father had not died from natural causes.

Eldon pointed to a chair by the window. "Please, have a seat. I honestly had not considered foul play. My father was eighty-four years old. He had heart disease, bladder cancer, crippling arthritis, and had survived two strokes. One left him in a wheelchair."

"How active in the business was your father, Mr. Babcock?"

"Minimal. He was on the founders' board. They met once a quarter. Other than that, he would come up here to roll around and snoop like most old people do."

"He made you work with William Marcantonio, didn't he?" Wolfe pushed.

"I don't know if I would say that," Eldon snapped.

"You're smarter than this, Mr. Babcock. Don't play games. You're in serious trouble. You have people coming for you."

Babcock's nervous eyes crawled up Wolfe's chest and stopped on his cold face. He saw a hardened homicide detective who had seen hundreds of gruesome deaths. Babcock saw the anger and the intensity burning inside the man who spent a lifetime hunting devious demons.

"I don't know what you think you know, Mr. Wolfe."

"You think you can find the Dario Group on your own?" he asked with locked eyes.

"The Dario Group?" Babcock looked away.

"Do you really believe you can avoid the Marcantonio family zealots, the fanatics, the young Turks who blame you for the patriarch's execution?"

"But I had nothing to do—"

"You didn't? You were the last close adviser on board, Mr. Babcock. You were the one who set up the meeting where Mr. Marcantonio's head exploded like a watermelon dropped from a ten-story building.

"Or maybe you are hunted by the crime families that believe you were the close confidant to the drug lord. These miserable excuses for people have waited a lifetime for this day to come. It's their turn, Mr. Babcock. They desperately want to fill the void created when Marcantonio's empty body dropped to the floor that night. They want to take over the businesses they've always coveted."

"Stop it!" Babcock exploded. "Okay. I'm worried about all of that. But I'm working with my team of private investigators to get to the bottom of the Marcantonio shooting. I know we must solve the case or—"

"—or you will die. Now, doesn't that feel better? It's called truth, Babcock. If you level with me, you may have a chance to survive this runaway train. If you lie, I can promise you and your PI friends, you will each die a very painful death."

"Do you believe my father was killed?"

"Yes."

"How do you know?"

"The medical examiner said time of death was between nine and ten last night. Your father was with someone when he died, yet they did nothing about it. It was someone who smokes expensive cigars and drinks expensive scotch," Wolfe said. "It was a woman."

"How could you possibly know all of that?"

"Your father's wheel chair was not centered on the window. It was positioned for a chair to be next to it, the chair returned to the conference table, the only chair wiped clean of fingerprints." Wolfe looked around Babcock's office for anything that could help him solve his latest puzzle.

"I smelled scotch on your father. I smelled cigar smoke on your father's blanket. There was no cigar or flask or glass of scotch."

"He could have had a cigar earlier. You're guessing, Detective Wolfe."

"Trace cigar ash on the floor, Babcock. The cigar smoker missed it when they tidied up. The CSI boys may be able to tell me the brand—I'm betting it's unique."

"You still don't know if he died of natural causes or if someone killed him. Even you need to wait for the medical examiner to complete the inquest," Babcock spouted.

Wolfe stopped scouring the office and zeroed in on Babcock. "Few people die with their eyes closed—unless they are asleep in bed. Someone closed his eyes."

Babcock leaned back. The reality of the simple observation sunk in. "If that's true, I don't know who would want to kill my father," he said.

Wolfe leaned closer. "What woman would close his eyes, Mr. Babcock?"

No man, he thought. "Only one person," Babcock gasped. "Margaret Sorensen."

"Now we're getting somewhere," Wolfe said. "Your father and the Sorensens, how well did they know each other?"

"They go back forty years. They were very close. Dr. Sorensen was strange. Margaret Sorensen and my father were close, maybe closer than they should have been. I think they had an affair. It was love. My mother never said anything about it, but she knew. Pretty sure Jacques Sorensen knew too."

"Are you looking for Dario?" Wolfe threw a curve and looked for a reaction.

Babcock moved from memory lane to Wolfe's question. "Dario, I don't know the name. But we are looking for someone. We think there's a guy out there hunting the snipers hired by a vigilante group."

"Vigilante group?" Wolfe repeated without emotion.

"The victims of the snipers are similar," Babcock said.

"So, you and your PI friends surmised a group of law abiding citizens came together to right these wrongs?"

"Yes. We believe a well-meaning vigilante group has been formed to rid the world of the demented serial killers who beat the legal system. They are doing what they believe our justice system was designed to do but does not do. They are focused on truth. They don't give a flip about legal process or the rights of a killer."

"What makes you so sure about all of this?"

"Because I helped one of those monsters beat the system. I'm a damn good lawyer. I can tie up the legal process and achieve my goals regardless of guilt or innocence." Babcock dropped his head. "Not a day goes by I don't regret putting Pender on the streets."

"So, this vigilante group is operating in Chicago," Wolfe said. "They contract with snipers to kill these monsters. And now some crazy guy is running around out there hunting their snipers. Is this your theory?"

"Yes. It is theory. We have video of a man at two locations that also involved snipers. One was a vacant lot on the South Side where Pender was killed by a sniper. The other is the parking garage on Washington where a sniper was killed."

"Tell me more about the man you believe is hunting

snipers."

"We have him on POD video. We have experts in enhancement technology working on it now. We have a face and biometrics. This guy is strong. If we find him, we will have a path to the vigilante group. He may be the Dario guy you asked about."

"How good are the facial enhancements?" Wolfe asked. On his last word a bullet pierced the window on the 97th floor and hit the ceiling sprinkler head above Babcock. It began to spray. Wolfe dove over the table and pulled Babcock to the floor before a second bullet shattered the window and pushed Babcock's chair to the wall. Wolfe began to drag Babcock to the window.

"God no!" Babcock screamed. "Let me go. What are you doing?"

With a single thrust Wolfe whipped Babcock toward the windows like a ragged doll. The attorney in the three-piece suit slid across the polished floor like a hockey puck on fresh ice. He collided with the three-foot wall beneath the shattered windows and started to get up.

Wolfe yelled, "Don't stand. Put your face on the floor and lower your butt or get hit." The next bullet shattered more glass and buried in the wall. Wolfe elbow-crawled across the expansive office to the corner of the northeast windows. He peered over the three-foot ledge and saw the last flash of light above the observatory deck on the John Hancock Center. The sniper dropped out of view.

I'm impressed, a daytime shoot. Got your gear up there and used a silencer. Nice technique, but you're still a rookie. This is the second target you missed. Someone's not going to be happy with you.

"Are you gonna call the cops?" Babcock yelled across the room, his head still glued to the floor. "We gotta catch that sniper. You're wasting time."

With second thoughts, Wolfe looked over at the attorney he should have left for a bullet. People like

Babcock were the root cause of Wolfe's latest unfolding mess. "The sniper's gone."

"A missed opportunity," Babcock squawked.

"Not really. You will see him again. The good news is we know who wants you guys dead. The bad news is we still don't know where to find the vigilante group."

I must admit, I'm a bit surprised Dario had not yet neutralized the sniper. Maybe he had a full schedule today. Wolfe got to his feet and walked across the office kicking broken glass and holstering his gun. He pulled Babcock to his feet. "Let's go."

"I guess I should thank you," Babcock said.

"Don't thank me. When we get downtown, call your PI buddies. You boys need protection. If they think they can go it alone, you tell them Wolfe knows everything and they won't last twenty-four hours."

***

The next snow entered the city in the early morning hours of the first Wednesday following the Dario Group meeting on Birch. Robert Mason and Charlie Dunn sat on their bench in Lincoln Park looking out over the frozen lake. This time it was Robert's idea to meet.

"You read the newspaper this morning," Dunn asked.

"Nope. Didn't see it," Mason said. "I'm not interested in all the bad news anymore."

"Considering what we have gotten ourselves into, you should keep an eye on what's happening around here, Robert. There was a shooting, the Willis Tower downtown."

"Probably some office skirmish that got out of control. They got their own little world going on up there in the clouds, Charlie. Most are insurance companies or law firms—all crooks making all the money."

"No. There you go again. None of that is correct,"

Dunn said as he struggled to find a match for his dead cigar. "I start reading the newspaper, and you stop. A sniper on the John Hancock Building was taking pot shots at people in the Willis Tower. It all took place on the ninety-seventh floor. The John Hancock was the only building in the city tall enough to get a bead on people at the top of Willis Tower—a law firm."

"You think it was our new sniper?"

Dunn lit his cigar and puffed. "I guess Margaret found one. I don't like that Barry Woods was killed. He was a broken young man. We didn't sign up for that."

"Did they say who the sniper shot at?"

"Nope, but they did report a man named Jennings Babcock died in the Willis Tower earlier that morning—cause of death pending. The Chicago homicide people were out there investigating. It said the guy was in his eighties, nothing out of the ordinary, looked natural."

"Then why were the homicide people out there?" Mason asked. "With all the goddamn killings going on in this city, they got no time to be checking on some eighty-year-old man dead due to natural causes."

"Don't get worked up over nothing," Dunn said. "I don't have the answers for anything. Tell me why you dragged me out in this cold. We said we would stop doing this for a while, at least until the weather got above twenty. I froze the cheeks clean off my backside last time."

"It's about the Dario Group," Mason said as he cleaned his wire glasses with snow.

"I don't want to talk about it. I'm pretty much burnt out on the whole thing."

"Easy for you to say. You got justice. Pender is dead."

Dunn stopped sucking his cigar and turned to the man who had become his best friend over the last five years. "What has you all riled up, Robert?"

"You are ready to chuck the Dario Group because you have gotten justice for Beth and Billy. I get it. I understand it. I just—"

"Slow down. We're in this together." Dunn patted Mason's shoulder and puffed faster. "Since we've been doing this, the Dario Group has eliminated nine monsters. Remember, it was about killing all the monsters." Dunn turned to the lake. "Eric Ramsey, James Pender, Frank Pazrro, Jake Newman, Charles Bordon, William Marcantonio, two bodyguards they will not release names on, and Jack Noway. These people were monsters, Robert, but they were still human beings. I can't get them out of my head. I never knew that was gonna happen."

"What about Barry Woods? What about Paul Timberman?" Mason muttered.

"Those hurt, especially Barry Woods. Timberman went nuts. He got what he should have gotten. He tried to kill a homicide detective. But Woods was struggling over the death of Ellen Dumont. He had failed her." Dunn turned to Mason. "At least we had some life with our wives. Those two were so young. They had not even gotten married yet. Then the Dario Group founders make a unilateral decision. I thought we had a vote on such matters. I never believed breaking a bylaw would really get you killed."

"I have something to say," Mason whispered.

Dunn turned. "I know. We gotta call it a day. We gotta leave this group and move out of Chicago to a place where we can live out our lives in some kind of peace."

"Not yet," Mason said. He stopped cleaning his glasses and slid them into his coat pocket. Dunn sat up straight. Mason had worked up to the moment. "Mathew T. Whitten is getting out of prison tomorrow."

"The son of a bitch who killed Susan?"

"Yes."

"You want the Dario Group to terminate Whitten," Dunn said.

"Yes. I can't leave until that's done."

Dunn pitched his soggy cigar butt into the snow. He

could not work with the Dario Group anymore. The nine kills had made it impossible for him to sleep, and he just read about the death of Frank Peters. Mason did not know that the man in the cowboy hat by the fire on Birch was a serial killer. The bastard had infiltrated their secret club and targeted a female member. Dunn knew the monsters could be anywhere. Mason did not know Frank Peters' DNA had linked him to a dozen rapes and kills.

"Are you going to say something, Charlie?" Mason asked.

Dunn was slow, but he was not stupid. He knew things were not good for the Dario Group. After Dr. Sorensen got killed by a delusional patient with multiple personalities, the vigilante group started to drift off course. Margaret Sorensen tried to hold it together, but she did not know how to stop Dario, and she stuck with bylaws that killed innocent people. Dunn knew Detroit, the CPD, and Dario were closing in. It was no longer safe. It was time to go.

"Are you with me or not Charlie?" Mason asked.

Dunn turned to his friend, the last person on earth who meant something to him. Mason was there for him when no one else was.

"Yes," Dunn said. "We get Whitten terminated fast, and then we get out of Chicago."

"Thanks, Charlie."

TWENTY-EIGHT

"The next ten seconds of silence were like ten hours in hell."

Margaret Sorensen thought she was safe on Birch. Nobody had the address except the members of the Dario Group. A bylaw spelled it out—revealing the location was punishable by death.

"Thank you for seeing us," Mason said as he took a stuffed chair next to the fire, the one Frank Peters often chose. From it he could see out the three windows and through the archway into the kitchen and dining room. Charlie Dunn took a seat on the sofa across from the fire.

"I made adjustments when I received your message," she said. "Please, Mr. Mason, tell me more about Mathew Whitten."

Outside, sleet pelted the window panes. Inside, the fire popped and candles flickered—Mrs. Sorensen preferred it to electricity. The darkness and chill reminded her of the winters she and Jacques spent in Marquette Park years ago, their Indiana escape from the big city. When the property across Birch went on the market, they snapped it up to further secure their slice of privacy in a dangerous world. The two Birch properties were their secret—they kept them from family and friends for three decades. Now old, she sat alone in her dead mother's favorite stuffed chair knitting by the fire and wondering if she and Jacques had lived a good life.

"Mathew T. Whitten sexually assaulted and killed my wife seven years ago. He was on the run for two years and on trial for one. He was represented by Marcantonio attorneys. Whitten fits the Dario Group profile. The man's a serial killer and there is no question as to his guilt."

"I read his profile, Mr. Mason. Did you discuss Mr. Whitten with my husband?"

"Yes. Whitten is why I joined the group in the first place. Dr. Sorensen agreed Whitten would be placed on the kill list if the man was released from prison. He got out today after four years. Look at the termination protocol. It has both our signatures. That document demands the attention of the Dario Group within days of release."

She fanned through the file and pulled out the single page. "This is the protocol." She laid it on her lap and read every word as Mason and Dunn stared at the fire.

Nobody saw the tall black man wearing the knit cap and sweats—he stood at the edge of the den in the darkest shadow. It was the glint off the knife that caught Dunn's eye. Without moving he found the man's sick grin and froze as Sorensen finished reading.

"I am satisfied this is an official document. The Dario Group shall honor your initiation agreement. I'm certain Jacques would want it that way." She slid it back into the file and smiled at Mason. "However, at the moment the Dario Group has a few business matters to resolve first."

The creaking board moved her eyes to the archway. She saw the black man and slid her hand between the seat cushion and chair arm. Her fingers frantically searched for her gun. "Who are you?" she asked, but already knew the answer.

He held up her derringer. "Lookin' for dis, ole' lady?" He stepped into the den like he owned the room—he did. Another black man stepped out of the shadows. They spread out. "We from Detroit." He pocketed the derringer and ran his thumb across his shiny blade. "They call me Jevon. This be Deke. And da big man behind ya be Andre'. Ya can see—he big. You know Andre' the Giant. His mama watched wrestlin'. Named her first boy, Andre'."

"You are from Detroit," Mrs. Sorensen said. "I assume you work for Mr. Doran."

"You is one smart ole' white lady," Jevon said as he moved closer to the fire staring at Mason. "That'd be a correct assumption." He looked back at Deke. "Where Liddell? He posed to be here. I told 'em ten minutes."

"Liddell outside runnin' 'round," Deke said. "He securin' things."

"We in da boonies, fool. We on a dead end motherfuckin' road, in da woods in a snow storm. Ain't nobody gonna be out in this shit snoopin' 'round for some black men with knives and guns doin' home invasion shit, man. Get Liddell. Tell him ta get in here."

Charlie Dunn had physical limits. He lost the ability to damage anything and anybody years ago. Robert Mason worked out. His strength came in short bursts. Arthritis and a bad heart would allow for one wild swing, but Mason would miss the target and drop out of exhaustion.

Margaret Sorensen had zero physical skills to call upon. Without her derringer or the shotgun from under the bed, she could only sit and hope for the best. Like Jacques, Margaret could talk her way out of most situations. The intellectual capacity of her invaders made talk an unlikely route to resolution. Regardless, she had to try.

"Gentlemen, we owe Mr. Doran $100,000. I am sure that's what you are here for. Please understand that we have had some unfortunate developments and a recent unexpected event. The money for Mr. Doran is tied up in a bank account now under the control of the Chicago police. Realizing the release of those funds could be further delayed, I made arrangements for another $100,000 to be sent. It will be in Mr. Doran's possession early next week. I know this is not compliant with our agreement. We certainly will accept any financial penalty Mr. Doran feels is appropriate."

Jevon put the point of his knife under Mason's chin and pressed, standing him up from the stuffed armchair.

"Please don't do this," Sorensen begged. Dunn stared at the fire. "There is no need for anyone to get hurt. We are paying the money we owe a week late. We expect to pay a lot more as we continue our business arrangement with Mr. Doran into the New Year. He knows the Dario Group is a reliable profit center. We have a solid history. Please, Mr. Jevon, do not hurt this man. He's done nothing to you or Mr. Doran."

With the knife under Mason's chin, Jevon walked him to the edge of the sofa. If Mason hesitated anywhere along the way, the knife would have sunk into his neck and sliced open his jugular. Mason would bleed to death in less than a minute.

At the sofa, Jevon lowered his knife and pushed Mason down next to Dunn. He leaned into his face. "I ain't killed nobody for a week. I don't like you."

"I beg you to stop," Sorensen said. "We are business partners. We have never had a problem before. My husband died. I am taking over all business matters he managed for the Dario Group. Please work with us. We are in transition, that's all."

Margaret's eyes narrowed and her tone hardened. "I hope nothing bad happens here tonight, nothing that could stop the substantial flow of cash from the Dario Group to Mr. Doran. I do not think Mr. Doran would be pleased to lose a million dollars in annual revenue."

"You threatenin' me, ole' lady?" Jevon exploded.

"I'm educating you on the extent and magnitude of an error. Failure to recognize it could be costly to Mr. Doran, and could change your future."

Jevon jumped to the window. "Did you see that, Andre'?" He leaned and looked both ways. "I saw somethin' go by this window and it was not a brother. It was a big white guy."

"I don't see nothin' out there," Andre' muttered. "A tree branch full of snow hit the window. Damn sure ain't no white guy." They kept looking. Mason and Dunn kept staring at the fire. Sorensen stared at her primary problem—Jevon.

"What will it take for you to leave us alone?" she asked.

"We not here to negotiate," Jevon said.

"Why did you come?"

"We here to terminate our relationship," Jevon said with an odd smile.

"What are you talking—?"

Before she could finish her sentence, Jevon threw his knife across the room. Dunn and Mason did not move. Sorensen turned to the sofa in confusion—the aggressive action did not make sense. A log dropped and sizzled in the bed of hot coals. Where was Jevon's knife?

Mason leaned forward. He had something to say. When he opened his mouth, blood streamed from his lips and down his chest. The fire popped and new light filled the room. They saw the handle of Jevon's knife in the center of Mason's chest. His eyes fluttered like he came upon a swarm of gnats.

Mason turned to Dunn. "I'm dying, Charlie."

Dunn reached for his friend, but Mason stopped his hand. "No. It's okay. It doesn't hurt. I don't hurt. I'm not scared, Charlie." He blinked and spit more blood. "I miss Susan so much, Charlie. I need to go to her now. It's okay. It's—"

Mason fell back on the sofa. His eyes rolled into his head. His arms relaxed and hands opened on his knees as life left him. Mason died in seconds. His shirt filled with warm blood until his heart stopped pumping. Charlie and Margaret sat in shock. Then it registered.

"You miserable bastard," Dunn yelled as he struggled to get up from the sofa. But Andre' had an eye on the other old man. The clenched fist moved through the dark room like a hundred-pound log swinging on a rope. It found Dunn's face. Dunn collapsed—out cold or dead.

Sorensen watched Jevon and the twisted smile cross the room. He pulled the knife from Mason's chest and wiped the blade on the arm of the sofa. "Where my boys Deke and Liddell?" he asked as if he had just come for a visit. "They been out there long enough." Sliding the knife back into his belt he turned to the fire. "Go get 'em, Andre'—ain't nobody goin' nowhere."

Andre' left through the kitchen. When the backdoor closed, she started to work on Jevon. "You killed a good man, a much better man than you could ever be." She wiped her eyes and tried to slow her breathing and heart rate. "I don't know why you would be so mean. Mr. Mason did nothing to you. None of us did anything to you. We did business with Mr. Doran, that's all. You're a sick person. You're nothing but a miserable animal. I pray to God that when you die it is with great pain."

"You think you better than me, don't ya ole' lady?" Jevon said.

"I do not have any idea what you are talking about," she said. "I don't kill innocent people for the fun of it. I don't revel in anyone's death. You killed a man for no reason. You enjoyed watching him leave this world. You are a sick person who needs to be put down."

"You the sick one, ole' lady. You kill people, too. You think you got better reasons than me to kill?" He looked over at Mason's corpse. "It was time for him to pay for killin' people. Nobody allowed to kill, not even you. No. We ain't different, old lady—you an animal, too."

Margaret glanced down at the unfinished pot holder

hanging from the top of her knitting bag and realized she would never finish it. She also realized Jevon had it right—she was an animal. She had people killed. In the end, her reasons were no more important than the twisted reasons of any killer. Her final minutes of life had arrived and she cringed as the truth washed over her. What she thought mattered was evil all along.

"Andre' must be runnin' 'round in the snow, too. Maybe found some beer or somethin' out there." Jevon returned to the ice covered window and leaned close to the cold glass panes looking for anything that moved. But the white in the night was flying in too many directions to make out anything.

"I'm supposed to kill all of ya and get back to Detroit tonight," he mumbled into the glass window. "One of ya is dead—I know 'cause I stuck him good. I think Andre' killed the other old guy. I ain't no doctor, but he ain't been movin' for a long time. That's dead in my book." Jevon studied the ice crystals on the window panes. "Ain't no more Dario Group people 'round here. That leaves me and you, ole' lady. I can take my time; have a little fun on a cold night before we all get back to Detroit."

Her heart crawled into her throat. She gagged on the thought of being touched and then butchered by Jevon. Her new reality continued to close in around her. She would die by the hand of a real monster, the single terror she most feared in her life, and the very reason she joined Jacques in creating the Dario Group.

When Jevon put his hand on the glass, the bloody hulk crashed into the window. Jevon fell back pulling his knife. He watched Deke's bloody face slide down the crystalized glass, eyes opened wide, and his head undulated like an over-filled water balloon. When Deke's face reached the window ledge, it stopped below a ghastly trail of frozen blood and brains. Jevon stared and squeezed his knife.

"Looks like we're not alone," Margaret whispered.

"Maybe you're going to die tonight, Mr. Jevon. Maybe all of you are going to die tonight for what you've done. Did you really think killing members of the Dario Group would be that easy?"

"Shut up, ole' woman," he said as he pulled out the derringer and backed into the dark shadows of the dining room to think.

The body crashed through the window and landed on the dining room table. Jevon jumped back and flattened against the wall. He shot his only two bullets into the night. Now, the shattered glass, splintered wood, and snow filled the room. Jevon stared at the hole in the wall with his knife ready. He would throw it at anything that moved. It was his only talent—he could put a butcher knife in the center of a quarter at twenty feet.

"Go ahead and look at your dead friend, Mr. Jevon. Which one is on my table?" Sorensen pushed. "Is it Liddell? Probably. I don't think they could throw Andre' the Giant through the window like that."

Jevon ignored her. She wasn't going anywhere, and he had bigger problems. *Someone out there killed Deke and Liddell,* Jevon thought. *I still got Andre' somewhere. He's a smart guy. He wouldn't walk into no trap. Yeah. Maybe he be waitin' for me to make my move.*

The snow whipped into the room and snaked through the house. Now there were more ways into the house: the hole in the dining room, two windows, and the kitchen back door. Jevon returned to the den and positioned himself behind Sorensen—the person they would try to save.

"You like being hunted?" she pushed.

"Be quiet ole' lady, or I'm gonna take time now for you." *Whoever got Deke and Liddell, they had to get 'em one at a time. Ain't no way they take both of 'em at the same time. And ain't no way they take Andre' down easy. That ain't ever gonna happen. That boy's smart and strong as five. He'll fight after he's dead.*

SERIAL INTENT

"You want a chance to live, Mr. Jevon? You want me to call off my people?" she asked.

Jevon came up to the back of her stuffed chair. He reached over her shoulder, smelled her hair, and put his blade to her throat. Watching the archway and the dark entry to the kitchen he whispered, "You gonna call everyone off, old lady. You gonna do it now or I stick my knife in ya belly. I don't care what happen to me. I ain't afraid to die. But you, it gonna hurt bad and ya gonna live a while. The next stick gonna be in ya chest. It gonna hurt, too. And while you be thinkin' 'bout that, I'm gonna carve my name on your face."

"I don't think that's going to work," she said.

He dragged the tip of his knife down her shoulder. Blood flowed from the four inch cut in her skin. "Oh God!" She gasped. Her eyes watering as she struggled for air and her surroundings faded. Then he put the metal tip on her other shoulder and pushed. Blood broke to the surface. A drop rolled down her chest. "No," she screamed. "Please. I can't take—"

"Ya get ya people to back off. Tell them to send in Andre' and they go home now. We gonna go back to Detroit. We got two and ya got two—we be even. I tell Doran we worked it out, reached agreement. Ya good for the money."

Stunned and lost, Margaret Sorensen shivered in pain.

"If ya don't want the deal, the next place you feel my knife is ya belly." He cackled in her ear. "Ya think ya shoulder hurts, ole' lady? I promise ya the belly hurts more. Ya don't want me to—"

"Okay. I accept your proposal. I will do it your way." *I'm not made for this. I'm too old. I can't handle the pain.*

"Tell 'em back off—go home. All's good here. No one else dies. Tell 'em to send Andre' in here, now. No tricks, ole' lady." Jevon leaned over Sorensen and put the tip of his knife to her stomach. "One mistake, one surprise, the knife goes in. I do it before I die, ole' lady."

"Please stop out there," Sorensen yelled into the night. "Stop now. We have reached an agreement. No one else dies. Go home now. They will let me go when you leave, and only if you send Andre' in here now, alone. Please. No tricks. No surprises. This is an order."

The next ten seconds of silence were like ten hours in hell. The frigid winds transformed the warm cottage into a walk-in refrigerator. The fire battled to stay alive, candles flickered, and shadows danced.

The back door whined. Jevon leaned over Sorensen and readied his knife for a deep plunge. If they varied from the deal in the slightest, he would push the blade into her abdomen so hard that the point would stick out her back. Then he would dive out the window and disappear.

They both saw the enormous shadow in the kitchen doorway. It was Andre' the Giant. He paused, and then lumbered forward through the wavering shadows. When he reached the archway, he stopped and stared at Jevon and Sorensen by the fire.

"Ya okay, Andre'?" Jevon asked. "They hurt ya?"

Andre' nodded and took an awkward step into the thin light of the den.

"What's wrong with ya, Andre'?" Jevon asked.

Andre' nodded again, but not from his neck. The fire flared. The flash of light fell onto Andre's face. His eyes were open but empty, his head bloated like Deke's.

Jevon studied Andre'. Then he saw the arm wrapped around his waist, an arm holding up his giant friend. The arm moved. Andre' fell forward like a dead tree and crashed to the floor. The wind fed another flare. Jevon saw the larger man standing alone in the archway, the man strong enough to walk a dead behemoth into the house, the man unlike any man Jevon had ever seen before in his life.

None of it surprised Margaret Sorensen. She had had her suspicions when the first body slid down her window.

Her suspicions were confirmed when the second body crashed through her dining room window. It would only be a matter of time before Andre' and Jevon would die.

In the space between seconds of shock, her fingers found her weapon. Margaret sunk her steel knitting needle through Jevon's carotid artery and deep into his brain stem. His heart stopped immediately. She removed the knitting needle and pried the knife from Jevon's paralyzed claw. Jevon slid off the back of her armchair dead before he reached the floor.

Most knew Margaret had met Jacques in medical school, but few knew she was a medical student specializing in brain surgery, a career she ultimately chose not to pursue. However, she was an expert on the anatomy and function of the human brain. When Jevon dropped to the floor behind her, Margaret had a short moment of sadness. From her position in her stuffed armchair, it had been impossible to place the tip of her knitting needle in the most ideal region of Jevon's brain for the production of unbearable pain.

STEVE BRADSHAW

TWENTY-NINE

On the horizon, the top of the orange molten ball pushed out of the purple morning haze. Its fingers reached across the frozen tundra and touched each of the infinite crystal prisms left behind by God. Yet there was another presence in the cold dark night. On the loading dock of the Cook County morgue, seven frozen bodies were left behind by a monster.

Detective Aaron Wolfe had left the city—the message said he had to go to Detroit on a long shot. Detective Joe Hutson did not answer his phone—still on medical leave following the Sorensen brownstone incident. Commander Landers lay in a bed in ICU—vitals improving but still in a coma. Detective Ben Crowley, senior homicide detective, had been made interim head of the Bureau of Detectives, a position he would hold until Landers returned or top brass made a decision on a replacement. When the call came in from the medical examiner's office, Crowley drafted the greenest detective to ride along. Zach Huntsman's mistake was being the only homicide detective on the floor when Crowley put down the phone.

The toe tags read John Doe #1 through John Doe #7 with the date to differentiate between prior John Does. The naked bodies, covered in an inch of powdered snow, were lying face up in a line. There were four black males in their twenties, two white males in their sixties, and one white male in his thirties. After documenting the macabre scene on the loading dock and after CSI gathered all their physical evidence, the seven corpses were placed on gurneys and wheeled into the autopsy room to thaw.

"Thirteen please," Provost said with his head inches from the neck of another dead man on his table. The diener knew the doctor meant he wanted a thirteen-centimeter probe. The ME had his nose near a five-millimeter round puncture wound not caused by a bullet.

Provost adjusted his Ymarda magnifying specs hinged to his visor, and he looked over them at the suspended monitors a few feet away. "How's my ultrasound, gentlemen?"

"Good to go, Dr. Provost." The words flowed from a Siemens representative standing outside the lighted area.

Provost held out a bloody gloved hand. The diener slapped the requested probe onto his palm. Provost leaned in and inserted the metal tip. They watched the monitors. It moved on a line parallel to the neck vertebrae toward the base of the skull.

"I'm at fifteen-point-two-four centimeters, gentlemen. There is a slight narrowing of the canal. The change is from five to four millimeter diameter and narrowing more." Provost paused. He did not want to bore a new hole. His goal was to trace the pre-existing canal to its true endpoint, something that could not be accomplished by way of dissection. And the possibility of trauma-induced perforations in the canal made dye injection impossible—the precise depth of the canal could be lost.

Halfway into the procedure Provost realized the visual guidance provided by ultrasound was not enough. He had to feel his way. Switching hands and holding the probe in a fixed positon, he held out his right hand. "Somebody take off this glove, please. I need to feel the rest of the way."

After the glove was removed he held the probe with the tips of two fingers and pushed. His eyes were locked on the monitors as the probe moved deeper without interruption. Like disarming a bomb, Provost closed his eyes and relied on his experience and sense of touch.

Seeing the closed eyes and the doctor's hesitations, the dedicated diener had to ask. "Is there a problem, doctor?" He was eager to assist and not used to just standing and watching surgical procedures on the dead. But, although he had carved and harvested dozens of bodies a day over the last ten years, he did not possess the knowledge or skills necessary to do the probe. Provost opened his eyes and found his loyal diener. He winked and closed them again.

When the medical examiner is silent, the autopsy room is silent. When the medical examiner is speaking into his microphone or to his medical team, the autopsy room is silent.

Provost snapped open his eyes and watched the probe approach the heart of the brain stem. When it stopped, the room could not help itself—gasps floated in the dark and then returned to silence. At that moment Provost knew, and he knew his team knew, the cause of the man's death. But that's not why the gasps. Everyone in the autopsy room knew at that moment the killer could only be a brain surgeon.

Always teaching, Provost asked, "Who can tell us what we are seeing?"

Winston Foster stared at the body through his round wire glasses and pursed lips. Provost knew he knew first, probably even before the probe. And Provost knew Winston would not spoil the fun for the rest of the team. The answer came from the newest medical assistant. "I see perforation of the brain stem, sir."

"And what else do we see? Winston please amplify," Provost ordered.

"Perforation of the brain stem does not necessarily cause death. It can cripple a person and threaten death, but other areas of the brain can take over. In cases when brain stem tissue is scrambled and left intact, the heart often stops and respiration is inhibited."

"Well done, Winston," Provost crowed. *The man should be a forensic pathologist.*

Detective Crowley walked into the autopsy room and stopped at the feet of the deceased, a position often saved for homicide detectives who come and go.

"Detective Crowley. Hello, sir. I was expecting Wolfe."

"He's in Detroit on business. You're gonna have to put up with me."

Provost chuckled as he busied himself with the corpse and routine. "On the contrary, I've always preferred your more organized approach to solving crime. And I can say your timing is once again impeccable. We have some interesting information on John Doe #6 found on our back steps with the others—seven in total. The cause of death here may be more than helpful."

"I'm all ears," Crowley said as he watched Huntsman struggle with the smells and the visuals. The rookie homicide detective would learn to handle blood and guts one day.

"People have been dropping a lot lately," Crowley said. "Not typical gang kills."

Provost pointed to the puncture wound beneath the jawline of the naked black male on the table, his chest open and internal organs exposed. "We have a puncture wound here. It is not a bullet entry or exit wound. It is not a knife wound. The depth of this puncture wound is precisely twenty-point-one-five centimeters. The diameter of the distal canal narrows from a maximum of five millimeters to a gradual point."

"You think the guy was stabbed by an icepick?" Crowley asked.

"That was my first thought after eliminating projectiles and the possibility of a shallow puncture wound," the doctor said.

"Something changed your mind," Crowley muttered. Huntsman peered over his shoulder.

"The route of the canal is precise, not something the average killer could accomplish. It travels through the center of the right carotid artery and takes the shortest path to the midpoint of the brainstem, a well-protected anatomical structure."

"What are you saying, doc?" Crowley asked as Huntsman backed away to puke again.

"We are dealing with a weapon in the hands of a very lucky killer, or we are dealing with a lethal instrument in the hand of a brain surgeon."

"A brain surgeon wielding something other than an icepick," Crowley muttered.

"I believe it was a knitting needle."

"Just when I thought I was starting to understand life," Crowley teased.

Provost removed his other glove and wiped blood from his hands. He nodded for Winston to follow and issued new orders to the medical team. "Finish up here and let me know when you have the next ready." He signaled Crowley.

Winston, Crowley, and Huntsman followed Provost down the hall and into the walk-in refrigerator. There were forty naked bodies on gurneys, twenty on each side with an aisle up the middle. The group stopped at the feet of the other six found dead on the dock.

"I will give you my thoughts on all seven so you can begin to connect your dots. I will complete all inquests by the end of today. Although you can access my findings the normal way, Winston will be available to address your questions 24/7. He will bring me up on matters requiring my attention."

"I'm good with that," Crowley said. "And this is Detective Huntsman. He is new."

Dr. Provost acknowledged Huntsman with a nod. He

would not give the rookie any more of his time or attention until after a commitment to the profession had been demonstrated, and that would take two years. Over the interim, Huntsman would be a face in the room.

"Before we get started, give me an update on Louie's condition."

"Still in a coma. Vitals strong now. They say the bullet followed the skull and got in the best place possible. Don't know what that means. We need time and some help from above."

"I see. We must hope for the best." Provost flashed a smile. He knew precisely how the bullet could find a survivable course, albeit rare. "I will look in on him tonight."

Provost turned to the first body on a gurney. "This healthy black male in his twenties died from acute bilateral pressure to the temporal lobes—massive cranial fracture, brain tissue rupture, and hemorrhage." Pointing to defense wounds on the hands and arms, Provost continued. "The deceased put up a fight to no avail. Clearly his opponent was far superior in strength and agility. The deceased was demobilized in a matter of seconds. Death was instant."

Crowley rubbed his chin like he had just taken one in the jaw. "I think I know what you just said, but I want to be sure I understand. Can you dumb it down some, doc?"

"This man's head was crushed by hands compressed over the ears of he victim. The skull shattered. Brain tissue seeped through the cracks and out orifices. The jugular veins and carotid arteries ruptured. He bled to death, internally."

"That sounds like a terrible way to die," Crowley sighed.

"Yes. And it seems to be happening a lot lately," Provost said.

"The same for the others delivered to the dock?" Crowley asked.

"Not all and some prior. We've seen it two times before today. Our John Doe sniper killed at the parking garage on Washington Avenue—he had a crushed skull. And Frank Peters had a crushed skull. I'm confident after I complete the microscopic analysis today those two will be connected to three others from my dock."

"Frank Peters is the guy whose DNA submission to CODES got all the hits. Connected him to a dozen cold cases," Crowley confirmed.

"Yes, the man was a monster. Serial rapist and mutilating killer," Provost said.

"This black male died like the sniper and Frank Peters?" Crowley asked.

"Yes. He is one of four from my loading dock with identical head crushing morphology: three of the young black males and the one white male in his thirties."

"You had seven on the dock. Four crushed skulls and one killed with a knitting needle. That leaves two."

"Correct. One white male in his sixties was stabbed in the chest, a single thrust nicking the heart—but enough. I suspect the knife was thrown. There was evidence of bruising around the entry wound—we have a shield pattern. The man died in fifteen-twenty seconds, exsanguination.

"The other elderly white male died from a single punch in his face. His nasal bone collapsed pushing the nasal spine, supraorbital processes, lacrimal bones, ethmoid and sphenoid bones, and portions of the maxilla into the brain."

"Front of his face collapsed," Crowley said.

"Brain damage and internal hemorrhage. The blunt force trauma was significant, but not anything I have not seen before. The old man was hit by the large black male."

Provost lifted the hand of the leviathan on two gurneys against the wall. "These knuckles fit the damage to the old man's face. This clenched fist fits the topography of the contact wound and shatter pattern. I am 100% positive this black man killed this white man with a single blow to the face, the old man knocked unconscious and dead in three to five minutes."

Crowley stared at the huge black man hanging off both ends of two gurneys. "Please tell me this is the one crushing skulls around here," Crowley said.

"Sorry. This man is big and strong, but he does not possess near the strength necessary to generate the opposing compressive loads that would collapse a human skull like I see."

"Wonderful. *What* am I looking for?"

"You are looking for the man who killed Andre' the Giant," Provost said as he pointed to the tattoo above the dead man's breast. "I suggest you take a trip to Detroit. You may be able to get an ID on the four black men. They share a tattoo on their left shoulders."

Crowley shined his penlight. He and Huntsman leaned over the behemoth—DETROIT BLOODS. "That's where Wolfe is now." *How'd he get ahead of all of us on this?* Crowley wondered. "What about the white guy in his thirties, I'm sure he's not a member of this club."

"Cause of death is crushed cranium, same as the others," Provost said.

"He seems to be an odd participant."

"Good instincts, detective. He is an odd one. John Doe #2 died twenty-four hours before the others—their times of death were within minutes of each other. It appears the white male was dragged, stowed, and transported after death. He was killed somewhere else and brought to the site where the others met their demise. He was on the bottom of the pile of bodies transported."

"I'm not sure what that tells me," Crowley said.

Provost smiled and lifted the dead man's hand. "This man is different from the others. His finger and toe nails are manicured. His hair is cropped. His teeth are implants. His eyebrows are plucked. His legs, arms, chest, and genitals are shaved."

"That is peculiar, but what does it mean?"

"He has no fingerprints, Detective Crowley. They have been surgically removed. This man is stealth from a DNA, fingerprint, and dental record perspective. He does not exist and his movements would be difficult to monitor."

"Another sniper," Crowley muttered.

"I would say so. The physical condition and alterations I see here exist with our first sniper from Washington Avenue. Didn't Detective Wolfe share the information with you?"

No he did not. And I think I'm beginning to know why. "No. But that's not unusual. We are handling full caseloads and can't possibly talk about everything."

Provost looked over his glasses at the detective. He did not buy it, but it was not his problem. "Detective Wolfe told me he suspected the snipers were contracted by an unidentified group operating in Chicago—their mission unclear then. He said there are people in Detroit who provide discrete sniper termination services."

"Yes there are," Crowley sizzled. "Up until this year we've rarely seen them in our city. I'm speaking of shootings of the long distance .50 caliber variety."

Provost concurred. He had checked the history of large caliber ballistics in the city back on the day when Pender came through his doors from the South Side. "Where are we now?" he asked changing gears knowing he had his next cadaver waiting on his table.

"I would value your input, Doc. You're good with bizarre puzzles."

"Very well. I suspect the two elderly white gentlemen had contracted sniper services. The four black gentlemen were here from the Detroit Bloods, the group providing those services. They were in Chicago unhappy about something—possibly the loss of two valuable assets—two snipers—or a failure to pay monies due. I can only imagine the fee would be substantial. I believe the Bloods killed these two elderly white men. I think a third entity entered the picture for reasons unknown. This person killed the two snipers and three Bloods, crushing their skulls unlike anything I've ever seen in my forensic career." Provost pinched the bridge of his nose. "For the life of me, I do not know how Frank Peters fits in all of this, except the way he died."

"You said the third entity killed three Bloods. Who killed the fourth Blood?"

"I suppose that is the most baffling mystery of them all," Provost said as he turned from the corpse. "If I were you and Wolfe, I'd be looking for a brain surgeon."

THIRTY

"I have read the patient file, Mrs. Sorensen. I know about Dario." Lindsey Fetter stood in the shadows of the long narrow entry. This front door had been left unlocked for a reason.

Nobody had answered her knocks at the other house on Birch, the one where they held all the Dario Group meetings. Maybe if Lindsey had seen the demolished dining room, or the blood and chunks of brain frozen onto the window panes in the den, or the blood-soaked sofa where Robert Mason died, she would have turned around, gotten into her car, and driven away. But she didn't see any of it.

That night nothing felt right to her. The dead end on Birch Street seemed darker than usual. The surrounding woods were black stick trees in a black sky. The moon hid behind thick snow clouds, and the bone-chilling temperatures stopped everything—except Lindsey Fetter.

She had to find Margaret Sorensen before more people died. When Lindsey turned to leave the only house on Birch she knew, she saw the light across the road. They said the property was condemned. Dr. Sorensen said they purchased it for the land. He always intended to bulldoze the house, but that was more than twenty years ago. Curious, Lindsey crossed Birch and peered into the window through a sliver opening in the lace curtains. Margaret Sorensen was sitting alone knitting by the fire.

"Please come in, Lindsey," Sorensen said, her eyes locked on her hands and the precision gyrations of her needles. "I'm sorry. I did not hear you knock."

You said Lindsey. You never looked up. "I saw the light in the window," she said as she scanned the room. "There was no answer at your other house. I didn't know—"

"—that we used this old place for anything, right dear?" Sorensen said with an eerie tone.

"Yes. Anything," Lindsey mumbled as she eased into the room cradling her purse and a file to her bosom like a wounded rabbit she had just found outside.

The fireplace was much bigger than the other house. And the fire was popping and sizzling with a new log on top of the old. It had to be put there recently. *Who put the log on your fire?* Lindsey wondered. There were a dozen flickering candles scattered around. They and the fire provided the only light in the room of shadows. Lindsey eased up to the stuffed chair across from the old lady knitting.

Am I crazy? Lindsey thought. *She looks harmless.*

"Please sit down, young lady. You drove all the way out here in this terrible weather. There must be something very important to you."

"How long has Dario been a problem for you, Mrs. Sorensen?"

"Ah, you know more about Dario."

"I have his patient file. It was given to me by Detective Aaron Wolfe. Remember, he knows about my unfettered desires to fix a broken criminal justice system. He felt it was important for me to know about the man you call Dario. I have your husband's notes over three years. Dr. Sorensen was worried about this sick man. He did not turn Dario over to the authorities because you forbid him. He did not euthanize Dario like the others because you forbid him."

Margaret stopped knitting as if she heard the kettle

whistling in the next room. She set her work in her lap and looked up at Lindsey for the first time. Margaret's eyes were dark and puffy as if she had been in a fight. Her age lines were deeper and more pronounced. Her skin sagged as if she had aged another ten years in the few days since Lindsey had seen her last. When she attempted a smile, her face hung empty. Her eyes were barren. She opened her mouth, but nothing came out.

"The man your husband feared the most finally killed him, Mrs. Sorensen. The entity, who called himself Dario, born out of another man, a weaker and troubled man, should have been stopped. This Dario entity not only took over a sick man's mind, he took over his body.

"My God, I saw the pictures. It is science fiction. It is unbelievable. This man is grotesque. He looks evil. He is a monster. How could you justify protecting this killer? You had to know one day he would kill your husband. This Dario cannot be controlled. He is like a wild Bengal tiger walking the streets of Chicago. Dario should be in a cage or euthanized."

"I don't know what you think you know," Margaret said. "The medical records in my husband's files are woefully incomplete and impossible to understand unless you are a trained psychiatric physician. I think your comments are naïve at best, my dear."

Is what you say possible? Am I overreacting to something I am not trained to understand? No. This monster was protected by you against your husband's wishes. You were the founder of the Dario Group. You believed one day this Dario monster could be used to achieve your goals—the alternative to hired snipers. But something went terribly wrong. The monster turned on you. He had his own agenda, although it made no sense. He killed the man who gave him life—Dr. Sorensen.

"I know you are a doctor," Lindsey said with an accusing tone. "I know after receiving your medical degree you pursued a specialty in brain surgery. I also know you continued to study psychiatric medicine on your own to this day. You are a very smart woman, Dr. Margaret Sorensen. But why did you take a backseat to your husband's career. Why did you forgo your own promising career in medicine? Or did you choose a career in medicine and Dario was your only patient?"

"Very good, Lindsey Fetter. You have finally said something that merits my time and attention. Please sit. Let us talk this through. I am certain once you have all the facts you will be far less suspicious of me and far less concerned about Dario. If after we talk you still feel at risk, violated or compromised, you are certainly free to take your case to the police. I'm sure Mr. Aaron Wolfe will be more than willing to help you."

Still clutching her purse and Dario file to her chest, Lindsey sat on the edge of the stuffed armchair by the fire and across from the puzzling lady. *You are smarter than me, and you are up to something I cannot leave alone.* "I need to know."

"Jacques wanted to believe the story, the one that he came across a tortured stranger in an alley and decided to help." She closed her eyes. "I think he told that story so many times that he finally believed it himself."

"I don't understand," Lindsey said.

Margaret Sorensen stared at the fire. "He denied it most of his life. He refused to accept—"

"—accept what?" Lindsey demanded.

"—accept that the man in the alley was our son."

"Oh my God!"

"Yes. It is true."

"But the medical records say he is—"

Mrs. Sorensen held up her hand. "Please. Don't be fooled by written words in a dusty file. I am telling you the truth. The man Jacques found in the alley three years ago is our son."

"Please continue," Lindsey said sitting on the edge of her chair.

"Joseph left when he was twelve—he ran away. He was a troubled child. We knew. We were both psychiatrists. But even then we tried to explain it away—not our child.

"Twenty years passed. Our son grew up. He changed. We didn't know what he looked like anymore. We thought he was dead. But somehow he survived on his own. He had created a new identity. His old life had been lost to him like it had never happened."

"When did he return to Chicago?" Lindsey asked.

"When he joined the police department," she said. "You did not see those pictures. I have them tucked away. Jacques refused to accept it. Our son had grown to be a handsome man, and a quiet, patient person."

"You say handsome. The pictures I saw of your son are frightening. His face is grotesque, demonic. The muscles on his neck and shoulders are enormous. He looks deformed, monstrous. I cannot imagine that man as a Chicago police officer."

"You are looking at Dario, not Joseph," she said.

"Your son had multiple personalities?"

Mrs. Sorensen's face tightened. "He had moments when others inside him wanted to come out. He fought them but was not strong enough to stop them all. Our son suffers from dissociative identity disorder. It is a mental condition characterized by at least two distinct and relatively enduring identities that alternately show in one's behavior."

"You said behavior, not physicality."

"Our son's situation is unique—never seen before. His change into Dario is both a mental and physical event. The metamorphic nature of change needs study. We do not understand how it is possible, but the physical changes are medically feasible."

"And Dario's strength your husband wrote about, he

compares him to ten men. How is that humanly possible?" Lindsey asked.

"Temporary muscle tissue enhancements, unexplained endocrine secretions, changes in nervous system priorities, soft tissue manipulations, all contribute to the physical phenomena. It is not science fiction. It is unknown science. Dario has a rare condition that requires research and treatment."

"I don't know about this, Mrs. Sorensen. I must admit I am more frightened now than when I sat down. Dario—your son—is killing people with his bare hands. Detective Wolfe shared confidential information. Dario killed your sniper and Frank Peters. He is not working for the benefit of the Dario Group. He is killing people associated with the Dario Group. This puts your mission in jeopardy and the city of Chicago in danger. There is a monster loose that is capable of killing anybody at any time."

On Lindsey's last word, Mrs. Sorensen removed a knitting needle from her work and stuffed all but the needle into the bag next to her chair. Running her fingers up and down the long needle, she smiled in a new way. Her eyes widened, and for the first time she seemed younger and more alive.

"I'm afraid you do not understand the long term for the Dario Group, dear. You see we cannot continue to count on victims to participate in the removal of the monsters our criminal justice system cannot stop."

"I understand that reality. Remember, I was a victim. I failed to stop mine."

"We too cannot continue to work with lawless groups like the Detroit Bloods," Mrs. Sorensen said. "And we cannot continue to use snipers and other serial felons who will eventually expose our enterprise and jeopardize our mission. For us to reach our long term goals, we must put in place our own failsafe process to kill all the monsters."

Lindsey watched Mrs. Sorensen fondle her knitting

needle more than seemed natural. Lindsey shifted her weight to the edge of her chair in preparation for a quick departure. "You want Dario to kill all the monsters?" She had an odd feeling they were no longer alone.

"Follow the logic, my dear. It takes a bigger monster to kill a monster."

Lindsey shuttered when she heard the labored breathing and smelled the hot tainted breath pouring over the back of her chair. From the corner of her eye she saw the fat white fingers and dirty nails. But it was not dirt. It was dried blood.

THIRTY-ONE

"I think Wolfe could be the guy crushing skulls," Crowley floated.

Landers set down his cup of ice and rubbed his three-day old beard. "You would think they could have shaved my face when they shaved my head." He reached for his bandage.

Crowley slapped his hand. "You are not to touch, sir. It was the only order the doc gave you. If you mess with the head bandage, they're gonna tie you down again."

Landers squinted at the window and worked his mouth like he had taken one in the jaw. "Did the doc say I was gonna live?"

"Yes—again. He said you were too mean to die from a bullet in the head."

"That's right, I remember. I like him."

"Seriously, I can't tell you how lucky you were that bullet took the route it did. The doc showed me x-rays. Said it was a miracle."

"Doesn't feel like a miracle," Landers complained.

"He said if you woke up in a few days, you would live. If you stayed in a coma much longer, pneumonia would probably kill you if you didn't throw a blood clot."

"Wonderful," Landers sighed. "Okay, let's do some work. You said you think Detective Wolfe is crushing skulls in Chicago."

"I know it sounds ridiculous, but I think it's a real

possibility. A lot's happened while you were in your coma. Things seem to point to Wolfe as a suspect."

"Where are Wolfe and Hutson now?"

"Hutson's still on sick leave with his bogus head injury."

"Bogus?" Landers asked.

"I think Hutson's milking the assault at the brownstone. His head wound looks like a small bump on the noggin. Last three days his phone goes to messages. Says he's on sick leave and can't be disturbed. Reroutes his calls to the precinct."

Landers ignored the editorial. "Fine, what about Wolfe?"

"He's running around Detroit looking into the snipers."

"We have more than one?" Landers asked.

"Got two dead now. Got the second this morning," Crowley said. "He was delivered to the county morgue with six other naked bodies."

"I'll be damned, delivered?"

"Yeah. We got a total-service criminal element in our city now, Commander." Crowley chuckled at his own joke alone. Landers just glared at him.

"Ah, they were lined up on the dock at the county morgue this mornin'. Had been there a while, covered in an inch of powdered snow. There were four black males with tattoos—DETROIT BLOODS—and two old white guys, and one white guy in his thirties."

"The second sniper?" Landers asked.

"Yes," Crowley said.

"And that's why Wolfe's in Detroit—makes sense," Landers said.

"Wolfe did not know about the Detroit Bloods on the dock when he went. He left last night," Crowley said. "That's one of the things bugging me. How did he know to go to Detroit before we had these guys and another sniper?"

"Not enough, Crowley. He could have a good reason.

He didn't need the bodies."

"There's more. I have been over the POD video covering all angles of the parking garage on Washington Avenue after the shooting at the Burnham Hotel. I watched six hours on both sides of that shooting. Everyone going in came out except two, the sniper and Wolfe. CPD blocked off the area minutes after the shooting at the Hotel. I can't explain it any other way. Wolfe had to be the one who killed the sniper.

"Before you were shot, you remember Frank Peters was found dead in his Tahoe. We later learned through his DNA he was a serial killer wanted in three states. Provost said his cause of death was a crushed skull. Three of the four Detroit Bloods had crushed skulls. The second dead sniper had a crushed skull. In all cases Wolfe was the only one in the area or nowhere to be found—unaccounted for. I find the extremes suspicious and troubling."

"It's still not enough, Crowley. You're taking a giant leap."

"You saw Wolfe's hand at the CCLR meeting the day after Frank Peters was found dead. The edge of his fist was bruised. He acted like he did not know how it happened."

"Maybe he did not know. Maybe he fell on the ice, caught himself, and forgot about the whole experience. Everything you have can be explained. Let me remind you that Aaron Wolfe has been the top homicide detective in Chicago for more than a decade—I know him well. And you know him well. People do not suddenly turn into serial killers with super strengths."

"I hear ya," Crowley muttered.

Landers took a drink of ice water and set the cup down with his eyes locked on Crowley. "You're my senior guy. I got a bullet in my head and you're under a lot of pressure to run things. I will give you some valuable advice—slow down. Open your mind to all the evidence and go back to the basics. Investigate. Your frustration and worries have you fixated on Wolfe and pissed off at Hutson, the two most important guys on your team. Look, I'm gonna be tied up in here a while. I need you to keep your head screwed on right, Crowley. If Wolfe is in this, all the evidence will point his way, not just some."

Crowley nodded. He knew his suspicions were thin. It was mostly gut.

"I wanna talk about the CCLR conference," Landers said. "The shooting. When I got to that stage, I saw Margaret Sorensen's head disappear into the curtains. I do not know what she was doin' back there, but we need to find out. The death of Dr. Jacques Sorensen, the bizarre incident at the brownstone with Hutson, the doctor's diary, the snipers, the skull-crushing monster, and the CCLR are connected. I think Margaret Sorensen is in the middle of it."

"Great minds think alike," Crowley said. "Dr. Provost saw the same connections, but took it a step farther. He thinks the skull-crusher is hunting members of a vigilante group that has a mission to terminate released killers. He believes the snipers worked for the vigilante group and the skull-crusher is their nemesis."

"Go to Hutson's place. Get him back to work. Put calls out to Wolfe. You three need to get together and get on the same page. Ask Wolfe the question. He will be short with you, but I suspect he will tell you everything you want to know."

The phone rang next to the bed. Landers nodded for Crowley to pick up.

"We were just talkin' about you, Detective Wolfe. Yeah, the boss is awake and giving me orders now. Yeah, here he is." Crowley passed the phone rolling his eyes.

"Detective. Thanks. Yes, I am fine. What's going on out there? I get a bullet in the head and people start dropping faster than usual in my city."

"I'm returning from Detroit," Wolfe said. "The Detroit

Bloods are not real happy with their business arrangement in Chicago. They were eager to talk to me off the record."

"Let me put you on speaker. Crowley needs to hear this."

Crowley closed the door. "The Detroit Bloods have learned several of their people are in the Cook County morgue," Wolfe said.

"When did they hear?" Crowley asked.

"They got the call at 3:00 a.m. CST. The person said not to mess with the Dario Group anymore or they would be coming to Detroit for a bloody visit."

"The Dario Group exists," Crowley muttered.

"The Bloods were motivated to share what they knew. Obviously, they would deny any knowledge in a courtroom, and they do not intend on visiting Chicago for a while."

"Continue Wolfe. What did you get on The Dario Group?"

"They have been around a long time—several decades. Only in the last year did they enter into an agreement with the Detroit Bloods. Prior to snipers, the Dario Group used local felons to terminate their targets. The Bloods had a very lucrative contract, $100,000 a hit. They were not pleased when they lost one of their assets, and then learned they had just lost a second. They sent their people to Chicago to collect money and disengage."

"Looks like the Dario Group did the disengaging," Crowley muttered.

"Were we right on the Dario Group targets?" Landers asked.

"Yes. Serial killers," Wolfe said. "The worst of the worst. According to the Bloods, the Dario Group targets people with a long history of offenses against humanity—rape, assault, and murder, and released from jail in less than six years."

"That fits the CCLR mission—the injustices of the

criminal justice system. They are focused on the same monsters," Landers said.

"Crowley here. Did they say how this guy Dario is connected to the Dario Group?"

"They don't know about Dario, just the group."

"Who's running the Dario Group? Do we know where they are meeting in the city?"

"Hold on," Wolfe said. "I gotta take this call." He disconnected Landers and Crowley. The other line said Lindsey Fetter. "Yes," he said.

"We have Miss Fetter. This is what you're going to do."

***

Eldon Babcock left his father's funeral and sent his family home. He needed to be alone to think. Why would someone kill his father? Jennings Babcock was old and dying from prostate cancer. Anyone who looked at him knew he had only a couple months to live. Why kill a dying man? What possibly could Jennings Babcock do in sixty days that warranted such an action?

He didn't realize it until he turned the key in the deadbolt. Eldon had not been in his father's house for five years. There was never a reason to go. Jennings had servants and caretakers seeing to his every personal need, and Eldon saw his father at the office almost every day. The old man would wheel into meetings sipping his coffee and looking out the window. He never interrupted his son's work or took part in the discussions. Old man Jennings just sat in his wheelchair and watched his son, the man he adored.

On this cold day, Eldon sat alone in his father's home office. Everything was neatly arranged and recently dusted. Eldon opened a desk drawer and fiddled with the pens and pile of paperclips. He remembered the days when he ran around the house without a care in the world. Now everything was different. Now his father and mother were dead, he was a terrible lawyer, and someone was hunting him. Running BB&B no longer meant everything. Making money no longer meant everything. He was more alone than ever before.

When he pulled his hand from the drawer, his little finger snagged something sharp. Eldon sucked the blood looking for the culprit. He saw the little nail, but it was in a place that made no sense. He leaned closer and saw it was connected to a sheet of wood matching the bottom of the drawer. He pulled and the sheet of wood lifted. He removed the wood panel and opened the drawer to its fullest extent.

I'll be damned—the old man had a secret compartment. Eldon leaned closer. *What's this?* He removed an aged coffee-stained vellum envelope. It was fat with folded papers inside. On the front in bold ornate font it said—DARIO GROUP CHARTER. The words sucked the air from the room. Eldon carefully opened the unsealed brittle flap; he had to see the papers inside. He unfolded the stiff parchment. There were four pages and a cover sheet.

At the top of the cover page he read—DARIO GROUP CHARTER. Below the header he read—formation: July 4, 1986. Centered below that were five names and positions:

Chairman of the Board

Jacques Sorensen, M.D.

Director and Chief Operating Officer

Margaret Sorensen, M.D.

Director and Board Council

Jennings Babcock, J.D.

Director

Joseph H. Sorensen, Jr.

Director

W William T. Marcantonio

Staring, Eldon pulled out his cell phone, scrolled, and tapped Wolfe.

"Chicago Police Department, Homicide, how may I direct your call?"

"Yes. This is Eldon Babcock. I need to talk to Detective Wolfe, immediately."

"I'm sorry, Detective Wolfe is unavailable. May I take a message?"

"No. This is an emergency. Well, not a 911 emergency. No one is dying at the moment. This is about a homicide case Detective Wolfe is investigating. I have just come across some significant information. He will want to know about it immediately. I cannot leave this information on a voice mail, it is too delicate. Mr. Wolfe must call me, Eldon Babcock. He has my cell number."

"Can Detective Crowley help you, Mr. Babcock? He is the acting head of the department. I can connect you to him now."

"No. I prefer to speak to Detective Wolfe."

"I can locate Homicide Detective Joe Hutson. He was working cases with Detective Wolfe. He was on temporary leave. I believe he is taking calls now, Mr. Babcock."

"I don't know Detective Hutson. I want to talk to Wolfe, only Wolfe. Please tell him I'm at my father's house. I found something he must see."

"Yes sir, Mr. Babcock. I will pass this information to Detective Wolfe immediately." Babcock leaned back in the desk chair and flipped the cover sheet. He started to read.

SERIAL INTENT

My God. You were killing people most of your life . . .

Mission—We THE DARIO GROUP exist to remove the serial predator (murder of human) from society regardless of past/present/future American (and/or other) established and accepted criminal justice system ruling, action, intention, goal, objective, explanation, rationalization, excuse, or perceived limit. We THE DARIO GROUP exist to accomplish what established criminal justice systems fail (or are unable or unwilling) to accomplish on behalf of the society they were created to serve. We THE DARIO GROUP exist to eliminate without malice all known serial monsters permitted to prey upon society. We THE DARIO GROUP will use all resources and knowledge and expertise to do proper investigation of serial monster life and activity prior to conclusion, processing, and the issuance of said termination order. We THE DARIO GROUP will access and utilize the most sophisticated execution methods and tactics to end the life of a serial monster and to protect the organization and its mission from discovery. No effort will be made to choose a method of execution to minimize pain born by a serial monster in the death process.

Termination Factors—We THE DARIO GROUP opposes all forms of parole for convicted murderers. Provisional release of a prisoner who has taken a life is forbidden. Failure to complete maximum sentence is forbidden. We THE DARIO GROUP opposes probation for all convicted of murder in all degrees. Any court-ordered release of a criminal who has committed murder qualifies that killer for DARIO GROUP termination consideration. The only acceptable alternatives to incarceration of a serial monster are limited to death by hanging, lethal injection, electrocution, starvation, or any and all other forms of executing a painful death by the designated executioner . . .

Babcock leaned back in his father's desk chair and looked around the dated study. He saw the polished leather spines of the law books no longer needed in a computerized world. He saw the awards and trinkets collected over the years. He saw the legal degrees and continued study suggesting an honorable commitment to the law. Eldon Babcock could still smell his father in the room, the place where the old man spent much of his life when at home.

How do you justify the Dario Group? How could you abandon the law and your oath to obey the rules of law? What changed? What made you seek something other than to improve the criminal justice system we know?

Or are you right? Is it possible you and others know the better way to protect society? Is your solution better? But you knew it could not be amended to the current legal system—it had to stand alone focused and free acting. It would only address the inexcusable sin, the release of known monsters back into society. You differentiate, there are killers and there are serial predators—the most hideous monsters, the wild animals who feed on society, their appetites never satiated.

Eldon looked down at the next page. He did not need or want to read each paragraph under each heading. He knew the Dario Group saw each legal maneuver as an

SERIAL INTENT

unacceptable trick designed to serve the criminal element disguised as the innocent until proven guilty. The Dario Group saw all legal maneuvers as the root cause to the larger problem. A procedure that allows tossing out evidence or minimizing eyewitness accounts or moves charges for a heinous crime to something less do not serve the silent people, the victims, the too soon forgotten. The victim is not in the courtrooms of America, not enough. They are in the courtroom of the Dario Group.

> Double jeopardy, the exclusionary rule, fruit of the poisonous tree, violation of search and seizure, rogue jurors, hung juries, mistrials, elimination of the death penalty, minimizing the eyewitness, failure to inform accused of rights . . .

Eldon closed his eyes and leaned back to stretch his sore neck. He tried to justify his father's actions. *If I understand your thinking, the only justified homicide is self-defense or the execution of a known killer regardless of the legal process or rulings of a court.*

When he opened his eyes the last time, he had read everything on the four parchments. More than an hour had passed and Wolfe had still not called. Eldon had digested each line in the Dario Group Charter and was tired of waiting. He had to take the document to Detective Wolfe tonight. He had to put it in the man's hands.

Margaret Sorensen is alive. You have a son! Who is he? Did I ever know you had progeny? Damn, I just don't pay attention to menial things. One or both of you are at the heart of the executions in the city—Ramsey, Pender, Pazrro, Newman, Bordon, and one of your directors, Marcantonio. And now I know why you killed my father.

Eldon folded the papers and slid them into his coat's breast pocket. He turned out the lamp on his father's desk and realized it had turned into night. The cold house sat dark, but he knew every room. It was the place where he grew up. He knew the smells—the polish on the library paneling, and the dust embedded rugs and furniture. He remembered the tall windows that whistled on windy nights, and the doors that breathed. He remembered every creaking board and every whining rafter. Now, feeling his way down the dark hall, he thought about the nights he went drinking with friends. He remembered the whining boards to avoid.

As he moved up the hall toward the front of the house, he heard a creaking sound in another room. Was that a floorboard inside, or was it the wind pushing through a new crack in an old window? Eldon took another step and the high-pitched whine seemed closer. He stopped and it stopped.

"Hello?" He called out. His words echoed and died. "Is there anyone here?" He asked with a hard swallow, darting eyes, and a hand on his chest protecting the new found documents.

Eldon Babcock froze. Through the archway ten feet ahead, the living room came into view. On the other side of the dark room, the curtain sheers waved on tall windows. *There you are,* he thought. *Just the wind pushing on the old window—thank God.*

Eldon took another step and heard another whine. This time he saw the curtain sheer in the living room lift several feet into the air. This time he saw the center window wide open. What he thought was a large piece of furniture, moved. He froze.

His phone vibrated. He pressed it to his ear. A towering shadow stopped in front of him.

"Detective Wolfe, is that you?"

THIRTY-TWO

"This is gut-wrenching awful," Crowley gasped with a hand over his mouth. Rookie Detective Zack Huntsman had already stepped outside twice to puke in the bushes. "You say you saw Aaron Wolfe's car pull away when you rolled up?"

Crowley didn't wait for the answer. He turned away and pressed speed dial for Wolfe. He breathed through his mouth avoiding the smell of the bloody carnage. *Come on . . . come on . . . answer damn it!*

Crowley saw the young detective in the bushes. He yelled, "Huntsman, get in here with Winston Foster, the medical examiner field agent. You can learn something." He then watched the young detective climb the porch steps like he had just finished two marathons. His drawn face was white as snow, and the poor guy's shirt was soaked—nervous sweat.

Pick up, Wolfe. Shit! He lowered his cell and stared at the body—*Okay. Do not jump to any conclusions. Pace yourself. Louie is right. Do not overreact. Damn, I'm paddlin' like a duck in Grand Rapids, freaking big time—all this responsibility and the boss in ICU and me surrounded by dead bodies with zero damn answers.*

Did they say they actually saw Wolfe pull away? I don't think he would have left. And all us detectives drive the same black unmarked cruisers.

"Officer Tully, come here a minute," Crowley ordered.

"Yes sir." The well-built CPD officer got in Crowley's face.

He backed away. "Are you one-hundred percent positive you saw Detective Wolfe pull away from the curb when you guys rolled up?"

"Only saw from behind. It looked like Wolfe to me. Could have been the other guy, the one who looks like Wolfe," Tully said. "I've seen both around the city. Get 'em mixed up."

Couldn't be Hutson. He's on sick leave. "Okay, thanks Tully." Crowley hit speed dial for Hutson. *Still not picking up. I'm gonna go to your apartment and knock down your door. You better be in bed. If you're at the movies, I'm killin' ya.*

"Detective Crowley, I think you need to come here," Winston said pushing up his glasses and backing away from the body.

The hallway was sprayed with blood and pieces of skull bone and oozing chunks of brain matter. The floor was streaked with clotted blood where most of the struggle had taken place after the victim was caught. Crowley approached like a ballerina at an overstocked buffet.

"Watch out for the eyeball, detective," Winston warned.

Crowley froze and looked down with his penlight. The eyeball was perched at an angle looking at him. "What are the chances of that? Holy mother of God, this is terrible. How does an eyeball get this far from the body?"

"Actually the other eyeball went farther. It was by the front door," Winston said. "I almost stepped on it. I documented location and collected it in a forensic bag. I was concerned it would get crushed. It was so far outside the ground zero."

"Ground zero! Good to know," Crowley mumbled trying to avoid the blood on the walls.

"I don't think it's too much of a reach to conclude

whoever killed this man also killed the two snipers, the three Detroit Bloods, and Frank Peters." Winston said jotting notes.

"The victim—Eldon Babcock—is the son of the man who owns this house. We have confirmed he came here from his father's funeral."

"Tully gave me that information," Crowley said. "Why did you call me over here? I can see the guy's dead. I know he's the son of our unsolved homicide at Willis Tower."

"I know you do," Winston said pushing his glasses back up his nose and patting Huntsman on the back. "Don't worry, you will adjust to this. It takes a few times."

"Foster!" Crowley boomed. *Damned kids.* "Why did you call me over by this God-awful mess? I don't know why we can't discuss matters outside."

"I asked you here to point out a few things that may be relevant to your investigation. First, the 'Skull-Crusher'— the name the ME gave him—did this and was very mad at this victim. The forces applied to Eldon Babcock's head were much greater than those applied to the others. That could be significant. It could suggest a closer tie, greater motivation."

Crowley turned away to suck in some fresh air from the nearby room. "Okay. I get it, a closer connection. That may be important. What else?"

"I believe the deceased had something important in his possession, something that fueled the rage behind this vicious attack. I believe it was a document the Skull-Crusher wanted for purposes unknown at the moment." Winston flapped open the deceased's suit coat and looked up at Detective Crowley. "Every pocket is torn."

"Okay. The Skull-Crusher was looking for something. A document fits in a pocket. I get all that, but it doesn't help me when I don't know what was taken."

Winston got up pulling off and dropping his bloody gloves on the body. "It's something that might make sense later. Follow me." They stepped over the body and went to the study at the end of the hall.

"The desk chair is by the desk and turned away," Winston said. "Someone sat there."

"That's what you do at a desk, Winston," Crowley scoffed.

"I think the deceased sat here last. I know the owner of the house is wheelchair bound. He would not use the desk chair." He pointed. "It's normally kept over there, indentations in the carpet."

"Okay. You think Eldon Babcock sat in that chair before he walked down the hall and met his murderer. Continue Mr. Foster. Provost told me about you, a regular Sherlock Holmes."

Winston opened the center desk drawer with a newly gloved hand. "This was the only drawer open a few inches. All the others were closed, the layer of dust on the wood handles undisturbed. Look here. There's a fake bottom in the top center drawer, the one opened by Eldon Babcock. I think he knew about or found the secret compartment while going through his dead father's things."

Winston aimed his penlight. "You can see something's still in there. It's an envelope. It's been tossed in there, like an afterthought, possibly tossed there after the contents were removed. I think Mr. Babcock had the contents of this envelope in his possession when he was attacked, the contents now missing."

"Let's take a look at the envelope," Crowley said.

Winston removed it with tweezers and grasped one corner. Winston laid it on the blotter.

"THE DARIO GROUP CHARTER," Crowley read. *I'll be damned. That group name keeps coming up.* Winston flipped the envelope. Crowley leaned closer and squinted. "You got a magnifying glass on you, Foster? Can't make out what's printed on the flap."

"Always," Winston said pushing his glasses up his

nose and pulling it from his pocket.

"The print on the flap—looks like a faded address."

They leaned closer, noses in the magnifying glass. "It says—Sorensens. I can't make out the street number, but it says—Birch Avenue, Middle Beach. That's all we gonna see without the proper equipment," Winston said. "Have you heard of—?"

"—It's not Middle Beach. It's Miller Beach. It's in Indiana, northeast of Gary on Lake Michigan. It's not too far from the city." Crowley turned to Huntsman. "We gotta go. Keep up, son. Thanks Winston."

Crowley ran down the hall and jumped the corpse. Huntsman followed holding his mouth and tie. They piled into the cruiser. Winston and Tully watched the cruiser fishtail down the icy road clipping snow piles until it disappeared."

Officer Tully turned to Winston. "I should give the man a ticket, right?" he said with a soft chuckle. "You must have come across somethin' that fired him up."

"An address," Winston said. "Probably my next death scene." He waved at the morgue clerks waiting on the porch with a crash bag.

"That sounds creepy, young man," Officer Tully said.

"Sorry. I'm just anticipating." The morgue clerks approached. "We are ready to bag and transport. Don't want to lose the brain hanging out, so be careful."

Winston slid the Dario Group envelope into another evidence bag and stuffed his last clean pair of gloves in his pocket. Unlike the surgical arena, it was more about protecting him than the body.

***

She opened her eyes. The white room came into focus. Then she saw him leaning over her. The man's face was swollen, eyes black and blue, he was unshaven, and his head was wrapped in a bloody bandage. When he smiled, only half of his mouth went up. His face was dead and white.

Please don't kill me. I won't tell anyone. Please. I don't want to die. Sally day closed her eyes, cringed, and pulled her covers up to her chin.

"Ma'am..."

That word was not what she expected to come out of the face leaning in her face. She opened one eye a sliver. He was leaning closer. She closed it and played dead. *He knows I'm awake. He knows I was looking at him when I pulled my sheets up. Oh my God.*

"It's okay, ma'am. I'm a friend. Nobody's gonna hurt you."

She opened her eye again. She found him, and then looked around the room. "Where am I?" she asked.

"Miss Day, you are in intensive care at Northwestern Memorial Hospital. You have been shot, but you are going to be okay. A large caliber bullet hit you in your shoulder. You have lost blood, ma'am. They gave you more. You have been unconscious, shock I suppose. The doctors said you were never in danger of dying and you will heal completely."

"I've been shot?"

"You were shot. You will not die, ma'am. Do you know your name?"

She opened both eyes and focused. The man had on a hospital gown and a head bandage. "Who are you?" she asked. "Are you a patient, too?"

"I am Commander Louie Landers, Chicago PD, Bureau of Investigations, homicide. Yes, I am currently a patient here too."

"How do I know you're not lying?" she asked. Landers held out his badge case with the shiny gold star and photo ID.

"Okay, I suppose. I am Sally Day."

"Good. I wanted to know if you knew, because I know," Landers said as he offered to adjust her bed. "You mind? I hated being flat on my back. I'll give you some incline. You'll love it." He pressed. She went up and then held a hand up for him to stop.

"Why are you here, Mr. Landers?" Day asked.

"I think you know why I'm here. People are dying in the city, and you have information I need. The carnage must stop, Sally Day."

She looked away and avoided the commander's eyes. "I don't have any information. I was shot by someone. I have no idea why. One of your detectives came to talk to me about my friend, Ellen Dumont. I think he brought bad people into my neighborhood. I think they were trying to shoot him, and I got in the way."

Landers did not have time for games. Wolfe, Hutson, and Crowley were on a collision course. They knew the Dario Group existed, but had no idea where they met or the magnitude of the problem. The monster crushing skulls in Chicago had to be stopped.

"Okay, if that's how you want to play it, Miss Day." Landers turned and headed for the door. He paused. "When I leave this room, there's a very good chance you will be eliminated by the same people who eliminated your friends, Ellen Dumont and Barry Woods. I'm sorry you have to die young, and in such a terrible way. This time you were lucky—the .50 caliber projectile that tore the hell out of your shoulder only nicked you. The one that hit Barry Woods in the nose blew off the back of his head." Landers left the room.

As the door slowly closed, Sally Day's heart beat faster and harder. *Margaret Sorensen is going to kill me. She knows I talked to Wolfe. I broke the rules. Ellen and Barry are dead. I was only in this thing because of them. After a few meetings, I didn't even believe in anything those people were doing, but I couldn't get out.*

"Commander Landers," she yelled. *Please don't leave me here,* she thought. *I know they will come back for me. They will never leave me alone. I know too much. They will do everything necessary to protect the Dario Group.* "Mr. Landers," she yelled louder.

The door opened.

"What have you decided? Are you going to waste my time with part truths, or are you going to tell me everything you know and have a chance to live?" Landers spoke with cold eyes.

Sally Day felt the unbearable terror and found the courage to speak. "I will tell you everything."

"Is the Dario Group targeting convicted killers released early from prison?"

"Yes. It is their mission to kill all the monsters. The Dario Group has been around since the 1980s. The members are broken-hearted survivors, their loved ones sexually abused and killed. The predators responsible beat the legal system."

"What is the involvement of the Sorensens?"

"Dr. Jacques Sorensen started the Dario Group. His wife Margaret now runs it. I think he was killed by Dario, a man with a terrible mental disorder, multiple personalities. The 'Dario' personality is dominant and dangerous."

"How are Dario and the Dario Group connected?" Landers asked.

"I was told Dario took his name from the Dario Group and adopted his own twisted mission. Mrs. Sorensen will not discuss the matter. Since her husband's death, she's been running the group, but I think she's confused and frightened."

"Is Dario killing the snipers?" Landers asked.

"Yes."

"Have you ever seen Dario?"

"No. I heard he is very different," Day said.

"Different?" Landers asked.

"He's a monster, bizarre physical changes accompanying the mental changes."

"Sounds like an extreme medical anomaly. Is it your understanding the Dario personality comes and goes as it pleases?" Landers asked.

"Yes."

"Do you know why a sniper killed Barry Woods?" Landers asked.

"He spoke to the Chicago police about the Dario Group. That action broke a bylaw. That's why he was terminated."

"They terminate members?"

"Lindsey Fetter is a member. At the last meeting she said she told Detective Wolfe about the Dario Group. She said Mr. Wolfe understood. He was tired of seeing monsters return to the streets to kill again."

Wolfe said that, Landers thought.

Sally Day watched his eyes narrow. She said, "The members voted Lindsey not be terminated because of a bylaw infraction. I don't trust them. They will kill both of us."

"The behavior fits a predictable pattern for control-crazed people. They think they can do a better job than the professionals assigned to the difficult tasks. They get in over their heads. The self-aggrandized crusaders turn on the very people who share their beliefs."

"I feel terrible about the whole thing," Day said.

"Do you know if Dario is part of the group? Could he be a rogue factor?"

"I don't think anyone knows but Margaret Sorensen. I get the sense he is out of control and unpredictable. She cuts off all discussion about him. She said she would handle Dario."

Landers scratched at his bandage looking out the third floor window at his city in the snow. It seemed that looking out windows was the place where he did his best thinking, but this time he struggled to hold onto a line of thought. His head ached and the drugs kept him on the edge of groggy. He kept losing his place in the discussion. He knew he was going somewhere, but he kept getting sidetracked.

"Meetings!" He exploded. *That's what I need to know.* "You had meetings."

"Yes. I attended four. Well, that was after they screened me like a cancer patient. After I was approved, I went to a meeting every sixty days. That changed when the targets increased."

"Targets?"

"People with serial intent, Commander."

"Serial intent?" he asked.

"Serial intent to kill," she said. "Like a Bengal tiger has serial intent to kill. It's an animal born to kill efficiently and often to eat. It must. It can't stop."

"Right—a Bengal tiger." *There is a metaphor that captures the true sense of terror I've witnessed my whole career.* "Tell me Miss Day, were all the members of the Dario Group required to attend meetings?"

"Yes. No exceptions. We heard cases and voted. There were a slew of convicted killers released over the last six months—end of term governor pardons, I suppose."

Landers muttered walking small circles at the end of her bed. *Where was I going with this? Think. Shake the cobwebs out. Wake up.*

"I hope me telling you all this means I will not be charged with a crime. I did not participate in any of the killings. I did not take part, Commander Landers. Every time I parked my car, before I went in the meeting I said a prayer. I said—"

"—Right," Landers shot back. "I don't care about that. I'm focused on keeping people alive, Miss. Day. These crazy people are still running around out there." *That's it— where did you meet!* "Tell me all the places where the Dario Group met."

"We met at the same place every time," she said.

He spun around. "I need an address, now!"

She closed her eyes. "I don't recall a street number," she said. "But it's an old house on a dead end road. I believe it is Birch Avenue. I remember the sign—Miller Beach. Yes. It's on the lake east of Gary, Indiana."

When Sally opened her eyes, she saw her hospital room door muffle closed.

THIRTY-THREE

"An eternity passed in a handful of seconds."

Crowley pulled over and gave rookie detective Huntsman precise instructions. "I'm leaving. You're staying here. I'm going on foot."

Huntsman had puked three times in one hour, twice at the Babcock murder scene and once on the side of the road at North Lake and Birch Avenue—but that one was because of Crowley's terrible driving.

"Give me a half hour, then call SWAT—they move damn fast and I need time to locate the house. I will leave one of my gloves on the road in front of the place. Tell them no lights or sirens, and look for my glove. Tell them we got the vigilante group responsible for at least a dozen kills. I don't know what we're gonna run into, but SWAT knows how to handle most anything." With a wink, he slapped Huntsman on the back. "Wish me luck, son. One day you'll be doing this and someone else will be waiting for back up."

Huntsman nodded and watched Crowley disappear into the night on the snow-covered road. Crowley's coat flapped in the waves of sleet that moved off the lake across Miller Beach. "Good luck," he said with little thrust.

When Crowley opened his eyes, he did not know where he was or how much time had passed. His head was sore. His hands and ankles were tied tight. Lying on his side, he struggled to look around the (apparently) empty room. The first thing he saw was the candle flickering on a windowsill about twenty feet away, and through the torn curtains he saw bars on the windows. Ragged strips of wallpaper hung from the walls, and the ceiling had large water stains and dirty cobwebs in the corners. Crowley thought he was alone with nothing but a roll of carpet against the far wall—then it spoke to him.

"Who are you?" The words seemed to slide across the wood floor and mildewed carpet like a rodent scampering for food. Crowley reeled. "I'm Chicago PD. Who're you?"

There was a long silence. "Ya know they're gonna kill us don't ya?"

"Who am I talkin' to?" Crowley pushed.

"I'm Whitten," he replied. "I think I know why I'm here. Don't know why a cop—"

A door opened. More light fell into the room. Crowley smelled a fire. He closed his eyes and watched through slits—being unconscious would be best.

The large shadow of a man filled the doorway. He had a thick neck and bulbous shoulders. His arms touched the door jams, and his clenched fists hung like sledge hammers. "Shut up or I'll kill you, Whitten." The fuming anger and sour breath filled the room.

Crowley waited a few minutes after the door closed. "Why're you here, Whitten? And who the hell was that?"

"I just got out of prison. That was some kind of friggin monster they call Dario."

"And why were you in prison?" Crowley asked.

"Murder, but I didn't do it. I had bad lawyers. I was in the wrong place and got blamed. The system screwed me good."

"Who'd they say you killed?" Crowley asked.

"They said I raped and killed a lady—Mason. Yeah, I raped her alright. She wanted it, but I didn't kill her. She just stopped breathing. They say I beat her. I didn't touch her.

"Her old man's been buggin' me every day since—get a life, man. He's gotta be behind all this shit. He said he'd get me, the little punk." Whitten's words trailed off. "I should have killed him, too," he muttered.

Now I remember. I read the weekly update on Landers desk before going to the hospital. Whitten was released early. He was convicted of raping and killing Susan Mason. I worked the case five years ago. Robert Mason was left for dead, beaten like his wife, but survived. Whitten was a Marcantonio bottom-feeder. The high-priced lawyers on Marcantonio's payroll worked the legal system like Toscanini works a symphony orchestra.

They got Whitten's charge reduced—second degree. Not premeditated. Not committed in the heat of passion. Death caused by dangerous conduct. Some legal technicality tossed out the DNA evidence, and Whitten had an alibi—albeit lies from other bottom-feeders. They put the prosecution in a box. Didn't have enough legitimate evidence to get a conviction on murder one. Forced to plea bargain just to get him off the streets. Whitten got out in less than five years . . .

Crowley closed his eyes. *Maybe these people have a legitimate beef. Maybe it takes a Dario Group to shake things up, to make change happen. Human garbage like Whitten should not be allowed to walk the streets—happens too damn much.*

"Detective Crowley." This time the words came from inside the wall by his head. He squinted trying to understand if he was imagining things. Then he saw the vent, and then the shadow, and then made out the head looking in from another room.

"I am Lindsey Fetter," she whispered.

Crowley did not respond. He knew about Lindsey Fetter, but was she a victim or a member of the Dario

Group. Was this a trap?

"Aaron Wolfe is here," she said with desperation in her voice.

Crowley's heart beat faster as he struggled to understand the situation. If she saw Wolfe, he is either dead or he's one of them. Maybe everything Crowley suspected was true. Maybe Wolfe is Dario.

"Detective Crowley, I think he is the man they call Dario. I know it sounds crazy, but I saw him, Dario. He resembles Aaron Wolfe. I know Aaron Wolfe."

Can it be, Crowley thought as he struggled to make sense of why they tied him up and put him in a room with a convicted serial killer, and why was Fetter in another room?

"Although Dario's face is swollen and twisted in anger, it is Aaron Wolfe's face," she said as if she too struggled to rectify in her mind what she saw with her own eyes.

"The man's as tall as Aaron Wolfe, but he's much more muscular," Fetter said. "And his strength is shocking. He lifted me off the ground with one arm as if I weighed nothing. He handled me like a minor irritant, something unworthy of his time or attention. He acted like he did not know me."

I can't believe any of this is possible, Crowley thought. *It makes no sense. No man can change like that. He can't just turn into some kind of monster.*

"You are imagining things, Miss Fetter," Crowley said.

"You may be right," Fetter sighed. "I don't know what I'm saying anymore. I don't understand any of this. Maybe something's wrong with me. I'm scared. They won't let me leave here." Her words melded into the echoes of the tin vent as her hopes for survival waned.

The door opened. Crowley continued to play dead. His ankle ropes were grabbed. He was dragged from the room.

When he stopped, his collar was yanked up into the air, his body raised off the floor. Crowley stayed limp—the only strategy left to him. When he was let go, he dropped. His sunk into a sofa cushion. Crowley slumped back. Through slits he saw he was across from an empty stuffed armchair and fire. He saw large silver knitting needles sticking from a canvas bag filled with yarn.

The ultrasound, Dr. Provost, the person who sits in that chair killed the Detroit Bloods and probably had something to do with all the others. I get it—you have an organization and a sacred mission. You believe you can do better than our criminal justice system. But how are you going to justify killing me—a Chicago police officer?

Out the corner of his eye, Crowley saw moving shadows at a table in an adjoining room. *There you are—Dario Group members. Is court about to be in session?*

The man called Dario dragged Whitten into the room and flipped him onto the sofa like a small child.

Who has that kind of strength? Crowley wondered. *Is that Wolfe in some kind of altered state?* But Dario never gave Crowley enough to be sure. The face was always shrouded in shadows and the body covered in bulky clothes. *I never should have said a half hour. SWAT needs to get here now! I called Wolfe and Hutson three times on the road coming out here. They never picked up.* Crowley's eyes found his glove draped on the arm of the chair by the fire.

His pocket vibrated—his cell phone. *They never took it, only my gun.* But he could not get to it. *Take the hint. I need you now, people. Get your asses over here!*

The old lady walked into the room and sat in the stuffed armchair. Margaret Sorensen picked up Crowley's glove and smiled. "I think we can begin, now," she said. The shadows in the adjoining room stopped whispering and moving.

"Detective Ben Crowley, you can open your eyes

now," Mrs. Sorensen said. He did not move. "Pretending to be unconscious will not help your situation. Although I understand the strategy, pleading your case is all you have left. I suggest you take part in your defense."

Crowley opened his eyes and sat up. "I don't need to plead my case, Margaret Sorensen. You have committed more than enough heinous crimes to die in prison along with your members who believe somehow they will avoid prosecution for mass murder. I don't care how guilty you think someone is. You have no right to kill anybody."

After the gasps ceased, Mrs. Sorensen said, "It's not your time to talk, Detective Crowley." She threw his glove into the fire and watched it become engulfed in flames.

"Are you serious about this—holding a Chicago police officer captive? Your members may want to rethink their involvement. They may want to revisit the reasons why they joined your little club in the first place. I believe your charter says something about stopping the monsters. That would be you, Margaret Sorensen, not me. This group needs to stop you!"

On Crowley's last word the meaty hand swept through the air and smacked the side of his head. Blood dripped from Crowley's ear as the impact rocked his brain. Blinking through the pain he straightened his head and smiled at the old lady. "This will be over soon."

Margaret Sorensen pulled a knitting needle from her bag and ran her fingers down to its point. "You are right. This will be over soon, Detective Crowley." She turned to the room of shadows around a table. "Next to Benjamin Crowley we have Mathew T. Whitten. As you know from our last meeting, Mr. Whitten qualified. Among others in his twisted world, six years ago this man sexually abused and then killed Susan Mason, the beloved wife of honored member Robert Mason, may he rest in peace."

"I served my time," Whitten exploded. "I got rights. You can't do nothin' to me 'bout a crime where's I already did time. They call it double-jeopardy—tried, convicted, and sentenced. I'm a free man, lady. Those are the rules. Don't you know the law?"

"There's not much more to be said." Margaret Sorensen ignored the outburst as if the man was already dead. She turned to the table of shadows. "A show of hands will do. Those in favor of implementing the Dario Group sentence, raise your hand." She looked. "Thank you. It is unanimous. Mr. Whitten will be removed from society and do no others harm."

Dario walked up behind Whitten and held his head. Stunned, Crowley watched.

"At this time sniper services are unavailable to us," Sorensen said. "I cannot predict when we will have a new contract, or if we will continue to do business with other external services. I recommend Dario carry out the termination order at once."

Members were unaware of Dario's action—his hands firm on each side of Whitten's head. It was not until Whitten's words turned into desperate screams and he began to squirm like a worm being put on a hook. When Whitten's skull collapsed, the bursting of bone quieted the man and the room. In a casual sweep, Dario pulled the limp body over the back of the sofa and onto his shoulder. He left the silent room. The front door opened and closed.

Crowley muttered, "What are you people doing? You have no right." He shook his head in confusion and disbelief. Crowley saw Dario's face. Now he knew, but did not want to believe.

Margaret Sorensen stroked her long steel knitting needle like a musical instrument she knew well. "Justice, Detective Crowley. Mr. Whitten is an animal. He's too dangerous to walk among us. No more cages to escape from. We would rather he die than another innocent person."

"We have a process to find and remove these people

SERIAL INTENT

from society. You have no right to decide who dies. You have no right to kill anybody. You and your members are the monsters."

"Enough," she shot back. "You do not speak, or you will be gagged. If that happens, you will not be able to defend yourself. It is your choice."

He leaned back on the sofa with sizzling eyes. Crowley could do nothing tied up and surrounded by unknown numbers. They were in so deep they had no choice but to eliminate everyone who could hurt them—and Dario was unstoppable.

Crowley's head throbbed and he could not hear out of one ear. He remembered entering the last driveway on Birch. He saw the cars on the edge of the woods in the dead end. It was a perfect place for meetings to go unnoticed. He had just dropped his glove in front of the house that he knew belonged to the Dario Group. When his glove hit the ground, a crashing blow came from behind. He awoke tied up in a dark room.

It's been more than a half hour, now. Crowley thought. *Where's my back up? Where's my SWAT, goddamn it! Huntsman, are you just puking out there? Did you forget what we came here for? Damn rookies can't keep up. You'll never amount to anything.*

"The Detroit Blood," Sorensen said, "The one sent here to find the others, we need to return his body to Mr. Doran tonight. Maybe they will learn to leave us alone."

You killed another. You're going to start a war you can never win, don't you understand? Crowley watched Dario lumber back into the room, but something was different.

Still holding her knitting needle in her boney hand, she said, "We have two matters to attend to this evening. We must deal with Detective Crowley and Miss Fetter." Sorensen turned to the members. Dario stopped in front of the fire and turned to her chair.

It's you, Crowley thought as he looked at Dario's

profile in the flickering firelight. *How is this possible?*

Sorensen's eyes found Dario, but she spoke to the members. "These terminations will be difficult, but they are necessary to protect you and me. Detective Crowley and Lindsey Fetter have exposed our group and jeopardized our mission. If we do nothing, they will end everything we have built. They will stop true justice from growing in the world."

Crowley saw the angry look on the side of Dario's face. He saw the lip lifting and the teeth. He heard the raspy growl. *Was this sick man controlled by Margaret Sorensen, or was he wild? What was happening?*

"Stop," she ordered. "Stop now," she said with a tight grip on her knitting needle.

But Dario did not stop. He stayed in front of her by the fire looking down at the old woman. "You are the monster," he said. The room gasped. "You are like him. You both are the monsters in my world."

My God. He talks. Crowley thought as he struggled with the knot behind his back. *Is this how he changes? Is this the split-personality?*

Dario grabbed the sides of his head and dropped to his knees, the crash to the floor sent a spray of sparks from the fireplace. "You do not listen," he groaned. "I stopped your assassins. I stopped the bad men—the killers, and you still hurt good people."

Crowley could only stare at the man's titanic trembling body and huge arms.

"Who am I now?" Dario bellowed. "What's happening to me?" He slid his massive hands over his face and dropped his head. Whatever was happening, Crowley sensed the pain had to be unbearable if it crippled a giant.

"No, Dario," Margaret Sorensen yelled. The shadows in the other room stirred. "None of what you say is true. You are a good man. Your father and I are good people. We only want to help victims of horrible crimes, the people who lost everything in a world that has proven to be unable to protect them. You will be okay, son. Trust me, like always."

Son? Crowley sighed.

Margaret Sorensen's hand slid down her knitting needle. At that instant Crowley knew she was the brain surgeon who had killed the Detroit Blood. With Dario struggling in some sort of transition, possibly she was preparing for her next surgical strike, the one that would end Detective Crowley's life.

But before she could do anything Margaret Sorensen had to regain control. The beast was unraveling before her eyes and the members were stirring. Maybe the evolving dynamics can provide the window of opportunity Crowley needed. Maybe he could turn the man on his knees against the killer brain surgeon. Maybe she did not have the control she thought she had. After all, Dario killed Jacques Sorensen. He may have the ability to stop her, too.

"Don't allow this to happen—Aaron Wolfe," Crowley yelled.

Dario stopped trembling. His hands dropped from his face and he lifted his head. Staring at Margaret Sorensen he said, "I am not Aaron Wolfe." When he turned his head to the detective, Crowley froze—he had no words for what he saw.

Cold air entered the room. The fire popped. "I am Aaron Wolfe."

This time the words did not come from the man on his knees in front of the fire. Crowley searched for the voice he knew well, the man he had doubted. Crowley struggled to shift his broken and bound body to see more. He found Huntsman, the skinny detective he left on Birch. The rookie was entering behind a SWAT team pouring into the room of shadows with arms going up. Then Crowley found Aaron Wolfe standing behind the stuffed armchair with a gun pressed to Margaret Sorensen's head. Behind Wolfe,

Lindsey Fetter stood with a soft smile.

"Joe, it is over, my friend," Wolfe said, his eyes on the man they called Dario.

Joe Hutson looked up at Wolfe. "I can't live like this anymore, Aaron."

"We can help you," Wolfe said. "You don't need to go it alone anymore. You're a good man. You're my friend. We will get you the help you gotta have, the help these people have kept from you."

Margaret stared down at her son at her feet, Joseph Hutson Sorensen. She always thought he looked like Aaron Wolfe, but she knew he would never be half the man. "Joseph, don't let these men mislead you. They won't help you. They will put you in prison for killing all those people. Your only chance is to stop them here and now. Let Dario do it for you. Dario is special. He was sent to us to right the wrongs in this world. We must kill all the monsters, Joseph."

Maybe Margaret could not hide the contempt that oozed from her lips, the cold emptiness Joseph had felt every day of his life. Joe had believed them—he would never get better. That's why he ran away. But Joe returned. On that snowy night at their cabin in Algonquin, Joe saw his father's syringe. At that moment he knew he had to stop them. They never wanted to help him. They only wanted to find a way to keep Dario alive so he could serve their twisted mission.

An eternity passed in a handful of seconds. Detective Huntsman reached behind Crowley to untie the knot. Two SWAT members leveled guns on Joseph and Margaret. Wolfe began to back his gun from her head—it was over.

When the front door opened, all heads and guns turned to the plume of snow and the next unknown. When Commander Landers broke from the frozen mist, Dario lunged for Margaret's throat. In an instant her knitting needle plunged into Dario's neck and slid into his brain.

Before anyone could react, and before Dario could be stopped, Margaret Sorensen's neck snapped with a suffocating crack. Her body fell limp in her chair. She was dead.

Commander Landers cradled his head in his arms. He had less than ten seconds to say goodbye to the detective he loved like a son.

Next to the fire in the quiet room Commander Landers, Detective Crowley, and Detective Wolfe saw Detective Joe Hutson in the eyes and the smile of the dying man.

Dario let Joe die alone . . .

EPILOGUE

Summer – Ten Years Later – Sheridan Beach, Lake Michigan

The sapphire water edged the southern banks of Lake Michigan under a hot afternoon sun. The laughter of children and calls of Red-throated Loons and Whimbrels were only interrupted by the occasional car crawling down Lake Shore Drive. Aaron Wolfe sat on his favorite dune with tan toes dug into the sand and Ray-Bans keeping his long shaggy hair out of his eyes.

"I appreciate the opportunity to talk to you, Mr. Wolfe," The young true-crime author said as he squinted at a legend and got comfortable on the sand. "Do you mind if I record this?"

Wolfe did not turn from the sparkling water. He nodded.

"Commander Zackery Huntsman said you have never met with anyone to talk about the Dario Group and the events at the house on Birch. Just for me, why did you agree to this meeting?"

"I've read you. You get things right. Maybe it's time."

"Coming from you, that means a lot, sir." He pulled out a small leather notebook and flipped a few pages battling the gusting wind. "Three months after that night on Birch Avenue, Commander Louie Landers died. There were unexpected complications, the shooting at the

Congress Plaza Hotel. It's not clear who shot the commander that day or why. Can you help me with that?"

Sand sprayed as a small dust devil jumped their dune and slid up the bank toward the house fifty yards away. Wolfe ignored the brief visitor—he was used to them.

"Louie was looking for me," Wolfe said. "Margaret Sorensen shot him. She shot me, too." He smiled touching the scar on his arm. "I would take a closer look at the Timberman file."

Wolfe rubbed his three-day beard and said under his breath, "Paul Timberman was a member of the Dario Group. However, his actions that morning were his alone."

"Are you saying he went rogue?"

"He was not acting on the orders of the Dario Group."

"How can you be so sure?"

"Logic and facts," Wolfe said. "The weighing of the two made it possible for me to solve hundreds of homicides over two decades."

"Please continue." The true-crime author put down his pen and leaned closer.

"Fact—the Dario Group terminated thirty-seven people over a twenty-two year period. We have supporting evidence from the crime scenes, and we have documents from the Dario Group archives. In all cases, the terminations were well planned and meticulously implemented.

"Logic—if the Dario Group had intended to terminate a Chicago PD homicide detective in front of 500 people at the national CCLR meeting, their executioner would have been a professional trained in the use of weapons. A high caliber weapon would be used to ensure success.

"Fact—Paul Timberman was a novice with guns. He missed me twelve times from fifteen feet away. He used a .22 caliber pistol. Even if I had been hit several times, the chance of survival was high.

"Fact—the Dario Group knew their member Paul

Timberman was not a stable man. They knew he despised the homicide detectives and defense attorneys.

"Logic—they would have never approved Paul Timberman sitting on the front row at a lecture given by a homicide detective or defense attorney."

"Why did he despise you?"

"He lost his wife a few years earlier—sexual assault and beaten to death in front of him. They beat and left him for dead too, but he survived. I worked the case. The man found guilty served only five years."

"We had DNA, blood, and semen. We had video of the guy entering and leaving the Timberman's home. Smart lawyers did their jobs. There were processing errors made. Legal technicalities threw out key evidence and created enough doubt that the state had to negotiate. He got murder-two and was released early for good behavior."

"Could you have done more as the lead investigator?"

"I struggled with that question for many years. I could have done some things a little differently, but after working hundreds of homicides over two decades, and after sitting in hundreds of courtrooms watching the process, I know I could not have made a difference in the outcomes. You see, in today's world there is too much quicksand between the victims and justice."

"Do you mean legal quicksand?"

"As a homicide investigator, I walk into a crime scene faced with countless details and conditions without knowing anything from the start. If anyone at that crime scene makes a wrong move, the case can fall apart in a courtroom down the road."

"Errors and uncontrolled variables?"

"Weather conditions, the people at the crime scene, the killer's cover up, and human error are just a few things that open the door for a multitude of interpretations. That stark reality creates endless opportunities for reasonable doubt. Any good lawyer can manipulate jury perception."

"I guess it is a well-known fact that people see the same things differently. I believe it is a human condition."

Wolfe smiled. "And when that *truth* enters the criminal justice system, guilty people can go free. To get back to your question about who shot Louie Landers, I need to set the stage. The Dario Group was surprised to see Mr. Timberman sitting on the front row of my presentation. They were desperate to get him out of there, but after I started speaking they had no way to accomplish that without drawing attention or creating a scene."

"So they had to accept Timberman could lose it."

"The Dario Group was forced into an unplanned containment operation. If Timberman lost it, they had to make sure he was not able to talk to authorities after the fact."

"That was why Margaret Sorensen went back stage."

Wolfe nodded. "After Timberman emptied his gun the second time, I had an opportunity to stop him. When I shot him, I saw him look back stage. I turned in time to see Margaret Sorensen move her gun from Timberman to me. She no longer needed to neutralize Mr. Timberman. Because I saw her with the gun, she now needed to neutralize me."

"You saw Mrs. Sorensen shoot you?"

"Yes. If I had not found her in the curtains when I did, I would not have moved enough to avoid a fatal shot. I went after her. Louie was jumping rows of seats to come help. He saw her too. He went back stage. Mrs. Sorensen shot him twice."

"Now I understand. It makes sense. Let me shift gears to possibly the most important question. When did you know Joe Hutson was Dario?"

"At the brownstone I had my suspicions he had some level of involvement. Those suspicions were confirmed on Birch Avenue the night he died."

"What triggered your suspicions?"

"The setup at the brownstone smelled. Joe's injuries were minor, could have been self-inflicted. The way he was tied—could have done it himself. Margaret Sorensen in the closet not tied and unconscious, very odd. The diary was a major clue. If Joe had been really working the case, he would have found it. The way Sorensen looked at Joe—seemed maternal."

"Was Dr. Jacques Sorensen's diary your first window into the Dario Group?"

"Not a lot about the Dario Group in there," Wolfe said. "More about Dario the patient and Jacques Sorensen's lifetime of killing patients he could not help."

"It never mentioned Joe Hutson?"

"No. Joe was a well-kept family secret," Wolfe said.

"When did you know the Dario Group was a vigilante group focused on terminating serial killers who beat the criminal justice system?"

"When I worked the Eric Ramsey homicide. He was killed by sniper fire—one shot between the eyes through an open window at night from a mile away. Nobody pays for that kind of talent to eliminate one scumbag. It had to be an organized effort with a broader purpose. A few nights after the Ramsey killing, Lindsey told me about the Dario Group. I believed she believed, but for me it needed more investigation."

"Only a few people alive today witnessed the physical changes that created the man called Dario. I'm having trouble getting any one to talk about it. Can you help me understand what happened to Joe Hutson that made him become this monster?"

"I was there when Joe died," Wolfe said. "We don't like to talk about it because it takes away from a guy we all cared about. Joe was a good man. We saw him as a man trying hard to be a good homicide detective. We didn't know anything about the battles he fought his whole life."

"I respect that. But his story must be told. It matters."

SERIAL INTENT

Wolfe slid his sunglasses to the top of his head and sighed. The young author was right and he knew it. "Dr. Jacques Sorensen explained the physical change as a metamorphosis. I suggest you go through Dario's medical records with a psychiatrist. The only thing missing is Joe's name."

"I will, but it will mean more if it is in the words of an eyewitness who knew Joe."

Wolfe rubbed his neck searching for the words. "I only saw him change from Dario back to Joe. I still can't believe my eyes. When I entered the room on Birch, I saw him on his knees by the fire facing Margaret Sorensen. His shoulders and arms were enormous, very muscular like a professional weight lifter. His face was deformed, angry. He looked dangerous. As I watched, his pronounced features melted away and the Dario persona left him. The anger and bizarre physical anomalies were gone in seconds, like relaxing a tensed muscle."

"Did Joe Hutson control the change?"

"No. He experienced it. Joe disappeared the last few weeks because he could not control Dario. That reality may have brought things to a head."

The young author turned off his recorder and closed his notebook. The two stared at the water in silence. The life and experiences of Joseph Hutson would not be fully understood for years, but the actions of the Dario Group were likely being played out in other cities.

"Do you think they were right, the Dario Group?" the author asked.

"You mean dealing with serial intent—private citizens taking on a mission to kill the monsters our system sets free?" Wolfe asked.

"Yes. Seems the legal system is not going to change enough on its own to better meet the needs of victims and survivors."

Wolfe smiled as he slid his sunglasses back on his

nose. Lindsey walked up, draped her arms over his shoulders, and rested her head on the back of his neck.

"When it comes to reform of the criminal justice system, all I hear about are efforts to reduce incarcerations and pull back law enforcement. I don't hear much about more aggressive penalties for serial offenders. We have become a more tolerant society over the years. I think that reality is out of line with most people who are not speaking up. I know it is not in line with the family and friends of victims. When a Bengal tiger walks the streets, society wants it removed. When it kills, they want it destroyed. It tasted human flesh. It will kill again."

"Is it possible your experience as a homicide detective has jaded you?"

Wolfe stared at the horizon as Lindsey rubbed his arm. She and Aaron were both lawyers and had real monsters in their lives. Under the stars above Lake Michigan, they often spoke about serial killers and the failing legal process.

"The United States accounts for five percent of the world population and twenty-five percent of the inmate population—that's over two million in jail. Every year more than a half-million people are released from state and federal prisons: parole, probation, and work-release programs or pardons independent of the law or the penalty. I have never understood the political fixation on releasing criminals early. To me it's a death wish. I may be jaded, but it is hard to ever envision a shift in the focus. The predators are out there."

Wolfe turned back to the young author as Lindsey sat up next to him. "I don't see our criminal justice system even catching up to current technology until I am long gone."

"I don't follow."

"Our criminal justice system is based on one premise—a person is innocent until proven guilty beyond a reasonable doubt. That made perfect sense over the last two-hundred years, but today we can catch a criminal on video committing a heinous crime. The video eliminates all doubt and questions of guilt. Now, the goal of a defense attorney is to remove that damning technology (evidence) from consideration in a courtroom. Does that action support our quest for justice? Is that what society had in mind when it sought to put in place a process to protect them from evil?"

"What are you suggesting?"

"I am saying in today's world some are guilty until proven innocent," Wolfe said. "Technology can be far more accurate than the courtroom. Do you ever see our criminal justice system embracing that reality?"

"Probably not in my lifetime," said the author.

"DNA should never be thrown out. New technology should always be incorporated and processes modified to deal with real facts. A criminal history should always be admissible. Eyewitnesses should give testimony in a manner that protects them first. Serial killers should be executed. Murder should be a life sentence at minimum—it is for the victim. For me, these are common sense if one seeks justice and to protect society," Wolfe said.

"Those are significant changes. Many fly in the face of human rights."

"It is a human right to live in a safe world. It is a human right to live! The mission of a criminal justice system is to deliver justice. Through that justice people are safer. I'm afraid ours is failing to keep up in important areas."

"You would agree that is your opinion. There's no proof society wants change."

"There are more guns in America than people," Wolfe said. "They can't all be collectors or sportsmen. That number tells me there are a whole lot of people out there who don't feel safe. Maybe if our criminal justice system did a better job, those numbers would be different."

"Well said, honey," Lindsey teased. "We need to move this conversation to the house and lunch? This discussion is good for you, even though you're no longer in law enforcement."

Wolfe smiled. "Not sure I know how it's good for me." He got to his feet looking down the beach. "Joseph. Liddy," he yelled. "Time to eat."

"Your kids—fourish and fivish?"

"Joe is six and Liddy five. Lindsey and I married when I left the Chicago PD. After Louie died and Ben Crowley retired, I had an opportunity to change my life. I'm glad I did."

"Your kids will have a great life growing up out here."

"Yes. And I intend for them to be safe," Wolfe said.

When they turned to walk to the house, the author saw the Smith & Wesson holstered in the small of Wolfe's back. Then the sweatshirt dropped.

A Bengal tiger won't get far on this beach . . .

STEVE BRADSHAW is a forensic field agent and biotech entrepreneur writing his unique brand of mystery/thrillers. Steve's training and experience investigating thousands of unexplained deaths for the medical examiner's office, and as the founder-President/CEO of an innovative biomedical device company enables him to put his readers on the front row in the fascinating worlds of fringe science, modern forensics, and the chilling pursuit of real monsters.

Steve enjoys sharing his experiences and perspectives as a forensic investigator, President/CEO, and mystery/thriller author. Visit his website and join MEMBER GUEST so you can interact with the author, get insider information and updates, arrange for an author visit, and to be the first in line for new releases.

Website stevebradshawauthor.com
Email steve@stevebradshawauthor.com
Facebook com/steve.bradshaw.9400
Twitter com/sbauthor
LinkedIn com/pub/steve-bradshaw/18/246/660